HAMPSTEADPUB.COM

OFFICIAL
STREET
CHRONICLES

Hampstead Publishing

www.hampsteadpub.com
www.illstreetz.com

To order additional copies of this book, contact
Hampstead Publishing Inc.
P.O. Box 33
Keasbey, NJ 08832

ISBN 0-9764907-0-6

Edited by Simone Wright

STREET TEAM

By

JOE BLACK

You know what it is.

Don't seem so surprised.

We live in a world where only the strong survive.

A world that presents two choices...

Ride or die,

And most of us choose the passenger side.

A world consisting of the have and have-nots.

A world of board rooms and crack spots.

A world in which you have the minor and major leagues,

And I ain't talking bout the Yankees,

This right here's...

The Street Team.

Dedicated In Loving Memory
To
Leila and Johnny Reddick

Acknowledgements

Off the top I'll have to give the crazy big ups to Susan of Hampstead Publishing. Thanks to Kevin Chiles for that connect. Ah yo, Sue, you betted on Black and put me back in the game. I'm forever grateful to you. Get ready to count the chips. And check this out, they say behind every strong man there is a strong woman. Well I got a gang of strong brilliant women behind me so how can I lose. Sue, Shae, Libre, Jessica and Racqual, with a starting five like y'all, niggas can't ball with us. And yo Richard, what up son, you that nigga for real. And I can't forget the special thanks I have to shoot to my man T.J. Carter, ah yo big homey, real niggas do real things.

I would like to acknowledge several individuals who've made my years, months, and days appear to be a lot shorter than they actually were. The entire Reddick family—I can't thank my family enough for holdin' me down from the very minute of my arrest and still doing it eleven years later. Your love and support is what has been keeping me strong, balanced, and focused throughout this struggle. I would like to thank the mothers of my children— Tonya Dunbar, Aretha Williams, and Claudine Hagigal— for being able to overlook my past immature, irresponsible behavior, and allowing my kids not only to continue to be a major part of my life, but in each other's as well. A lot of women feel like they're punishing the confined father and not the kids, and I'm just truly grateful that you three beautiful women were much bigger than that! Further, I have to thank my kids, Tyrone, Andrea, and Stephen, for always showing me crazy love and respect each and every time they speak with and visit me. The three of you keep doing what you're doing and stay focused! I'll be home in a minute. I love ya'all with everything inside me!

This is a special thanks to two people who have helped me bring Ill Streetz outside the prison. My mentor and good friend, Michael Santos and his wife, Carole. You've really helped me and I hope that some day my site will be half as big as MichaelSantos.net.

There have been a lot of special friends that have always been in my corner. My brother, James—yo kid, you're my hero! Keith Vaughn and Mashawn Simmons, you niggas are the realest! Darrly Boston, I know you mean well, get ya mind right famm. Carline, you know you're Drea's role model, right? Tonya, Ebony, and Vennesa Williams, check or bet Nessa, Ebony, only good things happen for sweethearts like you. Kim, Penny, Tina, Sonya, Regg and Monette Footman, yeah, ya'all thought I forgot. Kim Rollins, Kesha Carrington (do I still owe for missing that Thanksgiving dinner?), Lauren Ashford (hey Angel, I can actually feel all the love), my two nieces, Sharon and Sherice, you've both made your uncle proud.

Tiffany Chiles and the entire Don Diva family. Big ups to y'all for always bringing the streets straight to my dorm.

Last but not least I want to thank Diane Schulte, Daniel Robinson, Michael Norwood, Sam Harrel, Randy Robinson, James Flagg, Angela Foster, Kayle Mann, Tyrone Green, Jay Britt and John Cuff. These are all the people that patiently waited for their copy! I need y'all to know, that the delay was due to last minute adjustments Hampstead Publishing felt was necessary to deliver their readers quality material.

Joe Black
January, 2005

PROLOGUE

The moment Kelly and her friend Tonya stepped into build-ing 1839, Wu noticed the redness and swelling along the entire right side of Kelly's face. He bounced up off the wall and cuffed his blunt in one hand, "What the fuck happened to you?," he asked, searching their faces for an answer.

"This guy slapped her," Tonya eagerly answered after Kelly seemed unresponsive.

"Who?," Wu asked as he stepped outside of the building with anxious searching eyes. It was a hot early summer after-noon and there were a lot of people outside. "Where he at?"

"I don't know his name but he lives in that building," Tonya said as she pointed to a tenement building a few yards away. It was a six- story building identical to the one they stood in front of and on the same side of the street.

"That's his car right there," Kelly's friend angrily continued, pointing out a gold Mazda M.P.V.

Wu recognized the vehicle but couldn't immediately put his finger on who he'd seen driving it. "Damn, who shit is that?," he thought out loud while racking his brain.

"He just moved around here," Kelly finally spoke in between weeps.

"Oh, I know who the fuck you talking about," Wu fumed as his focus rested on Kelly's bruised face.

Though Kelly was no kin to Wu, they'd grown up in the same building, therefore, he considered her like family. Knowing she had no father, siblings or boyfriend she could turn to, Wu instantly decided he'd deal with the situation. "What happened?," he asked.

"He said I thought I was all that. Then he knocked the bag out of my hand," Kelly tearfully stated, directing Wu's attention to the busted open brown paper bag that rested a couple of feet away from the guy's building. The groceries it contained were shattered all about. "I cursed him out then he slapped me," she said.

"Word," Wu shockingly said. "You mess with him or something?," Wu asked making sure he wasn't about to get involved with a domestic problem.

"No. He's been trying to talk to me since he moved around here, but I never spoke back."

"He was just mad because Kelly wasn't sweating him," Tonya instigated.

"Come on," Wu said as he gestured for them to follow him.

A step behind Wu they marched down the block with a quickly growing crowd of nosey bystanders behind them. Kids and grown folks alike. It only took one person to spot Kelly's face and Wu's demeanor to know that there was about to be drama on the block.

D-Mac ran up beside Wu. "Yo! What's up?," he asked. He'd seen the small intense crowd from a house window and raced across the street.

"A nigga slapped Kelly," Wu informed him while they continued to pace forward.

"Oh shit!," D-Mac said as he looked back at Kelly's face. "Who did that?"

"Money right there," Wu directed D-Mac's attention into the M.P.V. that was parked across the street in front of D-Mac's house. "He just moved around here," Wu added.

"I know who you talking about," D-Mac responded as they

came to a stop in front of the building.

A girl handed Kelly the half torn paper bag. "Here Kelly," she said. It barely held the non-glass recovered items. "Are you okay?," she asked. She eyed Kelly's slight nod yes then stepped back.

"What apartment Money live in?," D-Mac asked the girl who recovered the items.

"They either live in 5-E or 5-D," the girl answered. "I know they live on the fifth floor," she added with certainty. She knew because she also lived in the building. Her response instantly reminded D-Mac of another dude he suspected to be the guy's brother.

"Who's the guy that be with him, his brother?"

"Yeah, it's them two and their mother," she said giving them the entire scoop.

Because they were unsure which apartment the guy lived in, Wu suggested that they lure the guy back outside. He knew exactly how to do it too. "Kelly, go chill in front of our building," Wu turned and said.

"Why don't y'all go up the block, damn!," D-Mac barked at everyone else. He then followed Wu across the street.

"Help me rock this," Wu said. Then they began rattling the Mazda, causing its alarm to scream.

They both were heated with dude. Not only because he slapped Kelly, but for also pulling a stunt like that on a block he'd just moved to. Even worse— their notorious block. The one they grew up protecting.

With their fitted hats pulled low and stooped behind the M.P.V.'s tinted windows, Wu and D-Mac looked up at a guy who had emerged out a fifth floor window. It was the 5E apartment. They suspected it to be dude once they noticed him aiming what appeared to be a remote. It silenced the alarm, but not for long. The second he disappeared Wu and D-Mac rattled the Mazda a second time.

Moments later, while remaining hidden behind the tints, they spotted dude hurriedly exiting the building and rushing towards the Mazda. They eyed him pulling on the driver's door handle. He made his way around to their side where they stood straight up with their backs resting against the Mazda. "Yo man. Y'all niggas gotta raise up off my joint," the dude said. His tone wasn't harsh but demanding. "Can't y'all hear that alarm keep going off?"

"Oh. My bad Dude," Wu said. Then they rushed him.

The dude was not as frail as Wu, but not as thick as D-Mac either. "What the fuck is y'all niggas doing?," the dude whaled as he desperately tried to free himself from D-Mac's steady hold. A hold that had his arms locked straight up about his head. It was a wrestling hold known as the "Full Nelson." D-Mac mastered it. "Let me go nigga. Give me a fair one!" Paying dude's request for a fair fight no mind, D-Mac literally began to drag the dude across the street while Wu stopped traffic.

Realizing that he wasn't going anywhere, dude gradually let up on his resistance until he was practically walking while still under D-Mac's hold. The moment they made it to the other side and he spotted Kelly amongst the crowd; he knew what was going on. "Yo Nigga. You betta let me go!" he warned.

"Kelly, come here," Wu called out. "Fuck his ass up!," he said.

"I'm telling you bitch. You betta not touch me!," Dude shouted as he threw a kick causing her to stop in her tracks.

"Shut the fuck up nigga," D-Mac said while tightening his hold. "And if you kick her, I'm going to slam the shit out of your fucking ass!"

"Fuck him up Kelly," her friend shouted, with tears of anger trickling down her face. But Kelly stood frozen.

"Hit 'em Kelly! Hit 'em," others in the crowd started yelling once they noticed she was not budging.

"You think your face is fucked up now bitch! Go ahead and put your hands on me!" the dude threatened.

As if a fuse had been lit, Kelly charged him and smacked the shit out of him. She hit him in the face with an open hand. "Oh shit!," the dude shouted angrily.

"Don't slap him Kelly. Punch his punk ass," Tonya yelled.

"Shut the fuck up bitch," Dude grilled Tonya.

"I got your bitch," she shot back as she rushed him. But before she could get a hit off, he kicked her in her midsection. "Ouch muthafucka," she raved falling backwards. Tonya was thick. It was hard enough to knock her down, no doubt keep her down.

As promised, D-Mac slammed him to the ground and everyone watched as Kelly and Tonya jumped on him like two wild animals. The blow he suffered from the ground combined with the immediate following blows of Kelly and Tonya stripped dude of any fighting power he might have had.

"What the fuck is up?" Butter asked as he walked up on Wu and D-Mac.

"That nigga slapped Kelly," Wu explained.

Noticing the puzzled look on Butter's face, D-Mac said, "Money just moved around here. You know, the nigga pushing the MPV."

"Oh yeah, aight", Butter responded. He raced over to Tonya. "Uhn uhn. What you trying to do, murder him?," he asked while snatching a stick out of her hand. "Yo, that's enough Kelly!," Butter said as he pulled Kelly up off dude. The dude's face was badly scratched and beaten.

"Aight y'all. It's over!" Wu yelled, gesturing for the crowd to disperse, which they slowly did. "Y'all didn't see nothing!," he jokingly said, drawing a few laughs. He really wasn't worried about anyone calling the police because he was sure that everyone had heard that the dude had slapped Kelly for no apparent reason. And that was enough for them to enforce their neighborhood security. Something the block loved them for.

"Check this out, Money" D-Mac said as he towered over the motionless dude. "You got your fair one. Next time we coming up in apartment 5E." D-Mac lifted his shirt slightly and exposed the handle of a Mac-Ten. "And my man Butter ain't gonna be trying to save y'all," he snidely added, letting the dude know that the threat was lodged against the entire family.

Seeing the seriousness in their faces, dude quickly decided that he didn't want to bring the drama to his mother's crib. Even if he'd gotten to the three of them first, he'd still have an entire block to deal with. That much drama he didn't' want, nor was he built for.

Chapter One

December '88

Butter, a short light-skinned kid stepped into the pinched hallway of building 1839 sporting his brand new all-black triple fat goose bomber. The puffy goose feather filled coat took his sort of pudgy figure and made it appear to be bulky. His three friends, D-Mac, Wu, and Flip, who were hanging out in the hallway, stared in astonishment.

D-Mac, a slim dark-skinned kid broke the silence. "Oh Dip!," he said as he and the other two guys began feeling on the coat as if real muscles were underneath its nylon material. "Where you get this joint from?," he asked.

Butter was an only child. A combination of his complexion and soft, pudgy appearance earned him his nickname. His parents were financially comfortable in the real estate game. He lived with them in the house they owned around the corner from 1839. He relished all the benefits of being an only child and was practically given everything he wanted.

Whenever something new came out, Butter was the first out of the bunch to get it. In the spring of '85 it was the New York Knicks starter jacket, in the fall of '86 it was the big gold chain. Though, he was only fifteen, in '87 it was the Honda Elite scooter, and now the winter of '88, the Triple Fat Goose. "Ma Duke," he answered with a slight grin, the same grin as in years earlier.

"I gotta get me one of these joints," D-Mac said, the same thing he'd usually say when Butter popped up with something new.

D-Mac at sixteen was an only child, too. At the age of three, his father took off and his mother was sentenced to three years in prison for her role in forging checks. So, D-Mac was adopted by his grandparents. D-Mac and his grandparents lived in a private house across the street from 1839. His grandfather was a retired gun-store owner who taught his grandson about guns at an early age. By the time D-Mac was twelve, he was stealing guns from his grandfather's basement and showing them off to the fellas. At the age of fourteen he removed a Mac-Ten machine gun from his grandfather's basement. It went unnoticed. So two days later he removed a Tech-Nine. The very next day his grandfather died of a heart attack and his grandmother closed down the basement, never noticing the missing guns that D-Mac never returned.

D-Mac would let any one of the fellas hold the Tech-Nine, but never the Mac-Ten, and that's how he earned his nickname. Like Butter, D-Mac was given everything he wanted, so when he said he had to get him a Triple Fat Goose, there was no doubt in the fellas minds that he would soon have one.

They often hung out in the narrow hallway of the meager six-story red brick-face tenement building, smoking weed and shooting dice. It was also the building where Wu and his mother resided. Wu's father was black and his mother was Chinese. They met while Wu's father was overseas with the Army, and one year later Wu was born.

Now at sixteen years old, Wu was almost the spitting image of his mother. He had straight hair, with slanted eyes, stealing only his father's tan complexion. The combination earned him his nickname. On sight, you knew he was Chinese but if you let him tell it, he was black. His father abandoned him and his mother before Wu got to know him. He left Wu to be raised solely by his welfare recipient mother who had recently started disappearing for days at a time, leaving Wu to fend for himself.

"Where she get it from," D-Mac quizzed, wanting to have all the information to take back to his grandmother.

"We got it from Jew man," Butter answered. The Jew man was the clothing store in the Hunts Point area of the Bronx. Nearly every kid shopped or wanted to shop at Jew man. If it was in style and you wanted it, Jew man had it.

"How much?"

"A buck seventy-five," Butter answered, drawing four wide eyes.

A hundred and seventy-five dollars was a lot of money to be paying for a coat, Flip and Wu thought, but D-Mac who apparently was not phased said, "Bet." Two nights later, Butter, Wu and Flip were in the hallway shooting dice when D-Mac kicked the chip painted red steel door open. "Yeah Boy!," he shouted stepping into the hallway with his arms folded as if he were a genie. He was wearing his new black triple fat goose. All four of their faces lit up with grins as he unzipped the coat. He then playfully pulled out the Mac-Ten from his waistband. "Who want static?," he yelled waving the small semi-automatic in the air. "Bring it," he added.

D-Mac's actions drew laughs from the fellas as they gave each other five. Flip who was facing the door's twelve inch square window that was protected by a mesh metal grill on both sides of the door, immediately stopped laughing when he spotted the black Cherokee pull up in front of the building. "Yo chill," Flip said, groping for D-Mac's arm. "Put that away. Here come Kelly and Bill," he warned. Without hesitation D-Mac tucked the gun back into his waist. He and Wu then quickly propped up against the wall on one side of the hall while Flip and Butter faced them standing against the opposite wall clearing a path to the three steps that led to the second steel door.

Like always, when they heard people coming out of their apartments or spotted people coming into the building, their raucous would turn into low chattering and sometimes silence as they were greeted by mostly all tenants. Practically everybody in the building knew them and nobody complained, especially after the muggings and robberies had ceased since they had been hanging out in the hallway.

Kelly lived on the first floor in the last apartment at the end of the hallway. She was twenty-one and gorgeous. Standing about five-eleven with a swim suit figure. She had a dark tan complexion with jet black, hip length, wavy hair. If you didn't look twice you would swear she was Lisa Ray with a suntan. The fellas had a huge crush on her. Always kidding around about who she liked best.

Whenever she was coming through, they all would try to impress her in their own way. Despite the fact that she was only into hustlers, she would purposely flirt with them from time to time.

"What's up Kelly?," they said in unity before hesitantly greeting Bill with a half a nod. Flip held the door open as she and Bill made their way in.

Kelly wore a sky blue pair of Guess jeans that looked like they were painted on; some black Gucci boots; and a zipped up, waist length, black Shearling coat. She pranced through the held open door, greeting them with her perfect smile. "Thank you," she said while pinching Flip's cheek. "What's up ya'll? Ooh, these are nice!," she commented, feeling both Butter and D-Mac's coats as she passed.

"Thanks," they both replied wearing a half grin.

The four of them watched as Bill did his usual, walking close up on Kelly trying to block their view of her phat ass. Bill stood at about six-four with a football player's build. He was in his early thirties, but the neatly shaped side burns and goatee, had him closer to forty. He was a correctional officer on Riker's Island, but he also had guys selling crack for him on 114th Street in Harlem where he lived.

Bill never had a problem with Butter and the crew, but it was evident that they didn't like each other. He didn't like how they looked at Kelly, and they didn't like the fact that she was seeing him.

"Yo that nigga a sucka," D-Mac said as they watched them from the second door's window entering her apartment. "Word to Mizz. If that nigga ever try and front, Im'ma buss off on 'em," he added lifting up his black Champion sweatshirt exposing his gun.

"Fuck that," Flip changing the subject said, with his eyes glued to the coats. "We gotta get us some of these joints," he added with cold beady eyes shifting from the coats directly on to Wu, who was nodding in agreement.

They called him Flip because he had different sides to him. He was nice when he was good, but hell when he was bad. At seventeen he was the oldest of the group.   His age and tacit ways made him the unspoken leader of the group.   Flip lived with both his parents in a six-story tenement building down the block from 1839. His mother worked as a nurse in Jacobi Hospital and his father drove trucks. When it came to money, his parents were more conservative than D-Mac and Butter's guardians. Asking them for the money was out of the question. Getting a hundred and seventy-five dollars from them for a coat would be like trying to pull an alligator's tooth. Flip knew it and so did D-Mac and Butter. So when Wu agreed, they knew what he and Flip had in mind.

"What's up, yall wit' it?," Flip asked as he and Wu faced the other two. Though they weren't into stick-ups, they had done it on two occasions and the last time was almost two years ago in '86, when Wu and Flip wanted gold chains. The only time before that was in '85, when Wu was the only one out of the three who didn't have a starter jacket. Butter had no idea that he had initiated a cycle of lust, envy, and greed every time he popped up with his latest prize.

D-Mac and Butter never had a problem helping their best friends obtain the same things they had, even if it meant going to jail—something they never thought about then, and weren't thinking about now.

"Bet! We wit' it!," they answered in unison.

Hampstead Publishing

Chapter Two

Christmas night

It was 2:00 a.m. Flip, Butter, and Wu stood in the hallway of 1839 watching through the open door as D-Mac backed his grandmother's Volvo out of the garage. He had stolen the car on numerous accounts for joy riding, but this would be the first time he had stolen it as a get away vehicle. D-Mac pulled the dark blue sedan up to the front of the building. Flip got in the front while Butter and Wu hopped in the back. All were dressed in denim jeans, black Timberland boots and over sized Champion hoodies. D-Mac and Flip wore black, and Butter and Wu wore blue.

They had planned the stick up for Christmas night because they knew that not only were half the city's kids going to have a North-Face by or on Christmas, but they'd be wearing them to the annual X-Mas party at the rollerskating rink that night.

When they pulled up to the roller skating rink, the scenery was just how they thought it would be, havoc. Mobs of people were standing around in packs in front of the entrance while a long column of people lined up along the building's lengthy façade wall waiting for bouncers to wave them forward.

Double-parked cars jammed both sides of the street, some occupied and others unattended. "It's mad cuties out here," Butter commented.

Their eyes scanned the site as they slowly drove by on their way to circling the block. "I seen about fitty joints," Wu exaggerated on the number of coats he spotted as they circled the block.

"Word," Butter agreed.

As they slowly pulled back on the block, two cars were pulling off from their double-parked spaces. "Yo, right there," Flip said as he pointed to an unoccupied spot that was a little beyond the rink's entrance. D-Mac made a quick U-turn and pulled into the space. Their eight cold eyes began piercing through the rolled up windows and into the crowd, in search of prey. Ten minutes after they parked, D-Mac noticed two guys straying away from the crowd. He gained more interest as they made their way past the end of the line, indicating they had either already been inside, or had no intentions of going inside. "Yo, look!," he said as he pointed, drawing everyone's attention to the two guys. "Down there. Headed toward the train station."

Seconds later all eyes were glued onto the guys as the duo conspicuously made their way down the street sporting their Triple Fat Gooses. They were about forty yards from the stairs that led to the elevated train station and twenty yards from the end of the rollerskating rink's extensive wall. Near the very end of the wall was the narrow dim alley. Just inside the secluded alley was the exit janitors used to discharge bags of trash. He knew it would be the perfect spot to pull it off, but they would have to move quickly. "Yall could bag them right in the alley," D-Mac suggested.

"Aight bet," Flip agreed.

Wasting no time, D-Mac pulled off. He drove ten yards past the alley before coming to a stop. "Meet us around the corner," Flip said. Then he, Butter and Wu calmly got out of the Volvo. They stepped onto the sidewalk, going unnoticed by the two boys who appeared to be lackadaisically goofing off as they headed their way. As the three of them gradually closed the gap between themselves and their potential victims, the butterflies began to twine inside Butter's stomach, just like they had done on the two previous stick-ups. Not out of fear, but because he knew what they were about to do was treacherous and unjustifiable. Bad enough they were about to attempt to take something that didn't belong to them, to make matters worse they were about to rob their own brothers, two young black kids out of the same ghetto they're from. It made no sense.

"Butter, watch the entrance while we strip 'em," Flip muttered. They pulled their hoods on, burying their faces. The butterflies quickly vanished. Right now it wasn't about making sense, it was about getting two Triple Fat Gooses. Whether it made sense or not had slipped to the back of Butter's mind as they accosted the two young men directly in front of the alley. "You know what it is," Flip said as the three of them pulled out guns from their waist. "Get in the hole!," he ordered. Their two boyish faces instantly flooded with fear.

The boys glanced at each other as the foolish thought of trying to run had flashed into their heads. Realizing that they wouldn't make it three steps before they would be gunned down, they made the wiser choice of doing as they were told.

"Yo, please don't kill us!," the taller of the two pleaded as they stood against the wall in the alley with their hands in the air and staring into the darkness of the hoodies.

"Close your eyes and shut up!," Flip snidely retorted. "Do what I say and you gonna live, aight?," he added, letting them know they had no interest in murdering them unless of course they had to. His last words brought a ray of light to grief stricken faces of their victims. "Now both of you take your gear off."

The two had surmised that the prize was their expensive coats, so they were caught off guard when ordered to take their clothes off. "Our clothes?," the shorter one asked.

"You heard! Take them shits off!," Wu interjected, raising his 9-mm to the head of the short guy standing in front of him.

Without hesitation the two boys frantically began undressing, starting with their coats and ending with their tennis shoes, dropping each article at the feet of Flip and Wu.

"Everything!," Wu said, gesturing for the two shivering boys to remove their underwear and socks. Butter remained at the entrance, his head rotating from corner to corner as if he were watching a tennis match. As he looked to his left he spotted a police car cruising their way. He calmly took two steps back into the alley, warning Flip and Wu who were putting on the coats.

"Jake on the move," Butter whispered causing them to freeze.

"Everybody get down!," Flip ordered. He and Wu never took their eyes or guns off the two freezing naked boys. "Now!," he emphasized to the two who looked as if they had other thoughts before wisely squatting down.

The five of them remained in the same position until Butter witnessed the patrol car pass.

"Aight they ghost," Butter said.

"Aight stand up!," Flip ordered while he and Wu towered over the naked duo while wearing their Triple Fat Gooses. "Listen. I want yall to count to a hundred. If any of you come out of this hole before then, we gonna start bustin'," Flip said then watched, as they nodded their heads.

Wu began tossing their clothing further back into the alley.

"Ready?," Flip asked.

"Yeah," Wu sighed.

They both looked to Butter, who gave the okay, then walked out of the alley. After only a few steps, they dashed around the corner and quickly filed into the Volvo. Then D-Mac peeled off.

Back in the alley, the two coatless guys were dressed but in no hurry to come out of the alley. Though they knew the robbers were a mile away by now, it was better to be safe than sorry. After all, they'd only lost their coats, which were replaceable—but their lives, never.

Chapter Three

'89, Six months later

It was two days before the summer break and D-Mac, now officially allowed to drive the Volvo, was enjoying the warm breeze as he, Butter and Flip zipped through the busy Bronx streets with the windows down. It was one thirty in the afternoon and as far as they were concerned, the break was already in effect.

"Make The Music With Your Mouth Biz," was the song coming out of the Volvo's factory system that had their heads bopping in rhythm as they turned up one street and down the other.

"Yo turn that joint up," said Butter, who sat in the back.

"That's as loud as it goes," D-Mac replied without turning to face him.

Minutes later they pulled up in front of the park, which was across the street from 1839 and right next to D-Mac's grandmother's two-car garage house.

"We gonna walk up the block and get some smoke," Flip said as he and Butter got out of the Volvo. D-Mac turned his radio off, "Aight, I'll meet yall in the park," he said before letting the windows up as he slowly rolled a few feet to the garage.

The all-inclusive six story brick tenement building around

the corner from 1839, on the opposite side of Butter's parent's house, was just one of the multiple buildings that allowed marijuana dealers to rent apartments to conduct their business. As D-Mac and Butter entered the decomposed building, they were met by the foul stench of urine and what could have been weeks of old trash. The smell caused them both to pinch their noses while covering their mouths with the palm of the same hand as if they were about to jump into a pool of deep water.

"Got damn!," Butter muttered as they hurriedly moved through the hall and up the steps to the third floor where the scent of a well-prepared Jamaican dish lingered. It was escaping from the apartment at the end of the hall— the same crib they were about to buy the weed from.

"Knock! Knock! Knock!", came the sound of Flip's knuckles hitting the door. "Yo, they selling food out this mothafucka too?," he whimsically commented as they stood facing each other in front of the only gray steel apartment door on the floor. It looked as if it had been primed for painting and either someone forgot or changed their mind.

Seconds later the light that seeped through the two inch hole in the door where the door bell once was, became shadowed by the wide eye of a human. "Wha' happen Star?," the guy's heavy Jamaican accent drilled through the closed door.

"Yeah, let me get three nicks," Flip said putting a five and ten dollar bill together before creasing them.

"We're out of trays and nicks. Me only 'ave dimes, Star."

Knowing a ten-dollar bag wouldn't be enough, Flip looked to Butter, questioning whether they should try another spot, or put five more with the fifteen. Without comment, Butter dug in his pocket and pulled out a small wad of money, handing Flip five more dollars. "Aight gimme two dimes," Flip said placing the money through the hole. "And a plate of that jerk chicken," he amusingly added, drawing a chuckle from Butter and the guy behind the door.

After taking the money and pushing the two small puffy clear plastic zip lock bags through the hole, the guy corrected Butter before disappearing, "Nah Mon, curry chicken," he said.

"Jerk chicken," Butter mocked.

"I knew it was one of them mothafuckas," Flip retorted as

they walked away.

When they arrived back at the park, D-Mac had a c-low game going on amongst himself and a few fellas from the block.

"Ah shit," Flip said as he and Butter approached the circle of eight guys. "Who got the bank?," Flip asked.

"I got it," D-Mac answered while holding a small fortune in one hand as he rattled the dice in a clinched fist. He raised his fist above his head, "4,5,6, c-low on the dice!," he chanted as he lowered his fist close to the pavement and released the dice. After gliding two feet away, the three dice almost simultaneously came to a stop, but instead of displaying 4,5,6 — the numbers that would have made him an automatic winner, they revealed the numbers 1,2,3, making him an automatic loser.

"Gimme them shits," Flip said, picking the dice up from the ground. " Let me show you how to work 'em," he added.

"How yoouu get the bank?," one of the guys whined.

"Cause he sold it to me, Junior," Flip said, handing D-Mac some money to make it seem official. He then began rattling the dice in the same fashion as D-Mac had.

"What's up? All downs a bet. Point seen money lost," he said.

"How much in your bank?," two guys chorused.

Pulling money out of his pocket, Flip announced, "The bank is open. Whatever you bet I got it covered Junior." He rattled the dice.

C-low is a dice game that is most commonly played among friends that live in the same neighborhood. As long as you show money, getting in the game is never a problem. But getting out is something different. Any New Yorker who plays will agree that it's safest played in one's own neighborhood, but every once in a while someone might cross the path of a c-low game on a block other than their own, and if he's lucky he loses, because if he wins, he lost. Once a guy from Kingsbridge Avenue was visiting a friend that lived in 1839. He felt it would be all right to shoot a little dice with D-Mac and the crew, who were playing in front of the building.

"All downs a bet!," Wu said as he rattled the dice.

"I got twenty!," Kingsbridge said flashing a twenty dollar bill.

"Put it down. I said all downs a bet, Junior", Wu charged.

After seconds of rattling, all bets were placed. "I'm taking off," Wu said before releasing the dice.

Fifteen minutes later, Kingsbridge, who had the hot hand, was controlling the bank with a hundred and seventy-five dollars in it, including the twenty he started with. "Bet it up! Scared money don't make money!", Kingsbridge poetically chanted as he rattled the dice while bets were being placed.

"How much in the bank?," Wu asked.

"Fifty."

"Fifty?"

"Yeah Fifty," Kingsbridge repeated more boldly.

"It can't be fifty in the bank," D-Mac disdainfully interjected. "It was a buck seventy five last roll!"

The rule is, if the banker rolls 4,5,6 — c-low — he has the option of passing the bank and pocketing all his winnings, or he could keep the bank and cut it down to the amount of his choice.

"I hit c-low, Junior," Kingsbridge retorted somewhat hysterically.

"Yeah aight," D-Mac grimaced

Kingsbridge rattled the dice again. "Fifty in the bank! Fifty in the bank!," he repeated, watching as bets were being placed. After all bets were placed, he rolled the dice, cooing, "Baby needs some shoes!"

"BOP!", was the sound of D-Mac's fist colliding into Kingsbridge's jaw as he stooped down to roll the dice that were now smothered underneath his stretched out body.

"What's up?," Kingsbridge frantically wailed, curling into a fetal position as they all began stomping and kicking him.

"You know what's up! Gimme this loot!," D-Mac said, ripping off Kingsbridge's front jeans pocket.

The only thing the friend Kingsbridge had come to visit could do was help him up and into a cab after he was sure the beating was over. Since they were now playing in the park amongst each other, things would turn out different this time. It would be fun, and who ever won would get to keep the money. An hour passed, and after Flip wiped out everybody with the exception of Butter and D-Mac who he split the winnings with, they stood around in the park passing around the last of the three blunts they had been smoking.

"Ayo here come them two frontin' ass bitchez," D-Mac said,

drawing their attention to the two girls who were on their way down the block—apparently coming from school.

"Oh, take this," Butter said, handing D-Mac the blunt. "Im'ma bag one of them today," he said while moving toward the steps of the park as they neared.

"Hello. Yall ladies still not speaking?," D-Mac asked them. Smiling down on them, Butter was leaning against the short black fence at the top of the steps of the park's entrance.

In the same fashion they had been doing every time they walked through the block, the girls, who were engaged in conversation, continued slowly walking, never acknowledging Butter or his comments.

"Oh it's like that?," he said, neither upset nor surprised.

"Fuck them bitchez!," D-Mac blurted out loud enough for the girls to hear him. His remark caused one of the girls to stop dead in her tracks. She backed up a couple of steps.

"Excuse me?," she demanded, with her tan complexion reddening. "I know you didn't call me a bitch?," she questioned as her brown almonds glared from Butter to Flip, then to D-Mac. "I know yall mothafuckas ain't tryin' to play yall-selves!"

"Fuck outta here bitch!," D-Mac ordered while fanning his hand.

"Your mother a bitch!"

"What! I'll knock you the fuck out!," D-Mac said as he started toward the entrance of the park, visually upset. He didn't like the fact that she cursed his mother, though; he thought nothing of it when he cursed her.

"Chill yo!," Butter said as he grabbed D-Mac and tried to exit.

"Let that mothafucka go! He ain't gonna do shit to me!," she raved, clearly unfazed by his tantrum.

"Come on Li-s-a," the dark skinned girl pleaded, picking up Lisa's purple leather backpack while pulling her by the arm.

The weed, getting the best of D-Mac, had him worked up and the fact that Flip and Butter weren't concealing what they suddenly found amusing wasn't helping the matter.

"Yo, let me go. I ain't gonna fuck wit' that bitch," D-Mac said, appearing to gain his composure.

"You know what?," Lisa fumed, taking her book bag from her friend. "I'm playing myself for paying your faggot ass any mind. But I want you to act like you wan' it when my brother come to see you," she added as they began walking away.

"Ha! Ha!," D-Mac howled as if to appear amused. "Check this out. If your brotha come thru here looking for drama, he gonna get murdered!," he called-out to the girls' backs and the elevated middle finger that Lisa responded with.

His last words *"he gonna get murdered,"* may not have effected Lisa, but they went off like a fire alarm in Butter's head. His mind immediately raced back to the previous summer, when a girl that Wu had thrown juice on threatened that her brothers would come looking for him.

It was about seven o'clock when the brothers pulled up in front of the park. In the back seat of the four door smoke gray Cherokee sat the girl. Through the dark tinted windows her eyes anxiously searched for a familiar face — primarily Wu's.

"You see any of them?," the brother who was driving asked. All six eyes gazed into the park from behind the dark tint.

"No," she answered.

"Let's go up in there," he said reaching back to grab her red and black leather book bag. He took two 9- mm handguns out, giving one to his brother before tossing the bag back. They tucked the guns in their waist before stepping out of the jeep followed by their sister.

D-Mac and Butter were in the hallway of 1839 waiting on Wu, who was upstairs, and Flip was on his way down the block. The girl and her brothers were in the park. Her eyes fixed on the guys playing ball and her brothers eyes were glued on her.

"You don't see 'em?," one brother asked.

"You know what they look like, right?," the other brother asked before she could answer the first question.

The girl, visibly upset because none of them were around, turned to her brothers and with much attitude said, "Yeah I know what they look like! I don't fuckin' see 'em!," she said bitterly as her eyes became glassy.

As Flip got closer to 1839, he noticed the Jeep double parked in front of the park. His eyes then gazed at the three making their way down the steps of the park. He thought nothing of it at first, but then a split second later, the girl's familiar face dawned on him. "Oh shit!," he said. About thirty yards away from the building, he pulled his gun from his waist and held it down to his side as he picked up his pace, trying to make it to 1839. He was twenty yards away when she spotted him.

"There go one of them right there!," she shouted, pointing to the opposite side of the street at Flip. Without panic he slowed up as he moved closer to the parked cars with his gun concealed down by his side.

The girl got back into the Jeep as the two brothers began making their way across the street. Flip, now only five feet away from the building, had thoughts of making a dash for the door but he noticed the brothers who were half way across and reaching for their guns.

BOOM! BOOM! Without warning Flip aimlessly fired two shots, sending them ducking and sprinting for cover behind the jeep.

BOOM! BOOM! BOOM! BOOM! BOOM! the two brothers simultaneously returned fire at Flip who took cover behind the parked cars.

The roar of the guns sent the people in the park scattering and screaming. It also alarmed Butter and D-Mac who scrambled to the door's window. With eyes scanning, they spotted Flip squatting behind a car a few feet away, then D-Mac gazed to the Jeep. "That Jeep!," D-Mac said, pulling out his Mac-ten.

"They squeezing at Flip!"

Butter, not one for always carrying a gun, stood empty handed and watched as D-Mac slapped a clip in the gun. "I don't have my joint," Butter said.

"I got this! Meet us up at Wu's crib!," D-Mac said before he *cowered* out the door.

BRUGGGDA! BRUGGDA! RRUGGDA!, went a rainbow of shots flying at the jeep. D-Mac took cover a couple of feet away from Flip. The bullets ripped into the Jeep and surrounding parked vehicles, busting out windows and taillights.

"Hurry up, let's go!," the girl deliriously cried as the brothers managed to muddle back into the Jeep before recklessly driving off side swiping vehicles trying to elude the trail of bullets that tailed them.

The distant sound of police sirens sent Flip and D-Mac racing into the building next to 1839. They didn't want to bring heat to their hang out so they zoomed to the roof and climbed back over to 1839 entering the building and safely making it to Wu's apartment.

Like always, after the drama had ceased and all potential suspects had fled the scene, N.Y.P.D. were everywhere.

"Here, you wan' it or what?," D-Mac asked, breaking Butter's thoughts as he tried handing him the blunt.

"Nah," Butter said while making a rapid exit out of the park. I'll be back."

"Where you going?"

"To catch up with them girls," he answered.

"Don't sweat them bitches," D-Mac called-out before he and Flip laughed, giving each other five.

Wisely ignoring D-Mac's last comment, Butter proceeded to catch up with the girls who had not been walking much faster than they were before the commotion. "Lisa!," Butter called, now only steps behind them. He thought what happened last summer was senseless. An innumerable amount of people could've gotten hurt, even killed, over some weak ass drama, and if there was any chance of preventing a recast of the previous summer's melee, it would be through his attempt of rational input.

"You don't know me!," she snidely retorted after glancing back realizing it was Butter, a guy she'd just seen with her most hated person on earth—D-Mac.

"I'm sayin' I heard ya girl call you Lisa so I thought that was your name," he said walking along side of her. "My bad if it's not," he said as his eyes fixed on her beauty.

Though her golden tan complexion was still tarnished by the redness from her anger, he was able to see that she was certainly a cutie destined for gorgeousness in her many years to come.

"Look at you. You still hyped up. Ya girl was on some real cool shit."

"I'm not her," Lisa shot back, never turning to notice how he was appreciating looking at her deviant chemistry of feistiness embodied with beauty.

"Listen, that bullshit that happened back there in front of the park—my man was just buggin'. He—"

"He said he'll murder my people," she charged. "We'll see."

"See what I'm saying. Listen to yourself. Just check out the science," he said before painting her a picture. "Aight say you get your people and they come through looking for me and my peeps. They strapped, we strapped, and the shit goes down. Everybody's lettin' bullets fly," he said then paused for a second before continuing. "You right, we will see. I don't know if you or your peeps seen it before but I have, and trust me it's not a pretty sight. And it never adds up."

"Listen, what do you want?," she asked as the three of them came to a complete stop.

For you to be my girl, he wanted to say, but instead he replied, "I want you to cool out and give a little thought to what I just said."

Glaring into his face for the first time, she noticed the way his dark brown eyes complimented his light skin, and the low cut waves in his jet black hair that made him seem younger than his seventeen years. For a second, she wondered if he had even been in the world as long as her eighteen years? Though, his mature attitude diversified with his juvenile appearance sent a pleasant chill through her body extinguishing the fire that D-Mac's unwarranted comment ignited, it was not enough for her to pretend it didn't happen.

"That's it? Are you finished?," she asked with less sting in her tone of voice.

"Well not really," he hesitated for a split second. "I was wondering if I could have your number?," he said as his thin smile exposed the letter B engraved on the gold cap of his front tooth.

"My what?," she said glancing at her friend then fixing her gaze back to him. "I know you buggin'!"

"I'm not buggin'," he said with a widening smile as he surveyed both their faces. He suddenly noticed the indented prints of dimples on the dark skinned smooth face of Lisa's friend and her cut short stylish hair, that made her easy on the eyes also. "I'm tryin' to maybe take you and your girlfriend out to a movie or something. Oh my bad. By the way my name is Butter. I know you're Lisa and you're…?"

"Denise," she introduced herself before he turned colors.

"Denise," he huffed, before ogling his dark brown ones back on Lisa, whose face displayed a credulous glow. "Aight check this out," he said while writing his number down on a piece of paper that he pulled out of his baggy jean pocket. "I'll just give you my number and you call me if you decide that the movie would be better than drama."

"What if I've already decided on drama?," she asked, while ignoring his extended arm with the number in his hand.

"That's cool, give it to your peeps and they can call if we're not around...nah I'm just bullshittin'," he smiled.

"That's cute," she said sarcastically.

"We'll call you," Denise interjected as she snatched the paper from his hand. "Let's go girl."

"I'll be sittin' by the phone," he called out while walking backwards toward the park as they bounced in the opposite direction.

Chapter Four

Two warm afternoons later.

Flip, Butter and D-Mac were hanging out in front of 1839 taking turns dragging on a blunt, when they were accosted by a man who's physical appearance incontestably indicated drug addiction. Since the Special Drug Task Force, "TNT," shut down the crack dealing operation on Montgomery Avenue which was two blocks up from 1839, hundreds of their crack addict customers probed nearby neighborhoods in search of the drug, and the man that now stood in front of 1839 was undoubtedly an ex- Montgomery customer.

"Any work out here?," he asked while, looking for the drug that was sweeping through the urban ghettos with lightening speed, destroying both those who used it as well as those who sold it.

"Get the hell outta here!," D-Mac yelled kicking him in the ass, causing the man to almost stumble as he hurried off. The man had been the fifth crack head within the last four minutes to ask such a question.

"Ever since Jake locked up all them kids from Montgomery, them crack heads been runnin' around here like zombies," Butter commented.

"I'm sayin'. Wu said the kid he be fuckin' wit down on 42nd Street told him that this block is a gold mine. And if we wit it, he'll hit us off wit some work," D-Mac said.

"Yeah I heard they getting mad cheddar down on the deuce," Butter emphasized.

"Word," D-Mac agreed.

"That kid frontin'," Flip said. "He been sayin' that shit for weeks…," he added as their attention was drawn away by the music that suddenly filled the area.

"Here I am—R-A-W. A Terrorist here to bring trouble to," were the Big Daddy Kane lyrics that poured out of the red convertible Saab. The bass traveling through the pavement as it slowly made it's way down the block. In the front passenger side sat Wu, and driving was his man Uptown.

It was a couple of weeks after the Skate Key stick up when Wu met Uptown, who called himself that because he lived uptown in the Bronx.

One day while aimlessly strolling the always busy 42nd Street, Wu witnessed Uptown who was being chased by a cop, throw a black shaving size bag full of crack underneath a parked car.

Before other cops arrived, Wu, not knowing what was inside the bag, dashed to the car and retrieved it. On his way to the train station he opened it, only to see contents unfamiliar to him. Wu quickly closed the bag with the intentions of taking it back to the Bronx to show the fellas, but his plan floundered when Uptown, who had eluded the cop, recognized the bag.

"Ayo Shorty, let me get that," Uptown said as they boarded the train together. Uptown the tall slender brown skinned guy towered over the shorter, and startled, Wu. Immediately recognizing him, Wu handed him the bag. "Where you headed?," Uptown asked him.

"Back to the BX, " Wu answered.

"Where your momz at? You by yourself?," Uptown asked firing one question after the next.

"Yeah, I could handle myself," Wu answered defensively.

"I hear you Shorty. I hear you," Uptown said while jokingly throwing his hands in the air as if he were being stuck up.

Uptown took an instant liking to Wu's spunky attitude. He was also impressed with his courage to fetch the bag.

Uptown, coming out of his baggy jean pocket, handed Wu two hundred dollars, "Here you go Shorty."

Wu didn't hesitate to take the money, "Good lookin' out," he said.

"You wanna make some more of that?"

"Bet."

"Aight chill wit me," Uptown said as they gave each other five, and since that day Wu had been a part of Uptown's 42nd Street crack operation.

"Cause I get raw," Butter sang along with the song as Uptown made the U-turn pulling up in front of 1839. "That Kane shit is right," he said giving Wu five as he got out of the car.

Normally Uptown would drop Wu off, acknowledge the fellas with a nod, then peel off. This time he turned off the music, then closed the top of the windows and got out of the car. "What's up fellas?," Uptown said as he made his way onto the sidewalk. He was dressed in a pair of black Timberland boots, Guess jeans, and a black Champion sweat shirt that made the Run DMC style thick gold rope chain he wore around his scrawny neck shimmer.

"Aight," they responded together, the three of them numbed by the extravagant gold crucifix pendant that dangled from the rope, and the Wonder Woman-style gold nugget bracelet wrapped around his wrist.

"Let's go upstairs," Wu suggested as he went in the building followed by the rest of them.

The one bedroom fourth floor apartment that Wu and his mother lived in was small. As you entered the apartment you faced both, the dinning and living room, which was separated by what at one time could have been an orange-rust colored carpet that started where the dining room ended and the living room began. Off to the right of the dining room area was the kitchen, and off to the right of the living room area was the bathroom, followed by the bedroom. The apartment was scantly decorated with what looked like second, maybe even third, hand furniture. In the dining room, sat a dark brown oak dinner table with four wooden chairs. In the living room sat a three-cushion sofa, an oak coffee table, an oak one-cushion chair and a stereo.

"So what's up? You fellas ready to make moves or what?," Uptown asked, as he took a seat on the single-cushion chair now facing Flip. Butter and D-Mac were seated on the three-cushion sofa. After turning the stereo on at a low volume Wu pulled up one of the chairs from the dining room.

"We waitin' on you, " D-Mac replied.

"My bad. I know I had yall on hold for a minute, but it's on now," Uptown quipped before going into further details.

For the next hour Uptown sat around explaining to them how there was a lot of money to be made in the crack game. During the conversation he was informed by the fellas on the shut down of the Montgomery Avenue operation, which made it seem that much more urgent that they set-up the operation as soon as possible. "I'm saying," Uptown concluded, standing up as if to bring the briefing to an end, "Wu, you and Flip can come to my crib about seven tonight if yall wanna open up shop tonight."

After glancing over at Flip who nodded affirmatively, Wu answered, "Bet, we'll be there at seven."

"Aight cool," he said. Picking his Motorola cell phone up from the table, he gave everybody five before making his way toward the door as Wu followed. "Aight later."

"Later," Wu said closing the door behind him.

The poorly lit cloaked street that Uptown lived on was in one of the least busy sections of the Bronx. The expanded tan brick six story flat in which he lived, occupied the cramped block nearly in its entirety.

It was ten past seven when the cab made it's way up the narrow one-way street. The street was bulging with parked cars on both sides that belonged to both occupants of Uptown's building, and the identical building it faced on the opposite side of the street. "Ho! Right here," Wu said, directing the cab driver to stop in front of the building.

After paying the driver, Wu and Flip got out of the cab, then Wu led Flip to the building on the left side of the street. He pressed the intercom affixed to the metal panel on the right side of the building's secured glass and metal trimmed door.

"This joint probably don't even work," Wu commented as he mashed down on the button a second time.

"Call him from the window," Flip suggested after getting no

response to the buzzer.

Taking a couple of steps back, Wu tilted his head back with his hands cupped around his mouth and yelled, "Aaaaaay yo!" After no response seconds later he called again, 'Aaaaaay yo!" Still no response. "The nigga probably got the music pumpin'. Im'ma go around the corner and call him from the phone. Stay here in case somebody come out of the building."

"Aight," Flip said, backing away from the building.

Flip leaned against a parked car and watched as Wu disappeared around the corner. As his eyes viewed the area's darkness, he found it kind of amusing that what would be considered one of the more decent buildings in the Bronx had intercoms that didn't work.

"Aaaaaay yo!," Uptown called-out while looking down at Flip, as his head leaned out of the window.

"Yo!," Flip responded looking up as he raised up off the car.

"Pull the door! Im'ma hit the buzzer!," Uptown said.

"Aight!," Flip answered as he hustled to the door. Seconds later he was buzzed in.

"You got it?," Uptown's raspy voice came from the intercom's speaker.

"Yeah, I got it!," Flip replied as he held the door until Wu made it back from around the corner.

"Damn. Money must be the only one that lives in the building. Nobody came in or out the whole time I was out there," Flip whimsically commented as they walked past the elevator and headed for the stairs.

When they reached the fourth floor, they could hear the music throbbing from behind the closed door. Halfway down the hall, they could feel the vibration of the bass quaking as they neared. By the time they made it to the door, the music was replaced by the sounds of a barking dog as Uptown opened the door.

"What's up?," Uptown asked as they stepped into the apartment.

"Aight," they replied.

From the opened door, they stared down the hall at one of the two bedroom's interior doors. Entering the apartment, they noticed the kitchen and adjoining dining room on the immediate left while further down the hall was the living room, followed by the bathroom. In the blind spot around from the bathroom was the second bedroom. Unlike Wu's apartment, Uptown's apartment was roomy and live. Each room was extravagantly decorated with expensive furniture. In the dining room was a glass and gold metal-trimmed dining table with matching chairs, and in the living room was a three-piece leather cream sofa set with matching glass coffee and end tables.

"That joint was thumpin'," Wu commented on the music as they followed Uptown into the living room.

"Sit down, sit down," Uptown offered as he flopped onto the three-cushion sofa. "Ya'll want a Heineken or something?"

"Nah I'm aight," Wu said, sitting straight up with his back to the hall in the recliner sofa that faced the big screen TV and stereo system.

"Nah I'm straight," Flip answered, sitting on the two-cushion sofa facing Uptown.

Flip's eyes wandered around the room taking in the two keys of coke, one key of crack, and the triple beam scale that sat on the coffee table. His eyes then glanced behind Uptown where a beautiful poster sized portrait of Uptown hung on the wall. He was arm-in-arm with a very attractive women while they both held the hand of a seemingly happy baby on a stool.

"Im'ma give yall half of this pie," Uptown said, picking up the key of crack and drawing both of their attentions. "I'm gonna pay yall on a weekly salary for a minute, then when shit blow up we'll go seventy thirty," Uptown told them.

Though Flip knew little or nothing about the crack game, he knew when something didn't sound right, and thirty percent divided by four people definitely didn't sound right. The look he shot at Wu said it all. "I'm saying, it's four of us, we ain't gonna see nothin' off of thirty percent," Wu said as if he heard exactly what Flip was thinking.

"Yo trust me Duke, in a minute the block gonna be doin' two, three pies a day. It's gonna be enough dough for everybody," Uptown shot back.

Flip was content with the way Wu spoke up and since Wu knew more about the game than him, he would go along with whatever Wu decided.

"Aight," Wu conceded.

Leaving the key of crack that filled a giant clear zip lock bag on the table, Uptown took the two keys of coke and disappeared to the bedroom. Quickly returning, he placed numerous packs of clear, empty crack vials, a large silver platter, and a few packs of single edge razor blades on the table. He then began weighing the crack—shaped like pancakes—until the scale displayed five hundred grams. "While I chop it up, yall bottle them up," Uptown said, gesturing to the empty vials while brushing the five hundred grams off the scale and onto the platter. "Let's go in the dining room," he added knowing more space would be needed.

Uptown was carrying the platter with two hands, followed by Flip and Wu who were totting all the vials. Uptown led them to the dining room table where they sat down and began to work. As fast as Uptown was chopping the pancakes down to pebble sized pieces, they were stuffing them inside ¾ inch clear plastic vials before sealing them with green caps and placing them into sandwich sized zip lock bags.

"Put a hundred in each bag," Uptown instructed. The team worked silently and rapidly, and in less than two hours they had managed to bag up twenty packs. Though, there were still ounces of crack left on the platter, Uptown felt what they had ready, would be enough to start with. Besides, it was getting late.

"Yo grab them," Uptown instructed. Clutching as many packs as he could, Uptown gestured for them to get the rest before leading them back into the living room.

After unloading everything on the table, Uptown retrieved a small calculator off the end table and they all sat down in the same seating arrangement they'd used before going into the kitchen. Uptown mumbled the figures out as he played with the calculator. "Five dollars a bottle,.... times.... a hundred.... equals five hundred.... times.... twenty packs. Ten G's," he concluded.

"Yeah," Flip agreed, doing his own calculation as Uptown began stuffing the packs into a black leather backpack that was on the other end of the table. "Yo who that?," Flip asked, drawing their attention to the sound of dangling keys unlocking the door.

"That's Cookie, his wife," Wu answered.

"Don't worry Duke, ain't nobody comin' up in here," Uptown said as he heard the door close and lock.

Seconds later, Cookie appeared holding a finger straight up across her lips, gesturing for them to be quiet. "He's sleep," she whispered after leaving the carriage in the hall. Wearing a pair of black denim fitted jeans laced with Louis Vuitton pockets that showed every curve, a pair of small Louis Vuitton boots, and a brown tee shirt with Mike Tyson's picture on it, she ran her hand through Wu's silky hair as if he were a five year old, while she passed him to give Uptown a kiss. Wu was like a little brother to both Cookie and Uptown, who were eleven years older than his seventeen years. After learning he had no family, they welcomed him with open arms.

"What's up Sis?," Wu asked almost whispering as he flashed his boyish smile. "This my man Flip," he said to her.

"Hi," she smiled.

"Hi," Flip half grinned. He couldn't help but glance up at the photo as he compared her to it. Though, she was dressed far less elegantly now compared to the full length red dress with a long split on both sides that she wore in the photo, she was no less gorgeous. *The face of a cover girl? The body of a Playmate? And dressed like a thug? What more could a man want?,"* Flip thought.

"Yall want something to eat?," she asked bringing Flip out of his thoughts.

"Nah I'm good."

"No thanks."

"I'm straight," Uptown, Flip and Wu answered in the same low tone.

Cookie stepped back into the hall and as she began to push the carriage towards the bedroom, the barks of the dog instantly awoke the baby. "Shit! Shut the hell up Rocky!," she yelled as she picked up the wailing baby and placed him in his crib in the second bedroom.

After checking to make sure that all twenty packs were in the backpack, Uptown stood up, followed by Wu and Flip.

"Huhn," Uptown said as he handed the bag to Wu. "Bring it back when you come to re-up."

"Aight," Wu answered.

"Beep me as soon as it's finished and I'll let you know what time to meet me here," he said while walking them to the door.

"Aight," Wu answered again.

"Later," Flip said.

"Later," Uptown replied before closing the door and securing it behind them.

Uptown then turned into the kitchen, took a giant zip lock bag out of one of the cabinets and placed the remaining crack into it before carrying it back toward the first bedroom where his wife met him. "Did you feed Rocky yet?," she asked as she opened their bedroom door.

"Nah. I'll feed him now. Put this in the safe," Uptown said as he handed her the bag.

The dark gray Rottweiler raced out into the living room, then into the kitchen in search of the strangers who'd been in the apartment while he was locked in the bedroom. After realizing that they were gone, he sat in the hall in front of the kitchen's doorway and watched while Uptown dumped dog food out of a fifty pound bag and into his big gray bowl labeled 'Rocky'. "Here you go boy," Uptown said as he sat the bowl in the hallway.

After walking three blocks over to Fordham road, it took no time for Wu and Flip to flag down one of the many cabs that galloped up and down the not so busy street during the night.

"It's on Duke," Flip exclaimed as the cab turned up one street and down another.

"I don't think we should crank it up tonight," Wu who was clearly not as excited said.

"Why?"

"I'm sayin' we gotta get pitchers an…"

"Pitchers?," Flip's puzzled voice interrupted.

"A nigga that's gonna stand out there and make the money drug transactions while we watch," Wu explained. "Plus we need look outs, a stash crib and the whole shit. That shit'll be ill if we just open up shop on some rush shit. Trust me, them crack heads gonna be like flies on shit."

Flip knew that Wu was talking from experience so it took no time for him to agree, "I hear you", he said.

From the park, D-Mac and Butter watched as they got out of the cab in front of 1839. After quickly crossing the street, the four of them went up to Wu's apartment. "We put the word out. The heads is fienin'," D-Mac said as they all took a seat in the living room.

"We not gonna open tonight," Wu said bringing a slight look of disappointment to the face of D-Mac, but not Butter, who really didn't care one way or the other. He rolled with the numbers.

"Why? What's up?," D-Mac questioned.

"We gotta find somebody to sell for us, unless you trying to do hand-to-hand combat. Cause I know I ain't sellin' a nigga shit," he looked at Flip before continuing. "You trying to do hand-to-...?"

"Hell no!," Flip jumped, before Wu could finish his question.

"What about you?," Wu asked, looking at the distorted disapproval on Butter's face before looking at D-Mac. "My man. What you trying to do?"

"I don't give a fuck. I'll sell all them shits."

"Yeah right," Wu amusingly replied as he reached for the bag that sat on the table. He pulled out a pack and removed three capsules. "Yo, let's go downstairs and give these samples out," Wu said.

"How much are they?," Butter quizzed as he held his hand out to get a better look at the two off-white pebbles that sat in each bottle. Though they were familiar with the term crack, this was Butter, D-Mac and Flip's first night actually seeing it.

"Five," Wu answered.

"Say word! These little joints is five dollars?," Butter asked while dropping them into the palm of D-Mac's extended hand.

"All day long," Wu replied as they headed for the door.

The thought of what would be their share of the take was the furthest thing from D-Mac and Butter's minds. Unlike Wu and Flip who were in it for the money, this was an action thing for D-Mac, and more of a groupie thing for Butter, Flip's protege.

The team stood in front of the building with their eyes scanning into the darkness as they studied the faces of people passing by in search of potential crack heads. A few minutes went by. "Damn, where all of them go?," Flip asked.

"D-Mac chased them away," Butter said with a chuckle, causing them to glance at D-Mac.

Knowing that crack heads can be pesky most of the time, and D-Mac's lack of tolerance combined with a gun happy attitude, Wu knew he'd better say something about D-Mac gaining more self-con-trol. "Yo duke. You gotta chill wit the Rah, Rah shit. Shit aw'ready gonna be crazy enough."

"Word," Flip agreed.

"My bad," D-Mac said, not wanting to let the fellas down.

"Yo Ike, c'mere for a second," D-Mac said drawing their attention to the dingy, scrawny light-skinned guy who came out of the building next to 1839. Ike lived on the block his entire thirty-seven years. He was once known as the best car mechanic in the area, working out of a tiny garage he owned on Webster Avenue. But between slow business and his crack habit, his business faltered. After losing his garage, in efforts to support his addiction, he roamed around in constant search of vehicles in distress with hopes that his services would be needed.

"Yeah what's up? The Volvo fucked up?"

"Nah," D-Mac chuckled. "We want you to check out some-thin'," he said while taking a vial from Wu and dropping it in Ike's engine-greased palm. "Oh bet," Ike said as his disfigured face lit up.

"We need two more people," Wu said, showing Ike the other two samples.

"Oh give 'em him here. I'll find somebody!"

"Yeah right."

"Hey Debra," Ike called stopping two women who were walking past. "C'mere. They want yall to try something," he said as they came over.

Debra was a tall brown-skinned woman with reddish-brown wavy hair that fell undone at shoulder length. Her haggard body still held its curves, unlike her short round-shaped light-skinned friend. It was plain to see that not too long ago, Debra had possessed beauty. "Check out what," she asked softly as her dark brown eyes briskly examined their faces.

It was obvious from the look on Butter, D'Mack and Flip's faces. They were stunned that Debra was a crack head. Wu on the other hand wasn't surprised in the least. After all, he had seen plenty of Debra's down on 42nd street.

"Huhn," Wu gestured as he gave each of the women a sam-ple.

"Listen, we gonna go up the block. We'll meet across the street in front of the park in ten minutes aight," he said, then watched as they nodded yes before hurriedly pacing towards Ike's building.

On their way up the block they decided to walk around the corner to the smoke pot. Instead of making a quick return to the block after buying the weed, they paraded through a couple of neighborhoods while passing the two lit blunts back and forth to each other.

Twenty minutes passed. The team made their way back towards their block. As they came around the corner, Ike met them. "There yall go," he huffed after spotting them. "I thought you said ten minutes," he said charged up, back pedaling in front of them.

"Don't be running up on us," D-Mac warned brushing him to the side. "And didn't we say in front of the park," he added as they continued to slowly pace.

"I know. I know. But yall got some more of that? I got a bunch of customers waitin' in the park," Ike said as he directed their attention to the mob of patrons that idled in the park's darkness.

"It's about thirty heads over there!," D-Mac said as the five of them came to a complete stop with their gazes viewing the park.

"I had them waitin' over there for a minute. It was more than that. They left but they'll be back, because Phellin Place and Davidson don't have work."

"Hol' up," D-Mac said as he gestured for Ike to back off as they huddled.

"I'm saying. Phellin Place and D-Street don't have work and Montgomery is shut down. We need to open up shop tonight. All that pitcher shit—I'll pitch them shits," he said with a grilling look. "Matter of fact, we can let Ike pitch," D-Mac suggested.

They all looked to Wu as he pondered the situation. He knew the most important reason that he didn't want them to rush into opening the operation was because without a pitcher it would mean one of them would have to do it. And that one would be taking a serious risk of selling to undercover cops that often posed as crack addicts to make a bust. But if Ike was willing to do it—like Wu was quite sure he would be—that would eliminate the biggest problem. As far as the minor problems, such as the look-outs and a place to stash the money and drugs that would be something they could get by with for the moment. "So what's up?," D-Mac asked as his question penetrated Wu's thoughts.

"Yo Ike," Wu responded.

"Yeah. What's up boss," Ike leapt up off a parked car and shot to the huddle.

"You wanna work?"

The only job Ike had ever known was fixing cars, so the question left him darkened. "What chew mean?," he asked.

"I mean pitch."

"You want me to pitch?," he repeated with astonishment. He was hoping for a free bottle or two for gathering all the customers, but being asked to pitch, it was almost too much to swallow. He had been on the receiving end for God knows how many times, and now to be the one dishing it out and knowing it would be rewarding for him at the end. He could think of nothing else he'd rather be doing. "Hell Yeah!," Ike answered rubbing his hands together like he was lotioning them.

"A'ight. Go tell 'em five minutes. And stay in the park until we come," Wu instructed.

"Got chew," Ike said before speeding off.

On their way down the block, Wu began explaining the best way he thought they should run the business. He was the only one with experience, so the others intently absorbed his every direction.

Wu ran upstairs as the team waited in front of the building for him. He promptly returned stuffing a pack in his front pocket. Then he led them across the street.

"Ike!," Wu called as they stood outside of the park.

"What's up baby?," he replied as he was coming down the steps.

"Check this out. Serve this pack. When you finish, give the money to him," Wu said as he gestured to D-Mac. "He's gonna be in the park with you and he's strapped, so you don't have to worry about nobody trying to stick you up." Wu paused as he watched Ike nod his head slowly. "Us three got yall covered out here. Butter gonna be halfway up the block, Flip gonna be halfway down the block, and I'm gonna be right here. If you hear one of us yell 'Jake' just break the line up until they roll past, aight?"

"Sounds good to me," Ike said.

"Aight let's work," Wu said, causing them to break out of the huddle like a football team on third and goal.

It took less than two hours to get rid of fifteen packs. Every time Ike finished one, he gave D-Mac the money. D-Mac in return would give it to Wu. Wu would then race up to his apartment and put the money away before returning with another pack.

The reoccurring line moved placidly and rapidly. By the time Ike was about done with the sixteenth pack, there was no longer a line. Customers were straggling in—one here, two there. Wu decided that it was time to close up.

"Ayo, D!", Wu called-out into the blackness.

"Yeah what's up?," D-Mac asked while looking down at him.

"Ask Ike how much he got left."

"Yo I need some more," Ike said as he walked up on their conversation, answering Wu's questions without realizing it. "I got two people waitin'. They want ten bottles and I only have three left," he said as his beady eyes shifted from D-Mac to Wu.

"Nah that's it. Shut it down," Wu said as he made his way up the steps and into the park. "It's goin' on one o'clock."

"It's still early," Ike commented. "And nobody got nothin'. I can move ten more packs easy," he said placing a wad of money and the three bottles in Wu's extended hand.

We don't have ten packs left? Wu thought to himself, *and the four we do have we gonna need for the morning crowd.* "Nah, tell him we're out," Wu said paying Ike a hundred dollars and the three bottles. "You can sell 'em those if you want. That's up to you," Wu added as he and D-Mac headed out of the park.

"How you say it boss? 'Yeah right'," Ike amusingly replied watching them make their exit. "You want me to be here in the morning?," Ike asked while hunching over the fence from the top of the steps.

"Yeah!" Wu answered.

"What time?"

"I don't know! Just be out here early!"

"Okay bet!" Ike yelled as they crossed the street.

The fact that they sold six thousand dollars worth of crack in less than two hours had the four of them baffled. Not even Wu expected that type of output on opening night. It was the most money any of them had been that close to in their young lives. Though, Wu had been around a lot of money when he hustled down on 42nd Street, he wouldn't have it for more than a minute before he'd pass it on to Uptown, and even then, it would be one,
two thousand at the most.

"We gonna be paid," D-Mac commented as they sat around in Wu's living room taking turns counting the money.

"Word. But that look-out shit is whack," Butter complained, slouching down in the single chair. "Standing there watching buses and shit go by," he added.

"Word. That is some bullshit," D-Mac agreed.

"Well, you rather pitch," Wu asked.

"Nah, we aight," Butter answered with a chuckle.

During the next few weeks, things got kind of hectic. The team quickly found out that running a crack spot wasn't just a headache, it was almost endless work, and without strict opening and closing hours they would have little time to do much of anything else, namely enjoying the money they were making. But things got a little easier once they hired one of Ike's smoking partners and broke the operation into shifts with set opening and closing hours. It allowed them more free time to themselves.

By the end of the summer, it was a beautiful thing. They were moving sixty packs a day and their individual pay fluctuated between five and seven thousand a week. It was enough to change the young boys' whole lifestyles.

They each had pagers and rigged cell phones. Though they still bought their Uptown Nike Air's and Timberland boots from Jewman, they had their clothes made by Dapper Dan, the Harlem seamstress that practically became rich by taking name brand materials such as Louis Vuitton, Gucci, and Fendi, then customizing them into outfits. Around their necks they sported big gold chains with huge pendants, and on their wrists and fingers were three-inch wide nugget bracelets and matching nugget rings.

Hampstead Publishing

Chapter Five

The last day of summer.

The gusty cool air and steadily pouring rain made the dull Saturday afternoon look like it was eight o'clock in the evening. The day had Butter and Lisa feeling more like it was the end of fall as they came out of the Loews Cineplex Movie Theater on Eighty Fourth Street.

Thanks to Butter's speech, and a heap of persuasion from Denise, Lisa was able to cool off and come to her senses after the night of the park incident. She had concluded that Butter's gesture was a nice one and made the wiser choice of the date he offered rather than the war he tried to avoid. Two days after that batty scene she called Butter. They hooked up that same weekend, and had been dating each other regularly. They also managed to hook Flip up with Denise.

"Hold this," Butter said while handing Lisa his white and Blue MCM pouch as they stood underneath the theater's mounted chart to keep from getting soaked. Seconds later he raced out into the street, stopped a taxi and hopped into it leaving the door open for Lisa who raced over and threw herself in before slamming the door behind her.

"Hey take it easy wit my door!" the dark Haitian driver bickered in his heavy accent.

His comment caused Lisa to instantly stop giggling which quickly angered Butter. "Fuck that door! Take us up to the Bronx!," Butter barked as he stared at the driver fixedly.

The driver slammed the car in park. "What do you mean? This is my cab!," he stated. "No. No. I don't take you nowhere! Please. Get out!," he said.

"Yo money, I'll tear this bullshit cab up if you don't get me up in the Bronx!," Butter threatened before slamming his balled up hand against the car's fiberglass partition.

"No. No I call the police," the driver fumed as he snatched his CB receiver.

"Come on baby," Lisa interjected while grabbing Butter's hand.

"Fuck that! I'm not going back out there!," he said, pulling his hand away. "He gonna take us Uptown!"

"No. No I call the police," the cab driver wailed, blabbering into the receiver.

Lisa, knowing Butter occasionally carried a gun inside his pouch, swept his attention by tugging at the bottom of his leather white and blue MCM jacket while directing his scrutiny to the bag she still held onto. "Let's go boo," she pleaded while opening the door.

Lisa slid out and immediately stalled a taxi that a couple had just gotten out of. Butter slid out behind her, leaving the door wide open and dived in the other cab nearly on top of a chuckling Lisa.

"Uptown. The Bronx," he told the Hispanic driver. He held his middle finger out the cracked window as they passed the Haitian's car.

As the cab made its way onto the Westside highway, Lisa looked over to Butter, who hadn't said a word since he told the driver where they were going. "Now was all that necessary?," she asked in a low sexy tone while lightly tugging at the big lion head pendant that dangled from his thick rope chain. After receiving a silent stare, she raised her lips closer to his ear and whispered, "You mad at me? "

Butter's anger quickly began to dissolve as he felt her hand rubbing the inside of his leg while the tip of her tongue flirted with the bottom of his earlobe. She then began to seductively caress his neck with her lips as her hand neared his penis, which was standing at full attention.

Not wanting a hickey, Butter slyly turned his lips to meet Lisa's as their tongues explored each other's mouths. Though, this was the furthest Butter usually got, it never stopped him from always trying to advance to home plate. He ran his hand up along the outside of her denim skirt, caressing her thigh as her hand ran once over his erection. He slowly motioned his hand down halting at the bare skin before sliding it up under her skirt. He could hear her lightly grunting as his fingers flirted outside the wetness of her panties. She let out a faint crow at the thought of them making out in the back of the taxi. Just as his fingers were about to enter where they had never been before, they were torn apart by the driver's call.

"We're in the Bronx Sir?," he asked in well spoken English as he focused on the giant green sign that read 'Cross Bronx Expressway ¼ mile.' "You did say the Bronx?," he asked while glancing back at the obviously anguished expression that blanketed Butter's face and the amused face of Lisa's.

Just drive mothafucka, Butter wanted to blow up, but instead he let out a long hiss and answered, "Yeah man. Exit right here. We going to Lorin' Place. You know where that is? "

"Yes. Yes," he answered, before he accelerated.

Lisa, who lived on Tiebout Avenue, didn't have to ask Butter why were they going back to his house so early. She knew what was on his mind. After all, she had started it like she had done a couple of times before, but this time she was ready to go all the way and in her soft sexiest voice she asked, "Did your mother and them come back?"

"Nah, they still in Florida—ho! Right here," Butter said as he directed the driver to stop in front of his house and paid before they sprinted out into the rain.

They were drenched before they made it up the short flight of steps and under the house's canopy. The little beige one family house was posted in the middle of the block in between a row of similar sized homes.

Butter and Lisa entered the front door, which led to a tight hallway that took them to another door. Once they entered the second door they were in the neat, well-furnished living room.

Butter wasted no time. He grabbed Lisa by the lower waist,

drew her to him and they began carrying on just as they were when they were in the taxi. Except this time, in chorus, they peeled the wet clothing off of one another. Seconds later he was easing her fully developed naked body past the living room and into the second bedroom on the left.

"MAKE-IT-LAST-FOREVER!," was the Keith Sweat jam that subdued his room. Butter couldn't thank 98.7 Kiss FM enough for its dedication to classic soul and R&B as they passionately kissed while exploring each other's sexually aroused bodies with uncontrollable roaming hands. Lisa eased herself onto the king size bed while pulling Butter down to her. She cocked her legs wide open while on her back. Butter, concentrating on caressing her nipples with his tongue, hovered over her. He then lowered his pelvis unresistingly as she firmly captured his erection in her hand and guided him inside her.

"SSS!" she inhaled throwing both hands back and clenching the sheets in her little fists as he began stroking into her gently, picking up speed with every flourish. Her body taking every inch of him as the hairs surrounding his genitals entwined with hers, her legs wrapping around his lower back as they picked up speed. Faster, harder, faster, harder, slowing down after several minutes of stimulus motions until they simultane-ously released the sensuous juices of life, each of them pausing every time their grind came together as one until both of their faucets were no longer dripping.

He rolled over on his back looking up at the ceiling while she lay cuddled next to him, fondling him with one hand. She wanted some more and her tongue swam inside his mouth until his dick got hard as logwood. She climbed on top of him as if he was a horsy ride at a carnival and rode him like she had put a dollar fifty in his ass.

By six thirty that evening the rain had fizzled away but the block was still deserted like it had been all day — all week to be exact since the coke drought that stagnated several big suppli-ers left many players sidelined.

At first Flip, who had just made it back from his car dealer in Brooklyn, was appreciative of the drought. He felt they need-ed a little break from the sometimes seemingly non-stop action surrounding the game. But, after the first two days, he found himself fiendin' to sell cracks just as bad as the drug addicts wanted to smoke it. His appetite for the money grew larger each day, that's why, unlike Wu, Butter, and D-Mac who spent their week off splurging through out the city, Flip was on a sly hunt for a coke supplier.

"Whomp! Whomp!," went the sound of Flip's Honda Accord horn as he and Denise came to a double parked stop in front of D-Mac's house. Minutes later D-Mac made his way out.

"What's up Duke," D-Mac said as he slid in the back of the white sedan.

"Aight. What's up," Flip responded, with an extended hand and gave him five. "Anything yet?"

"Nah," Wu said. "Hopefully tonight."

"Word. Aight. What's up with Butter?"

"I ain't seen money all day. He probably at the crib."

"Aight. Yo Im'ma drop her off and then meet you at Wu's rest."

Ever since Lisa and Denise had been seeing Butter and Flip, they had nothing good or bad to say about—or to—D-Mac, and by the same token he did not acknowledge them either.

"Aight," D-Mac replied while opening the door.

"Call Butter and tell him to meet us there," Flip added.

"Aight," D-Mac said before closing the door and heading back in the house.

Flip peeled off. He dropped Denise off in front of her building on Tiebout Avenue, made a U-turn and headed back towards the block. His demeanor was both fervent and urgent. His dealer had hooked him up with a potential supplier and he wanted to consult with the fellas before making a move. When Flip hopped out of the car he was met by Butter, who came from up the block, and they went to Wu's crib.

"Time Keep On Ticking...Ticking...Ticking..." was the EPMD sound that flooded the hall as Butter and Flip entered the apartment. "What's up?," Wu asked with a tone that rose a peek above the music as he closed the door behind them.

Wu had refurbished the apartment. His dining room and coffee tables were now glass. His sofa set was leather, and his big screen TV and stereo system were a high-end product of Mitsubishi. It was still a far climb from Uptown's crib, but it was a start.

"Aight," they both sounded as their heads bobbed in rhythm

with the thundering bass.

"Roll this up," Butter said as he flung a nickle bag and a blunt over to D-Mac who sat in the reclining sofa, before he himself flopped down on the three-cushion sofa. D-Mac caught the items and tossed them to Wu, who took a seat in the two-cushion chair.

"You roll better than me," D-Mac said.

Butter, cutting his gaze at D-Mac before springing up, uttered "Nah! Nah!" They all knew Wu liked sprinkling coke or crack in his blunts before rolling them. "I'll do it! That nigga wanna make a whoola!," Butter said as he rushed over to retrieve the weed.

"Oh word, I forgot this nigga be smokin' those shits," D-Mac chuckled.

Wu, who believed that a whoola was equal to smoking some potent weed, shot back, "I wasn't gonna put none in there." He let out a little chuckle of his own as Butter made it back over to his seat with the marijuana.

Flip, the only one in the room without a smile, turned the music down a couple of notches before getting right to the issue. "I found a connect," he vigorously stated, with his eyes sweeping their disconcerted faces.

"A connect?," D-Mac echoed.

"Yeah. I was talking to my man. This nigga got it like Al Pacino."

The four of them had built a good relationship with Uptown, but Wu's ties were a lot stronger. The thought of cutting out his man didn't set well. "We can't do that. What about Uptown?," Wu asked while sitting straight up.

"What about him," Flip's eyes searched D-Mac and Butter's faces. "The nigga ain't got no Coke."

"He said tonight," Wu defended, as Butter and D-Mac sat quietly watching and listening to the debate.

"He been sayin' that shit all week. Besides this is our chance to take it to the next level," Flip grasped all their attention as he began unloading what had been on his mind for several weeks. "We can cook and bottle our own shit up. And instead of making him house money while we make sneaker money, we can start seeing house money ourselves. Yo Wu, I know that's your man, but we famm and that nigga been jerkin us. We aint got paid more than seven thousand a week and we all sat here and counted crazy G's for this nigga."

"He said he was gonna hit us off with sixty-forty," Wu defended.

"Come on with that sixty-forty shit, Duke!," Flip said as his tone turned bitter. "He was supposed to have been hittin' us off with that. Yo, look at us. Yeah we running around here all geared out in our Gucci and Fendi shit, the trunk jewels. But that nigga is heavy. He rockin' Cuban links, pushin' the new BMW and a Ford Runner."

"Word. And the nigga got two mean eleven hundred Suzuki bikes," D-Mac threw in.

"Look at that shit," Flip said, taking the microphone back. "What we got? I got a bullshit Honda Accord that I'm almost finished paying for and yall niggas on foot patrol. Come on, how we livin' Duke?" The ringing of the phone interrupted him.

"Turn that down a little," Wu said to Flip as he reached for the phone, "Hello."

"Yo. I'll be ready by eight thirty," Uptown uttered.

"Aight bet," Wu said before hanging up. "That was him. "

"What he said?," Butter eagerly asked.

Wu, knowing Flip wouldn't be too thrilled with the news, concealed his excitement and answered, "It's on at eight-thir-ty."

Wu's response caused all eyes to travel to Flip.

"Yo, it's like this," Flip said in an even tone. "We famm, and if you wanna keep getting down like this, I'm wit' it."

Wu knew Flip was speaking the truth. He even thought about how unfair they had been treated but he never brought it up because he didn't want to rattle the cage. He appreciated the life Uptown gave him a chance at and didn't know how to separate business from personal feelings.

"Check this out," Wu said attempting to buy Uptown some time to play fair. "I just don't wanna cut the nigga off. That shit is bad business. I think we should move what he got for us now, and when we finish, we all go up there with the money and have a sit down. Let him know, we out if he don't come correct."

"Yeah that sounds good," D-Mac said.

"Whatever," Butter followed.

"I told you. I'm wit whatever yall wit," Flip said as they eyed him.

"Aight cool," Wu said trying to be appeasing.

Wu glanced at his watch and realized that eight-thirty was only an hour away. "I been up all day. Im'ma crash out for a little bit because I know shit gonna be going on all night."

"Word. Those jum heads gonna drive a nigga crazy tonight," D-Mac added as they made their way to the door.

"You got that?," *Wu* said, asking Flip to take one of them with him to pick up the work.

"Yeah. Butter and me gonna bounce up there," he responded on his way out the door.

"Aight cool," Wu said before closing the door.

At eight fifteen, Butter spotted the bright fog lights of Flip's Accord as it rolled slowly toward his house. When it came to a complete stop, he gave Lisa, who stood at the doorway wearing one of his big shirts like a dress, a quick kiss before dashing to the car. Though, she couldn't see through the car's dark tinted windows, she waved hello to Flip just in case he was looking her way. Flip let the window halfway down and returned her greeting before peeling off.

Like always, Flip parked on Fordham road. He and Butter walked one block over to Uptown's building where they stood in front pressing the buzzer. Getting no response, Flip used his Motorola cell phone and called upstairs. After the fourth ring, the throbbing base of P.E.'s Public Enemy Number One momentarily blitzed his ear. "Damn Duke! You tryin' to blow a niggas ear up?," Flip joked after Uptown turned the music down.

"My bad. I'm up here trying to do three things at one time. Im'ma hit the door."

"Aight," Flip said before hanging up.

"That nigga got a ass kickin' system up there," Butter added as they were buzzed in.

"Word to miz," Flip agreed.

When they got to Uptown's floor, they could feel the vibration of the music as they neared. Just as they arrived at the door, it opened letting all the music escape. It was like entering the Skate Key—music everywhere.

Flip couldn't understand how Uptown hadn't gotten thrown out of the building for noise pollution. Flip's tone was a notch higher than the music. "Your neighbors don't be riffin'?," Flip asked. "Man I take care of damn near everybody in this moth-afucka," Uptown replied leading them into the living room. "You niggas want a wine cooler or something?," he offered, turning the music down a notch.

"I'm good," Butter answered, taking a seat in the recliner with his back to the hall.

"I'm straight," Flip said, sitting in the two-cushion sofa across from Uptown.

All three of them were focused on the two and a half keys of coke and the half key of crack that sat chopped up on the silver platter on the top of the table.

"We'll finish bottling this half of brick up so we can put somethin' on the street until I cook the rest of this up for yall," Uptown said as they kneeled down to the table and started helping him stuff and pack the capsules.

The drought had caused the price of coke to skyrocket from eighteen-five to twenty-six thousand a key, and because it had affected Uptown, he had to let them know that it was going to affect them as well.

"Yall know this shit went up? So it's gonna hurt our pock-ets for a minute," Uptown said.

Nigga, you been hurtin' our pockets, Flip wanted to say. The sight of all the jewelry Uptown had on, combined with the lux-ury that surrounded his living quarters and the drugs that laid on the table, caused the rage that Flip illustrated in Wu's apart-ment to resurface. It was getting to the point where he could no longer look at the guy who he felt was pimping them. But because he agreed with what the fellas had planned, he man-aged to get a grip.

"Yo I gotta take a leak," Flip said rising up.

"You know where the bathroom at," Uptown said. "Go 'head. Nobody in there."

Flip disappeared around the wall that separated the living room from the hallway. On his way into the bathroom he could hear and sense Rocky' s rage as the dog barked and scratched at the door. "Shut the fuck up," he mumbled shut-ting the door.

Flip scanned the bathroom as he took a leak. *"This bathroom cost a few G's,"* he thought to himself as he viewed all the marble and gold that dressed the bathtub sink and toilet bowl. As he flushed, he couldn't help but wonder what a guy with Uptown's kind of money was doing still living in this apartment, this building, this neighborhood as a matter of fact. He then felt his anger building as he thought about the statement Uptown made about hurting their pockets.

He tried to chuckle it away as he threw the cold running water on his face. He froze in the mirror over the sink as his thoughts compared the thick hollow rope chain he had on, to the three thick solid link chains Uptown sat in the living room wearing. His rage instantly shot to the roof of his head, and the hotter his body got, the colder his eyes became. He tried throwing more water on his face but it did nothing to stop him from becoming overheated. Flip mechanically pulled his glock from his waist, cocked it, and like a robot exited the bathroom.

Boom! Boom! Boom! All Butter could see when he unburied his head from his knees was Uptown's body bent halfway backwards on the sofa. Butter was left frozen. He didn't twitch until two more shots drew his attention.

Boom! Boom! Flip put two in Rocky through the closed door. When he came around the corner his cold stare was met by Butter's blank stare.

What was going on had yet to register in Butter's head as he remained motionless in his kneeled position while his eyes followed Flip over to the stereo. Flip couldn't find the power switch so he just turned it down.

Flip then turned to Butter and barked, "What the fuck you waitin' for?!" Then he dropped to his knees and began stuffing the bag with the drugs. "Yo snap out of it Duke!," he shouted to Butter.

On that note Butter returned to earth. He, too, moved closer to the table and began tossing drugs into the bag. After taking everything but the half key of powder off of the table, Flip moved to Uptown's lifeless body and reached for the gold chains. But before he could feel the metal, he and Butter were frozen by the sound of keys jangling at the front door.

"Cookie," Butter whispered as their wide eyes met.

Flip handed Butter the bag then floated around to the door.

Seconds later, it opened. "Get in here!," Butter demanded as he gripped Cookie, snatching her by the chest area of her colorful leather eight ball jacket she sported. The force of his pull sent the baby carriage that was in front of her rolling in the apartment as her body hovered over it before she hit the floor. He closed the door, then dragged her while pushing the wailing baby further into the apartment. "Get up!," Flip demanded as his tug helped her to her feet.

Cookie's emotions began to unravel as she quickly came to grips with what was happening. Her face began to swell and her eyes became glassy at the site of Uptown's twisted body. "Oh my God!," she whimpered as the reality of her life ending rapidly began to sink in. "Please....!," she cried.

"Shut up!," Flip viciously replied, pulling her along as he headed towards her bedroom.

Using his shoulder strength, Flip pressed on the door moving the stiff and bloody Rocky to the side. "I hope you know the combination!," he said gesturing to the charcoal steel safe that was built into the closet's wall.

Cookie stood motionless as her blank stare fixed on Flip's grilling eyes. *It's no reason to tell him the combination. He's going to kill me anyway*, she thought to herself, as she was willing to accept the fact.

Their face off was interrupted by Butter's raucous entrance. "I got the jewels and everything," he anxiously stated. Flip knew Butter had no knowledge about the safe that Uptown sometimes bragged about in his presence.

"Nah, there's everything," Flip said, directing Butter's attention to the safe.

Cookie remained motionless as she watched the faces of two guys that her husband had mistakenly trusted, and she thought had treated fairly. Her heart began to shrink when she thought about the many times she cooked for all of them. "I don't know the number," she said in a stale tone.

Cookie knew there was no reason for them to kill a two year old. So she said a prayer to herself for her and the baby and was ready to get it over with. Flip looked fixedly into her lying, fearless eyes. "Yo, go get the baby," he said as his arm was tapping Butter's hip and his gaze held steady on hers.

After a brief stall, Butter left the room and returned with the carriage. He didn't want to witness any baby slaying. "Im'ma go wipe shit down," he said before heading out.

"Aight," Flip replied. He watched as the tears began to mount in Cookie's eyes again. "Listen, we not gonna play no games. You dying, and whether he goes to hell wit you or not is up to you," he coldly stated while nodding to the baby.

She was certain that the first part of his statement was true. As to the second part, she had her doubts. But she would rather have died knowing her baby had a chance to live. Cookie took one last painful stare at her son then turned to the safe. Nervously and sullenly she turned the black number knob right...left...right... "click!"

Boom! Boom! Flip pumped two hollow tips in the back of her fresh hairdo as he witnessed the safe's door crack.

The shots brought Butter dashing into the room. Though he was still uncertain about the entire episode, he was relieved that Cookie had done the right thing.

"Let me get that," Flip said, taking the bag from Butter. In the safe was a Mac-Ten, a forty-five caliber, and a large sum of cash. Flip hastily jammed it all into the backpack before moving over to the dresser drawer. He flung them open one after another until he came across one that had some tube socks in it. He snatched out two fairly new pair, handing one to Butter. "Put these on and wipe down everything you think you touched," Flip directed.

"I already did —"

"Well let's do it again," Flip said.

Five minutes later they were done. As they got ready to exit the living room, Flip picked up the half key of coke from the table and began dumping it all over Uptown's benumbed body. "You greedy bastard. Take this wit chew," Flip bitterly said before they hurriedly, but cautiously moved out of the apartment closing the door behind them.

As they walked down the hall, they took the socks off and stuffed them into their front pocket. They made a quiet and unnoticed departure from the unfrequented building.

Adrenaline flowed through their bodies like electricity as they hopped in the Accord. Flip tossed the bag in the back before pulling off. After turning up one block and down another, Flip called D-Mac and told him to meet them at Wu's apartment. He then hung up and glanced over at Butter who stared straightforward as silence filled the Honda. "You aight?," Flip asked.

After a short delay, Butter answered with a slight attitude, "Yeah I'm aight."

Butter accepted the fact that what happened had happened and there was no changing that. But he was a little distraught as to why Flip hadn't informed him on what appeared to be a plot. "Damn Bee! Why didn't you school me to what time it was?," Butter asked with a slight rage in his tone.

"Yo word to God, I didn't know it was going down like that," Flip replied in a sincere firm tone. "The nigga just started talking crazy and I lost it," he said as he made the left onto University. "Come on Bee, you know I would've pulled your coat if I was schemin'."

Flip desperately wanted Butter to believe him. He knew his words undoubtedly rang true with Butter. But now Flip found himself wondering how Wu was going to take the news, and whether or not they would be able to convince him that it was not something that they had planned.

"So how we gonna tell Wu we killed his man?," Butter asked, regaining his composure as they doubled parked in front of 1839.

The fact that Butter had used the term "we" instead of "you" pleased Flip because he now knew Butter believed that it was not premeditated. But he had no answer for Butter's question. He could only shake his head slowly while he hissed as they entered the building.

They were let into the apartment by D-Mac. The three of them entered the living room and Wu met them as he came from the bathroom. Flip routinely moved to turn the stereo down as the three of them took seats—D-Mac in the recliner, Butter in the three-cushion and Wu in the two-cushion. Flip opened the bag and turned it upside down onto the table.

"Oh shit!," D-Mac said, rising to his feet as he seized the Mac-Ten. Wu, instantly surmising the unimaginable, slowly rose to his feet and said, "Naaah maaan," with a blank face. His squint puffy eyes drilled back and forth at Flip and Butter.

"Ayo Duke, it didn't go down like you think," Flip quipped.

"Naaah maaan," Wu repeated as if he didn't hear a word Flip

said. "What happened to Uptown?," he frightingly asked, afraid of already knowing the answer.

After a split second delay Flip solemnly answered, "I lef' 'im."

"Wha'chew mean?," Wu asked, not wanting to believe the inevitable.

"I lef' 'im," Flip sternly repeated. He knew that simple answer was not enough so he decided to stretch the truth. "Look, the nigga said something slick. We got into it, and it was either him or me."

"What?," Wu distrustfully replied. "Come on Duke, what you and him gonna get into it over? The nigga was talking about handing us shorts."

"That's some bullshit!," Wu shot back.

"Ayo check this out Bee!," Flip said, as he became annoyed. "I don't think you heard me. I said it was either him or me. Now which one would you rather be here telling you the story?," he asked him. .

Butter and D-Mac fixed their stares on Wu's as his piercing eyes appeared to be searching for some truth in Flip's story.

"Ayo word to miz... The nigga was bugging," Butter interjected. He felt he could say that and it wouldn't seem like he was lying to Wu.

Whether Butter's statement was good enough for Wu was still in doubt. It was clearly enough for D-Mac who said, "Ayo Wu, I know he's your man but he tried to front on famm. Fuck that... Damn! I wish I was there!," D-Mac added, cocking back the Mac-Ten.

There was no doubt in Wu's mind that he'd rather have Flip standing before him instead of Uptown, as long as what Flip claimed had happened was the case. "What about Cookie?," Wu sorely asked.

"The baby aight," Flip indirectly answered, causing Wu to bow his head in sorrow. "Yo Bee she walked in on it," Flip added.

Wu stood lifelessly staring down at the carpet as he contemplated the entire ordeal. His mind played back Flip's story repeatedly as he tried to make sense of it all. *I wish I was there...maybe they would still be alive*, he silently thought.

"The baby!," his rejuvenated demeanor exclaimed. Wu suddenly felt the urge to make sure the baby would be found alive. That was the least he could do for Uptown and Cookie. "Yo let me get your keys," he said while extending his open hand to Flip.

"Save that shit!," D-Mac disdainfully interjected. "You can't go back to that crib!"

"I'm not goin' to the crib.   I'm goin' to call the police and…"

"You ain't callin' Jake…fuck outta here wit that shit!," D-Mac said as he started, unconsciously gripping the Mac-Ten firmly.

"Ayo listen! If Uptown and Cookie had to die that's one thing, but the baby don't have to die!," he said as he scanned all three faces. "Im'ma go downtown, make the call, and that's it."

Flip felt that Wu was genuinely concerned about the baby. He thought that if he were to say 'no', the only way to assure himself that Wu wouldn't eventually make the call would be to kill him. Something he felt was unwarranted at the time. Flip gave it a little extra thought and decided that it would be all right as long as Wu did what he said and nothing else. "Here you go," Flip said while tossing him the keys. His actions drew incredulous stares from both Butter and D-Mac as Wu raced away, and out the door.

"I'm goin' wit' 'im," D-Mac said, motioning toward the door before he was restrained by Flip. Flip knew Wu really needed to do that by himself. It would help to restore the trust amongst them.

"Nah he aight," Flip urged as he grabbed D-Mac by the arm. "Let's count this cheddar," he said, directing their attention to the money scattered on and about the table.

Hampstead Publishing

Chapter Six

December, '90

Seventeen months after the Uptown incident, the fellas were on top of the game. That night they walked away with fifteen thousand apiece from the sixty thousand that was in Uptown's safe. They spent the following couple of days getting rid of the two and a half keys, and taking the money and investing it into the re-up with Flip's new connect.

The team continued to sell between sixty and seventy packs a day as their individual pay skyrocketed from five thousand a week to twelve thousand. They added a new crew consisting of two lieutenants, three look-outs, and five girls from the block that were paid two hundred dollars apiece to help bottle up once a week. This new team allowed them ample free time to enjoy their riches.

Once again their lifestyles were affected. They went from hollow rope chains, to solid thick links, from triple fat gooses and sherlins, to short and full length furs and minks, and from a Honda Accord and foot patrol, to Flip's triple black BMW 850i, D-Mac's high-riding burgundy Land Cruiser, Butter's money-green Benz 300E, and Wu's cream Lexus 400. They also strayed away from their parents and changed residences, each living in townhouses within blocks of each other up in the suburb of New Rochelle.

It was five o'clock Christmas night, and Flip was having X-mas dinner in his extravagantly decorated townhouse. It was nothing too outgoing, just a little get together between he, the fellas, and their dates. Butter was there with Lisa. D-Mac was there with Regina — a Spanish girl he met in Spanish Harlem a month after the Uptown incident and Wu was supposed to be arriving with Kelly who slyly sexed Wu behind Bill's back until she eventually left him to be with Wu completely.

Denise, with the help of Regina and Lisa, traveled back and forth between the dining room and the kitchen that was behind a swinging door a couple of feet away. While placing prepared dishes on top of the lavish oakwood table, the fellas were huddled over the VCR and big screen TV trying to figure out why the bootleg movie, *New Jack City*, that D-Mac brought was not showing. "Ayo get this bullshit out my joint before it blow my shit up," Flip said as he hit the eject button before snatching the tape out.

"I know scrams didn't hit me off wit the dummy tape, " D-Mac said, scrutinizing the tape.

"That nigga seen you comin'," Butter amusingly commented.

"Word," Flip added.

"See you trying to make me lose the Christmas Spirit and go kill a nigga over this bullshit tape," D-Mac defensively stated before they were interrupted by Denise.

"Does anybody know if Wu is coming or what?," Denise asked.

Her eyes were frisking all three faces for a response. Out of respect for the seriousness of Denise and Lisa's relationship with D-Mac's two best friends and vice-versa, the three of them agreed to let bygones be bygones, and had actually became good friends over the past years.

"He said he was," D-Mac answered.

"Well can somebody call him or something? Because the food is almost ready," she added before walking away. She left the three of them standing around ogling each other's puzzled faces.

Flip thought maybe Wu decided to share the holiday alone with Kelly, while D-Mac thought he was just running a little late. But Butter, who had became a little closer to Wu since the demise of Uptown and Cookie, had serious reasons to believe otherwise, and he felt it was time to share them. "I don't think scrams' comin'," Butter said.

His statement drew inquisitive stares from both D-Mac and Flip. Knowing that "scrams" was a term they used to describe people who basically tried to get over— like the guy who sold D-Mac the blank tape—they both wondered why Butter addressed Wu with the term. "Why you say that?," Flip asked.

Shaking his head slowly, Butter answered, "Homeboy fucked up. I think the nigga on the glass dick?"

The news that Wu might be smoking crack straight from the pipe did not surprise D-Mac. But it rattled the shit out of Flip who said, "Say word!"

"Him and Kelly smokin'. He turned her out wit that whoola shit and now they getting' beamed-up," Butter gloomily stated.

Because it was winter, Wu and Kelly were able to conceal signs of their addiction by overdressing under excess size coats, and the drugs had yet to disfigure their faces to the point of immediate recognition, but Butter pieced it together through other signs. "You know that nigga sold his jewels? And he's waiting on the money for his townhouse."

D-Mac's mind instantly flashed back to the night a few months back when Wu beeped them and told them he had been robbed down by the Roof Top, the notorious Harlem skating rink. "I thought the nigga got stuck for his jewels—", D-Mac said.

"The townhouse?," Flip questioned before Butter could respond to D-Mac's question.

"That was some bullshit," Butter's face was drawn as he responded to D-Mac's question. "That night we was out huntin' niggas. That nigga shit was probably sittin' in the pawn shop," he added.

"What's this about the townhouse?," Flip eagerly asked.

"He sold it," Butter answered matter-of-factly. He watched their stunned faces before he continued. "Him and Kelly be staying at her crib or up in that nigga's old crib."

They thought it was a good idea to use Wu's apartment as a stash place for the amount of drugs they usually sold in one day. They kept up the monthly rent though Wu was no longer supposed to be living there. "They be sleepin' in the stash crib?," D-Mac asked.

"Hell yeah. That's what Al told me the other day," Butter replied.

He knew Al—one of their lieutenants— wouldn't dare fabricate something like that.

Flip jogged his memory and thought it was no wonder he hadn't seen Wu's cream Lexus parked in the drive way of the townhouse lately. His thoughts, along with D-Mac and Butter's attention, were pulled away by Denise's call. "I'm sorry Boo. But Wu and them will have to reheat theirs. So yall come on so we can get ready to eat!," she said. Denise then turned to Lisa, who stood at the table next to her and whispered," Okay, take him in the room and tell him."

Due to their negligence to have protected sex, Lisa recently found out that she was pregnant and told Denise but was afraid to tell Butter. She feared the worst in his reaction being he knew she was on birth control. Lisa told Denise that she would tell Butter at the X-mas gathering, not only because Lisa knew she was going to eventually have to tell him, but also to get Denise to stop pressuring her to tell him anytime sooner. She chose Xmas night because she hoped to catch him at a time when he possibly would not want to spoil the mood. "Not now," Lisa whispered back, as she searched for another excuse to postpone her announcement, "We getting ready to eat…"

Denise, fed up with Lisa's stalling, clinched her teeth. "Giiirrrlll, if you don't get your butt…," Denise said as she pulled Lisa away from the table. Then she placed Lisa's hand inside of Butter's as he made his way over.

"What's up?," Butter asked as his eyes suspiciously frisked their faces.

"Nothing," Denise said as her grim expression was turning into an adorable smile. "Just follow her," she added whimsically shoving them in the direction of the stairs that led to the bedroom.

"What was that all about?," Flip asked as they viewed the two climbing the stairs hand in hand.

"You'll find out," Denise answered, keeping Flip in suspense and directing them to their seats.

Instead of sitting at the head of the table set for eight, Flip sat in the first seat on the right, D-Mac sat next to him, and utensils were set up next to him for Butter. Directly across from each of them sat the utensils for their mates.

"I can't believe I got had," D-Mac said, referring to the tape as he tried to figure out if he had missed something. "Regina!," he called out to the kitchen, as his wheels began to spin. "Which tape did you grab from the glove compartment?"

Regina was a prize. She looked like a broke ass immigrant when she first got with D-Mac, but after D-Mac made their being together official, he had her looking like the lead singer of the Cover Girls.

Regina came from behind the kitchen's door carrying a silver platter full of cornbread. She was wearing a pair of brown leather pants that looked like they were poured on her viciously curved body and a matching tie-up top that exposed her belly button and partial cleavage of her firm looking breasts. "Wha'chew say poppy?," she asked in her sexy accent as she placed the platter on the table.

"Which tape did you take out of the glove compartment?," he repeated, with his eyes on one of his Cuban necklaces that swung from her neck.

"Oh, I took the one on the top."

"Come on Ma. I told you to grab the second from the top," he said as he rose up.

"Aaaaw. I only heard the top, Papeto," she teased.

Regina and Flip chuckled as D-Mac headed out. Butter stood with his buttocks leaned against Flip's long dresser while Lisa stood facing him between his spread legs. He could tell by the look on her face that what she had to tell him was urgent. He was thinking that maybe Denise talked Lisa into giving him an alternative on the issue of his unwillingness to live under the same roof with her.

"Don't tell me you gonna leave me if we don't live together?," he said, with a boyish smile on his face. The same one he had flashed when he first gave her his number two years earlier.

His comment pushed the jitters from her stomach straight up her chest and flying past her throat, "I'm pregnant," she blurted out.

It was like the Butterflies had flown right into his wide-open mouth as he searched for words. "How?" was the only thing he could ask. Giving him a gawky look, she placed her hand on his penis as if she had been passed a bowl of peanuts. "I mean...I thought you was on the pill," he spoke evenly.

"I am. Some days I forgot," she innocently stated.

Even if it hadn't been the season to be jolly, Butter could not find an angry bone in his body towards the adorable girl that stood before him. Actually, he wanted to jump for joy at the news, but he wanted to make sure they were drinking out of the same glass.

"We having it, right?"

"You're not upset with me?"

"Upset with you?," he said as he placed his thumbs separately in each back pocket of her tight denims, letting his fingers fall over the rhinestones that decorated them and pulled her up close against him. "Why would I be upset with you?," he whispered, before they engaged in a long, affectionate kiss.

They could've kissed all night if it hadn't been for Denise's call that had them break for air. "Come on, I have to tell the famm, " he excitedly said, leading her out the room hand-in-hand.

Everyone was seated at the table with their eyes glued on Lisa and Butter as they came off the last of the steps. "So what's up?," Flip eagerly asked as he watched Lisa take her seat and Butter move to the closet.

"Wifey's pregnant, that's what's up!," Butter exclaimed, walking to the table with five blunts in his hand. "Smoke up!" he cheered, handing one to D-Mac and one to Flip. Their faces lit up.

"Say word!" D-Mac said, standing up.

"Unt uhn, unt uhn. Light those up after we eat," Lisa said, as the cheers filled the room.

"Aight word," Butter agreed, "I want my baby's first word to be 'DaDa', not Buddha," he amusingly added, before taking his seat.

For a while they had actually forgotten about Wu's failure to show up. In fact, his name might have been mentioned one time during the dinner, and not at all while they bunched up on Flip's pricey five piece, cream leather, living room set as they watched the tape. It was the middle of the movie when the sound of a beeper had the three of them groping for their hip.

"That's me," Butter said, as he studied the number displayed on the pager. When he recognized the number of the public phone up the block from 1839, followed by the code 3-5-7 — the code only members of the team used — he moved to the closet, retrieved his phone from his short black mink, and dialed the number.

"Hello," the guy's scratchy voice sounded mid first ring.

"Who this?," Butter responded, never moving from in front of the closet.

"L.A.," the guy answered.

L.A. was Al's twin brother. They both basically ran the street patrol operation, but unlike the shit Uptown put Flip and them through, Al and L.A. were being treated fair. The only time they contacted Butter and them was if an out-of-towner buying several packs wanted a play, or to inform them that bail money was needed for an arrest that had been made. "Yeah what's up?," Butter asked.

"I need to see you," he said with a tone of urgency

Wanting to know if it was something he could say over the phone, Butter said, "It's like that?"

"Well I'm saying, ya man just flipped on my brother."

Butter didn't have to ask if it was Wu he was referring to, instead he asked, "For what?"

"Over some crills," came the answer, disguising the term *crack*.

"Word! Ayo, I'll be there in a minute!," Butter said, killing the conversation. He snatched his coat off the hanger and went to call for the fellas, but was startled by Lisa's presence.

"Who was that?," she intensely quizzed.

If it had been a female he would've smiled while thinking of a lie, but since he had no reason to lie, his adrenaline caused him to get defensive. "Not now Lisa, save that shit," he said while throwing his coat on.

"What?," she snapped with her hand in his mid section clenching a fist full of his brown Gap pullover sweater.

Her reaction caused him to think about her pregnancy, and the responsibility he would soon encounter. She was going to be the mother of his child and he had to start treating her as such. "Listen. Wu got into it with one of the workers," he calmly explained, loosening her grip, "and we gotta go straighten it out."

"So what was all that 'save it' shit for? You don't have to talk to me like that," she pointed out.

"Yeah you right," he said, cradling her in his furry arms. He was so wrapped up in her creamy body, he almost forgot his intentions, and if it wasn't for Flip and D-Mac heading his way, he might have very well forgotten.

"Yo, what's up?," D-Mac asked.

"We gotta jet. That nigga Wu is O.C.," Butter said, gesturing to Lisa to go back in the living room.

Without questioning Butter's comment that Wu was out of control, Flip said, "Let's motivate." He and D-Mac grabbed their coats, "We'll be back in a little bit!," Flip called-out to the girls before they parted.

The three of them climbed into D-Mac's burgundy Land Cruiser and were on their way to the Bronx.

It was fifteen past nine when the truck came slowly rolling down the block. Thanks to D-Mac's agile driving, the twenty-minute trip was reduced to ten. They scanned the obscure area and were pleased to see that whatever happened between Al and Wu wasn't grim enough to have interfered with the oper-ation as they witnessed the constant traffic in and out of the park's darkness.

"Why he be leaving his whip parked in front of the build-ing?," D-Mac complained as he surged into a U-turn, pulling up in front of the fire hydrant behind the Lexus.

"Told you the nigga O.C.," Butter said, as they came to stop.

During the cold or rainy days, Al and L.A. kept an eye on things from the hallway of 1839. They had it set up where they would bring two packs down at a time. They often left one in the mailbox to Wu's apartment, and would give Ike the other. When they spotted the truck through the door's window, they stepped out of the building.

L.A, the oldest of the two by fifty seconds, had Butter's com-plexion. He stood about five-eleven and had an athletic build. His short blow out afro and heavy eyebrows made him appear older than his twenty years. His brother was identical, well up until he came home from Riker's Island the previous year with a five-inch scar on the left side of his face from his ear to his chin.

Butter and them watched from behind the truck's tinted windows as the brothers neared. Butter sitting in the back passenger side let the window halfway down and said, "What's up fellas?"

"What up," the brothers greeted in chorus, giving him five before moving to Flip's rolled down window to repeat the gesture.

"Yo, get in Al," Butter said as he gestured for Al to walk around. "Can you hold it down for a minute?" He watched as L.A. nodded yes. "Aight cool," Butter added, before letting up the window and turning to face Al as he climbed up into the truck.

On their way down from New Rochelle, they decided that they wanted to hear Al's story first, and not in the presence of Wu, being sure to eliminate any intimidating factors. D-Mac drove up the block and parked in front of the U.S. fried chicken spot. "What happened?," Flip asked, getting right to the issue. Both he and D-Mac kept their bodies half turned, staring into Al's angered face.

"Your fuckin' crack head man pulled out on me!," he bluntly stated. "Ayo Bee, that nigga slapped me!," he added, clearly agitated.

"With the tool?," Butter interjected.

"Nah wit his dirty ass hand!"

"Yo cool out Bee," D-Mac said, trying to calm him down. "How did the drama start?"

As he began to play it back in his mind, Al found himself almost too upset to talk about it. But in order to expose their friend which he desperately wanted to do, he knew he had to collect himself.

After letting out a short, hard sigh Al began, "Yo for the last few dayz bottles been comin' up short. Two here, three there, and we wasn't really sweatin' it at first. Then crazy packs started havin' shorts and it was buggin' us out because we had started counting them, making sure a hundred was in each pack before we brung 'em down stairs. Anyway, to make a long story short, one day I played under the steps and I peeped ya man tappin' the mailbox stash."

"Say word!," Flip said, unable to believe that Wu would resort to such petty measured.

"That's my word," Al kissed his closed fist and raised it barely above his head. Realizing he had their full attention, he continued with his story. "So boom check it. I flipped the script on the nigga. I bottled up some unscented soap and put the pack in the mailbox. He fell for it. So when I seen him coming out of Kelly's crib looking crazy heated, I faked like I needed a pack. I couldn't help but gig on the nigga as I passed him and that's when he pulled out throwing me against the wall asking me did I think shit was funny."

Though Al may have found some humor in the story before Wu had put his hand on him, he certainly couldn't find a single thing to laugh about as he screwed the poorly hidden amused faces of Butter and D-Mac, who could no longer hold it in. "Pardon us Duke, we just got through smokin' some lethal," D-Mac said as he and Butter tried getting a grip. " I know shit ain't funny but…"

Flip cutting D-Mac off, looked as upset as Al. "You aight?," he asked.

"Hell no! I wanna shoot a fair one. I'm ready to fuck that nigga up!," he answered.

Flip could definitely understand why Al felt the way he did. But even if he allowed a fair fight, Butter and D-Mac wouldn't. "Slow down Duke. We got this aight," Flip responded as he brought his hand out of his pocket. "This should take care of the short," he said as he handed Al five hundred before adding, "and next time let one of us know before you pull that soap shit," *knowing that they'll be no next time, at least not with Wu, because he had made up his mind that something must be done.*

When they got back down the block, D-Mac let Al out in front of the park. He then rolled a little further and pulled up to the garage's closed door, next to the Volvo.

The two of them got out and marched across the street into the building. All the laughing had ceased as they approached Kelly's door like three marshals with an eviction notice. After a thunderous pound on the door by D-Mac, the door slowly opened, stopping a quarter of the way with Kelly behind it.

"Where he at?," D-Mac asked, with the three of them staring at her pale face and undone hair. It was difficult for them to believe that she was the same Kelly that any one of them would have shared their fortune with.

"He just went upstairs," she sorely answered, with a saddened expression.

Her information caused them to rapidly turn away and race up the steps. By the time they got up there, Flip had his key out. But before he could stick it in the keyhole, the door was opened by Wu who was on his way out. "What the fuck is up wit you?," Flip demanded as his two clinched fists landed on Wu's scrawny chest area, forcing him all the way back into the living room, then released him as he flipped backwards over the back of the two-cushion sofa.

Wu's eyes were desperately trying to focus through the dimness of the apartment as he began picking himself up. He dazedly searched their grimacing faces to make sure they were the guys he grew up with, before he barked out, "What the fuck did I do?"

"Nigga you know what you did!," D-Mac yelled, moving around Flip and shoving Wu onto the sofa. "Smokin' that shit!," he snidely added.

Wu knew it was no use denying it. He could tell by the look on their faces and the height of their actions. He was addicted to crack. "Why you niggas worried about what I do wit mines? I'm not fuckin' up your money!," he shot back.

"That's what you wanna do? Smoke your money away? Smoke your life away?," Flip boisterously charged. "You even got Kelly all fucked-up!"

Wu oddly flashed a wiry smile and replied, "Kelly was getting' high before I got wit her. Her and Bill was getting' skied up when we was broke," he said, breaking into a deranged chuckle. "That might seem like a long time ago to you niggas. His emotions started to surface through his teary eyes as he continued, "But it's like yesterday to me," He was glaring up at Flip. "I remember when we didn't have shit. We was fucked up until Uptown put us on.... And how you thanked him?" He studied Flip's expressionless face for a second before he continued. "You slayed him, that's how... you wanted what it took him years to get so you took it...He didn't get that overnight... Don't nobody get it like that overnight... Oh, my bad... Except for niggas like you...!"

"That's why you buggin?," Flip interrupted, expressing equal rage over Wu's dwelling of Uptowns' murder. "A mothafucka that got what he deserved...? Tell me something... How many little niggas he jerked to get what he had? How many niggas like you did he grease up into thinking he was really looking out for them?" Flip's sneer became repetitive as he continued, "You know what niggas like me do? We play fair with niggas that play fair wit us...Niggas like me go all out for famm... You see them niggas downstairs?" Flip's finger pointed towards the door as he referred to the twins. "Them niggas started out makin' more loot than we ever made fuckin' wit your man! You see us? We all caked-up in the same way...You know why?," Flip's grilling stare became colder, "'Cause niggas like me!," he yelled then paused letting his words linger into the silence.

"Yo get your things," Butter said meekly breaking the silence.

Wu, taking his eyes off of Flip and placing it on Butter replied, "I don't got nothing remember? I smoked it up," he reiterated with a wiry smile. "Oh I still got that bullshit Lexus I'm trying to sell...Any of you interested?," he asked while repeating the deranged chuckle.

"Yo man where your clothes at? Get some gear on," Butter demanded.

"Clothes? What I need clothes for?"

"Cause you goin' to a rehab," Butter said. "You fucked-up and you need help."

"Nah I don't need help. I need you niggas to leave me the fuck alone!," Wu stated as he dropped his head.

Butter knew Wu didn't mean a word he uttered as he moved beside Flip to stand in front of Wu's bowed head. Their anger fleetingly drifted into pity as they towered over him. They had been through too much to let it end on that statement, and if Wu meant it, he would have to show it. "If that's what you want, cool," Butter calmly said. "But before we walk out that door, let me say this. Once you and Kelly smoke up that Lexus and that townhouse, that's it...You can't get no more dough wit us to smoke up...That's history." He paused letting his words penetrate before continuing, "You still got time. It'll only take a minute. You go and come back to the riches."

"We gonna hold you down Duke," D-Mac threw in.

Wu was drowning as several different emotions filled his bowed head. Though he knew they had love for him, he wasn't sure if he could or should ever forgive them for what happened to Uptown.

He was also in love with a crack addict. The thought of him coming back to the world and leaving Kelly stuck with the zombies, was too much to grasp. He knew he needed help — and pronto, but so did she, and if he couldn't get help for Kelly, then there was no need to get help for himself.

Through the blur of his soaked eyes, he saw the hands of Butter and Flip waiting on him to take hold of them. He slowly lifted his stare to theirs and said, "I love Kelly. I need her to come with me." He studied their faces as they both unhesitatingly nodded yes. He then placed one hand in each of theirs and they pulled him up for an emotional huddle with the four of them.

At six a.m. the next morning Butter, driving D-Mac's Land Cruiser, pulled up in front of 1839. He left Lisa in the truck, went in the building and quickly returned with Kelly and Wu behind him.

"Hi," Lisa said, getting out of the truck helping Kelly load her Louis Vuitton suitcase in the back. Though, they'd never met, Lisa knew Kelly's story and now that she was looking at her, Lisa could imagine how gorgeous Kelly once had been.

"Hi," Kelly bashfully replied. She could tell by the way Lisa looked at her that Lisa knew about her. "Thank you," Kelly softly added.

Sensing Kelly's low self-esteem, Lisa surveyed Kelly's face while holding her hands and said, "You're still beautiful." Her smile drew a half smile from Kelly.

"Thank you," Kelly responded with a hug.

"What about me?," Wu interrupted as Butter tossed his bag in the back.

"You know you still a fly guy," Lisa said as she moved to give him a hug and peck on the cheek, followed by Butter who gave him five then a rugged hug. They all climbed in the truck and were off to the 150-day program at one of the most exclusive rehabs in upstate New York.

Chapter Seven

'91, One month later

The operation was still intact. Minus a few park raids and minor arrests, everything was moving along smoothly.

Wu and Kelly were doing well on their road to recovery. They were being visited four different days of the week, once by D-Mac, once by Flip, and twice by Butter and Lisa as they collectively made efforts at making the hundred and fifty day stay appear as short as possible.

"You jingling Baby—go 'head baby," was the L.L. Cool J. song that was thumping out of the stereo system in Flip's 850-I. It was seven o' clock Monday evening and Flip was flying down the Degan Expressway on his way back from his regular five hour visit with Wu and Kelly. The glow of the triple black BMW's fog and head-lights glistened in the rearview mirrors of the slower moving vehicles as he whipped from lane to lane, approaching then zooming past them as if they were standing still on a race track.

As Flip passed the 233rd Street exit, he felt the vibration of his pager dancing on his hip. He retrieved it. Recognizing his connect's code followed by an unfamiliar number, Flip reached for his phone. He dialed the number then turned the music down.

Flip had completed a deal with his connect Saturday prior to that Monday, and wondered why the connect was paging him so soon. "Yo my man what's up?," were the words that penetrated Flip's concentration after the first ring.

Recognizing that it was in fact his 'good English' speaking Dominican connect that answered the phone, Flip replied, "Yo-o what's up Bee?"

"I need to see you," the connect said in a tone that was not alarming.

"Aight where you at?"

"You hungry?"

"Aight," Flip said, before ending the conversation.

Flip knew "you hungry," meant to meet the connect at the Cuchi Frito on 135th and Broadway, one of the three Spanish restaurants his connect owned.

Zipping by the Sedgewick Avenue exit, the exit he had intended on getting off before the beep, Flip zoomed to the 161st Street exit, shot to and across the 155th Street Bridge, made the left on Broadway, then swerved into a gap between the bus stop and the restaurant.

Flip then placed his white fur hat on his head but tossed the full-length coat in the back seat before hitting the hazard lights and hopping out of the car. "What's up Papi," Flip said as he greeted one of the two Dominicans as they exited the restaurant acknowledging the other with a nod.

"Okay Papi," the first one responded.

"Todo bien Papi," the second one said gesturing to the dark tinted windows and chrome wheels that dressed Flip's BMW. They looked on as Flip thanked them with a smirk and nod before entering the moderately sized restaurant.

Flip was instantly embraced by the good smelling scent of fried platainos and low playing Spanish music. The restaurant almost had a club feel to it. When he arrived at his connect's table, he was promptly greeted as a comrade. "Hey-y my man!," the connect greeted, surprised by Flip's swift arrival. "Por favor, excuse me por uno minuto," the connect replied to the party he was entertaining before excusing himself from the table. The connect then turned to Flip and said, "Where was you at? Around the corner?," he joked.

"Nah," Flip grinned, as he followed the connect to the back.

Flip's grin quickly vanished as he spotted two Dominicans rising from a round table and nearing the back. His instincts sent his vision to the two skinny men's bulging waistlines. He could feel his stomach hardening up against the handle of the forty-five he had tucked in his waist.

The connect and Flip had a good relationship. Though, they knew each other's names, they only referred to one another as "My man" and "Bee." They never doubted each other's trust. The connect never worried about whether Flip was carrying a gun or not, and Flip never felt offended when the connect's men habitually stood around brandishing guns during a transaction.

"Damne unos minutes," the connect said to his two men, gesturing for them to take a walk.

Flip, who'd been around his share of Spanish people in the Bronx, automatically knew the matter was not life threatening since his connect had asked the guys with the guns to give him a few minutes. But he grew eager to find out what this meeting was about. "What's the deal, Bee?," Flip asked as his eyes shifted from the two guys leaving, then back to his connect.

"I want to show you something," the connect said, opening a locker that stood tall behind the table.

The connect pulled out a little machine about as wide and as thick as a Webster Dictionary. On the top of it was a three-inch wide, twelve-inch length slot with a small red bulb on one end and an identical green bulb on the other. Near the front bottom of the box was another slot that had three short flat plastic arms sticking out and upward at a forty-five degree angle.

"Do you know what this is," the connect asked.

Flip had seen a couple different styles of money counting machines but none like the one his eyes were now fixed on. "Yeah, but not like that," he answered flatly.

Flip's face was then painted by a frown as he viewed the connect take out an orange and white plastic Nike drawstring bag. It was the same bag Flip had filled with money when he delivered it on Saturday. But, this time it was nearly empty.

The connect plugged the machine in, then placed the bag on the table. He then reached in his front pocket, pulled out a wad of money and placed the unfolded stack into the top slot. "I want you to keep your eyes on the bulbs," he said as he hit the ON button.

They both stood and watched the existence of the green lit bulb as the money rapidly vacuumed down through the top, gliding out neatly stacked at the bottom. "You seen that?," the connect asked. Flip nodded yes. "Now watch this," the connect added. Taking the lump of cash out of the Nike bag, he repeated the routine. He surveyed Flip's drawn up face due to the existence of the red light.

"What that mean?," Flip questioned.

"That means, my man-n, that this five thousand is counterfeit!"

Flip went numb. The connect did not want Flip to think he was accusing him of foul play so he added, "Before you say anything. I'm sure this is new to you."

"You know I wouldn't—"

"I know," he said, cutting Flip off.

The connect unplugged the machine, then removed all but one bill of the money and pushed the arms in. "Take it with you," he said as he extended the machine to Flip after he stuffed it inside the Nike bag.

"I owe you five G's," Flip said taking the machine.

"No, no you don't owe me anything," he responded with a smile. "Please, just don't bring me no more," he added putting an arm around Flip as they walked out.

Flip, taking that as a fair warning over a threat said, "Thanks Bee," before departing.

Flip's anger jumped into his BMW with him. He started the car and paged both D-Mac and Butter as he peeled off. Because it was hard to receive incoming calls on the rigged phones, he paged them putting his beeper number in knowing that they would routinely page him back with a phone number he could call. As he flew across the 155th Street bridge, his pager went off and because he held it in his hand he only had to hold it up and glance at the numbers it displayed.

The phone number was unfamiliar, but he knew it was one of them by the 3-5-7 code that followed the number. "Yo," D-Mac's voice sounded after a half ring.

"Ayo, where you at?," Flip said as he recognized D-Mac's voice.

"On the Id' Ave," skeptical of saying Avenue. "Where Duke at?," indicating Butter.

"I think him and wifey still in the Poconos."

"Aight where the twid'ins at?," skeptical of saying twins.

"Doin' their thing. Why? What's up?," D-Mac asked while picking up on the urgency in Flip's voice.

"Shut it down and mid'eet me up stid'airs," leery of saying meet and stairs. "Yo and bring the Twid'ins," Flip added.

"Aight," D-Mac said before they hung up.

Five minutes later Flip was pulling up on the block. He could tell that they were already upstairs by the stranded customers that aimlessly paced about. Flip double-parked a little past the garage where D-Mac's Land Cruiser was sitting, and wearing just his hat, he hurriedly moved to 1839 with the bag in his hand.

"What's up fellas?" Flip asked while greeting the three of them as he entered the apartment, closing the door behind him.

"What's up," they chorused, watching Flip stop at the dining room table. Their puzzling stares focused on the machine as they neared the table, while Flip pulled it out of the bag and plugged it up almost in one motion.

"Bring out all the money you got," Flip said, watching as L.A. disappeared to the back room.

Flip learned a quick lesson from his connect and though, the counterfeit money could have cost Flip his life, he showed no hostility towards the twins, because he had trusted their lack of knowledge like the connect trusted his.

Flip waited until L.A. finished stacking all the money that covered a large portion of the table. He then explained to them what he had learned.

"Say word!," D-Mac said bewildered. "Five G's?"

"I'm sayin' watch this," Flip said as he placed the counterfeit bill in the slot. "Now if the red light comes on, it's fake," he said, figuring they knew what the green light meant.

They all intently looked on as the red light flashed. Flip then took a small stack and repeated the demonstration with some legit bills. The team continued to stare as the green light stayed on. Finally Flip placed the bill in the middle of the same stack and tried it again, this time causing the green light to turn red for a split second before turning back to green.

"Yo, who be buying the most packs," Flip asked, studying the twins' blank faces.

After turning to each other for a faint second, Al met Flip's stare and said, "A few custies. But there's some Jersey and Connecticut niggas that be coppin' heavy—like ten G's type shit."

Flip thought it had to be somebody who passed off a large sum of money at a time. "How often they come through?" he asked them.

"Every week, week and a half," Al said.

"What day they usually come?," D-Mac asked them.

"Jersey on Fridayz and CT between Thursdayz and Sundayz," L.A. sharply answered.

"A'ight. Go open shop back up. We gonna stay here and check this dough out for a minute, " Flip said as he dismissed them. The brothers went and retrieved some packs then left Flip and D-Mac behind to comb the money.

Twenty minutes later, D-Mac and Flip came out of the building. They had found no more counterfeit bills and had solely rested their suspicions on either the CT or New Jersey boys as the culprits. "What's up wit Wu?," D-Mac asked as they headed towards their automobiles.

"Yeah, he doin' good. Kelly too. They gonna be aight," Flip appealingly replied.

"What you about to get into?"

"A nigga madd tired. I'm about to go to the rest and clock some zeeze," Flip answered standing in between the two vehicles.

D-Mac, who had been sleeping all day, said, "I just came out. I think Im'ma go scoop my little Spanish mami and go parley up at the bowling alley."

"Aight," they said as they gave each other five before parting.

"Yo Bee, if you see little Miguel, tell 'im we need a van by Wednesday—a joint with the sliding side door," Flip said as he opened his car door.

"Aight. Im'ma go check 'em on my way downtown," D-Mac answered. Then they both held up the peace sign before getting into their vehicles.

Chapter Eight

Butter and Lisa returned from the Poconos Thursday morning, and by the afternoon Flip filled Butter in on the counterfeit money scam. By Thursday night he, Flip, and D-Mac were on the block playing it closer than they had been in months, which wasn't such a good thing for Butter, because while he and Lisa were soaking up the fresh atmosphere the Poconos had to offer, they had a discussion about marriage and Butter's departure from the game, something he had given serious consideration to the entire trip back. The minute he heard the news from Flip, Butter knew it was time to move on from the game. He decided to make Lisa his wife and build some other empire outside of the game, but he also made up his mind not to break the news about his departure to anyone until after things were straight with the counterfeiters. In no way did he want the fellas to think he was bailing out in the thick of things. It had to be after everything was held down.

The black van was parked two cars up from 1839's entrance. Butter was in the driver's seat. Flip was in the passenger seat. In between them, sat a white plastic five gallon jug of gasoline. In the back on a crate, the only other piece of furniture in the van, sat D-Mac. The obscure block and the way both Butter and Flip were slouched low in their seats, were the combinations that made it impossible for someone to recognize that the van was being occupied. However, they both were positioned to view everything that was going on out into the darkness.

Butter could see the pitchers serving the crack heads as they scrambled in and out of the park. He was also able to focus on the familiar and unfamiliar faces that pulled up, slowed down, or double parked in front of the park, even if they chose not to step out into the stiff cold winter air.

On Flips side of the van, he was able to view people who passed by in both directions as they strode in a rapid pace trying to get to where they were headed. Some bundled up with big scarves wrapped around their faces, others with big coats and hats. When glancing into the passenger's side rear view mirror, Flip had a clear view of 1839's red steel door, enabling him to identify faces as they entered and exited the building. D-Mac's dull view was the back of Flip and Butter's seats, the sliding van's door that he faced, the double windowless doors to his right, and the chip painted corroded van's floor.

Miguel had gotten the stolen van for them Monday night, just one hour after D-Mac's request. Miguel parked it on the block, showed D-Mac how to start it, received his two hundred and went about his business. D-Mac showed the twins how to start the van and paid them a few dollars to make sure it stayed parked on the correct side of the street each morning to avoid parking tickets that might bring unnecessary attention to it.

As silence filled the radio-less van, Butter thought it would be a good time to let the fellas know that he was about to become a married man. He turned his head to the right, slightly pulled his over sized, black Champion hoodie back and stared at the side of Flip's hoodie. "Yo Duke," Butter said. His call caused Flip's buried head to turn and face him. "Im'ma about to make wifey, wife," he said, letting a smile crease his face.

"Say word!," D-Mac interjected, sliding his crate as close as he could between them. Though, D-Mac and Lisa's relationship got off to a rocky start, it was all love between her and the famm, and he and Flip were genuinely happy for Butter.

"That's decent. Word, that's crazy decent," Flip said, following D-Mac in giving Butter a pound, their leather gloves clapping.

"I'm sayin," D-Mac was winking at Butter while tapping Flip's shoulder, "When you and Denise gonna do the do?," D-Mac asked Flip.

"When you and the Spanish mami gonna get married?," Flip whimsically replied.

Flip loved Denise, but growing up he heard too many arguments between his parents about one not paying enough attention to other because of their occupations. Since the game was his occupation, there was no doubt that it would demand and get most of his attention.

"Shi-it, that might be soon. She the truth," D-Mac boasted.

"If it's like that than you and Butter should hook up a double wed... Yo, I think it's on!," Flip abruptly stated after spotting L.A. through the rear view standing on the outside of the door with an over sized black hoodie on his head and his black and blue triple fat goose turned inside out — the signal that meant the out-of-towners.

The plans were, when L.A. came out wearing his coat backward, Flip was to go in the building and chill under the steps by the mailbox where L.A. would drop off the money on his way up stairs to get the work.

Meanwhile, Flip would run in Kelly's apartment where he had the machine set-up and check out the loot. Since Al always kept the out-of-towners waiting in the first hall, they knew it would be extremely difficult to witness the pass off through the metal mesh that covered the dull plexiglass window of the second door.

After retrieving the work, L.A. was to wait at the top of the first flight of steps until he witnessed Flip pass by. Five minutes later, L.A. was to hand off the work to the out-of-towners in a normal fashion without knowing whether they were the perpetrators or not. "Damn! I didn't see the plates," Butter said as he focused across the street on the silver, double-parked, four door Grand Am. He could see one guy in the back, one on the passenger side, and the chubby black guy that was getting out of the driver's seat.

"It should be them CT catz. L.A. said the Jersey catz come thru on Fridayz," Flip said before he hurried off.

Flip walked past L.A. like he didn't know him. Then he squatted under the steps. Minutes later, L.A. entered the second hallway, toting a block figure brown paper bag held closed by two thick rubber bands. Halfway up the steps, he passed it off. "Jersey catz. Twenty-three packs," L.A. whispered as he watched Flip's nod of acknowledgement before continuing up the stairs.

Sweating and eager, Flip flew into the apartment, went straight to the kitchen table and ripped the bag open. Knowing that they usually gave the out-of-towners a play charging them ten thousand for twenty-three packs, Flip surmised that each stack that neatly sat before him contained five thousand dollars. He placed the first stack in the slot but was pretty much disappointed when his eyes witnessed the steady lit green light and the red digital figures that displayed a five followed by three zeros.

Still amped up, Flip repeated his gesture with the next stack. This time his heart raced and his blood boiled when, seconds after he started the machine, he saw flashes of green, long periods of red, flashes of red, and long periods of green. He finally exploded with rage when the digital figures displayed a four followed by a nine and a seventy.

Quickly collecting himself, Flip placed a rubber band on the second stack, tucked it in his waist—opposite of his glock, then left the apartment. L.A. stood at the top of the steps. Flip calmly glanced at L.A. while walking passed him

"Yo you seen my little brotha?," Flip asked Al, being sure not to make eye contact with fat boy.

"Earlier," Al said as Flip exited.

Flip put his gloves back on as he slyly moved to the van and hopped in. "It's them Jersey catz," Flip said pulling out the money and placing it in his hoodie's pouch. "His fat ass thirty balls short too," he snidely added while pulling out the glock.

"They early huhn?," Butter said as he eyed Flip while lowering the glock underneath the glove compartment to cock it back.

"I don't know, but where ever they headed, they gonna be late," Flip coldly stated as he pulled the sawed off shotgun from under his seat.

"Crazy late," D-Mac grimly added, slapping a clip in the Mac

Ten.

It was already said, that if it were the CT catz, it was going down by the Cross Bronx Expressway, and if it were the Jersey catz it was jumping off by the 181st bridge next to the projects — which was five lights and four straight long blocks from 1839.

By the time fat boy came out of the building, the guy in the passenger seat had already made a U-turn. As fat boy made it around to the driver's side, Butter slowly pulled off. His gaze captured the Grand Am as it followed one car behind. When they reached the second light that had turned red, the Grand Am was the second car in the right lane and the van was the third vehicle in the left.

"Make sure you catch them at the light," Flip said as they began rolling again.

"I got 'em. The light gonna change again before we get there," Butter replied.

"Leave me enough room to bounce," D-Mac added, kneeling with one hand on the sliding door's handle and the other on the Mac ten pointed down.

"C'mon Bee. I'm not new to this," Butter fancifully quipped.

"My bad, my bad," D-Mac said as he flashed a grin.

With their heads buried in their hoodies, and cold eyes wide open, the three of them were charged up. They looked like extras in the Thriller video. The adrenaline rush almost began to overpower them as they neared the fifth light. With no cars in front of him and the nose of the van edging past the Grand Am's back bumper, Butter accelerated before slamming on the breaks dead even with the Grand Am at the red light.

"Clack! Clack! Boom!, Clack! Clack! Boom!, Brruggdaa!, Brrugggda!, Clack Clack! Boom!, Brrugggda!," came the thunderous roar of the shoty and Mac-ten after Flip and D-Mac simultaneously opened the front and side doors taking aim and opening fire at the startled Grand Am's occupants who never stood a chance. Hot metal tore through their bodies like the rivets in the bridge that they should've never crossed.

The sound of cars tires screeching and horns blowing saturated the area as Flip hopped out of the van before tossing a match on the spilled gasoline. Flip quickly located the blood stained vinyl backpack on the back seat of the car that held the drugs. He then reached through where a window once was, retrieved the bag, then tossed the counterfeit money onto fat boy's bloody corpse before darting off steps behind D-Mac and Butter. The three fled into the cold air on foot. Quickly, they moved through the projects as on lookers emerged from high windows and building exits with their attention focused on the grizzly scene. As they split up on the other side of the P.J.'s, they heard the screaming police, fire department and ambulance sirens racing to the scene just before the explosion.

The first week in February, a week and a half after the Daily News' front page described the hit as "*the 181st Street counterfeit slaying*," the heat was on. Police, DT's, undercover narcs and TNT commenced "Operation Pressure Point," squeezing drug spots, number spots, and hang out spots in search of pieces to the triple homicide puzzle.

By the end of the second week, "OPP" had died down and things gradually returned back to normal. That was the week Butter officially proposed to Lisa, who hysterically accepted. He announced to her that it would be his last week in the game, and that he was considering taking his money and investing it in the music industry— something Lisa's brother Mike had been desperately trying to persuade him to get with.

That same evening, Butter hung out with Flip and D-Mac, filling them in on his plans to call it quits. They were more stunned than upset with the fact that he was serious about walking away from the game—"free money" is what D-Mac even described it as. When they questioned him on his plans for life after the game, Butter shared the music industry idea with them. He then suggested that they move on it together.

"The four of us. We can leave the game behind," Butter added.

By using the Montgomery bust years ago, and the recent Phellin Place bust, Butter tried alerting them to the fact that it was impossible for the game to last forever. But instead of taking heed, they thought greed. "That's more dough for us," Flip replied as he and D-Mac laughed and slapped five.

The music industry was something they knew nothing about nor wanted to take the time and money to learn. Though at times they appeared to be intently listening, Butter's rationale fell way short in convincing them to leave "free money" behind.

"Nah, but good luck wit the music Berry Gordy," were their last amusing statements before ending the conversation.

Hampstead Publishing

Chapter Nine

One of the good things about having the type of loot Butter had was that relocating was never a problem. Wanting to be able to focus on his new venture without temptation of reentering the game, Butter made a tough, but wise decision to distance himself away from D-Mac, Flip, and 1839 for a while. He moved from New Rochelle and bought a townhouse in Yonkers. His next purchase was the leasing of a small recording studio on Boston road for Mike, and Mike's two artists.

The transition from the game to the music industry came rather easy for Butter. Not only did he have capital, he had Lisa's brother who had been pursuing the music game since the age of fourteen. Now, at the age of twenty, Mike was intimately familiar with everything the industry had to offer. There was no doubt in Mike's mind that, with his knowledge and Butter's cash, it would be no time before they'd both be millionaires.

Though, he'd only been a part of it for less than a month, the music industry was a beautiful thing, Butter thought. He had learned quite a bit from Mike and could easily see the both of them making tons of money — legally. Despite the few times he fought with himself to keep from going back to the Ave, Butter basically remained focused. When he wasn't at the studio, he was at the house, and when he wasn't at the house, he and Lisa were either up visiting Wu and Kelly, or out shopping for their much-anticipated baby.

It was 1:30 Saturday afternoon, the last Saturday in March. The return of sunshine kept the nippy day from turning cold. Lisa, with all the Benz's tinted windows rolled up, pulled up in front of their townhouse after the long drive from their early morning visit with Wu and Kelly.

"You gonna sleep in the car?," Lisa asked, shaking Butter before reaching in the back and retrieving her yellow goose down feather ski jacket.

Butter, who had been working endlessly with Mike selling their artist's singles out of the trunk of cars, let out a stretch and sigh then said, "Damn we here aw ready?" He checked his watch then met the sly gaze of Lisa's and added, "I told you about flyin'."

"I told you about flyin'," Lisa mimicked in an animated tone before playfully sticking out her tongue like a five-year-old. Losing the animation she added, "Who said I was flyin'?"

"Just get ya fat ass out," Butter whimsically said.

"Yeah and you'll be wantin' some of this fat ass tonight," Lisa shot back, patting her backside on her way out of the car. It was compounded by Butter's extended swat, "Ouch mothafucka!," she chuckled, popping Butter in the head as he slid in the driver's seat.

"Aight, aight, aight. Stop playin'," Butter said, gesturing to her small pop belly.

Things were going so right for Lisa and Butter, who seemed only in need of each other. They seemed to be in love with one another every minute of every day. The time he spent at the studio away from her was surely made up when they were together. "If your brotha call, tell 'em I'll meet him on 25th," Butter said as his words hit Lisa's back. He watched her nod then peeled off.

Butter and Mike had been selling for two weeks. They sold forty copies of their artist's single and close to three hundred by the end of the week. Since then, there was no turning back. They were traveling up, down, and around Harlem, Brooklyn,

Queens, and the Bronx. They dropped off the demos at every radio station, club, and record shop they could think of. This Saturday was making the end of their second week and they were close to having eight hundred records sold. As Butter slowly crossed 125th Street, he could spot the small crowd gathering around the open trunk of Mike's gold colored, rental Eagle Premier, which was parked in front of J&J variety record and tape shop.

"Money Mike!," Butter called. After double parking, he made his way around the trunk of the Benz. "What's up Bee," Butter said in a tone that was a pitch higher than the demo of their artist's track blaring out of the trunk's speakers.

"What up Duke," Mike cheerfully responded as he continued making transactions.

Mike's golden tan complexion was identical to his sister's. He stood the same height as Butter and carried a couple of pounds more in weight. It was easy to tell by his low, dark black, curly hair, that silky hair ran in the family.

"It looks like you been out here a minute," Butter said.

"Since ten o'clock Money," Mike answered in a matter-of fact tone.

"Okay famm. Get money," Butter replied as he gave Mike a pound before heading back around the Benz. "Yo, I'll be by the Apollo," Butter added. Mike acknowledged with a nod. Butter got in the Benz and drove off.

Butter was really fond of Mike, and both being twenty had little to do with it, nor did the fact that Butter was in love with his sister. Butter loved Mike's sense of loyalty, dedication, and determination. It often reminded him of his earlier 1839 days with D-Mac, Flip, and Wu during their strive to get money. He also couldn't help but appreciate Lisa even more every time he thought about how easily his crew and Mike could've been enemies if Lisa would've chose war instead of the date over two years earlier.

Butter parked his car in front of the McDonalds next to the Apollo. "Yo money grip," Butter said as he gestured for a guy to come over to the open trunk of his car. "Yo check this joint out for me," he said while turning up his car's radio. Butter watched the guy's bobbing head that expressed pleasure in the demo.

"Dat's the joint I heard on the radio the other day," the guy excitedly said.

"I'm sayin' Duke. You ca cop it right here for a pound," Butter said, while waving for other passing people to come over. "Good lookin' Chief," Butter said as he was exchanging the record for the crumbled five dollar bill the guy extended.

"Let me get one," said a young lady extending five dollars."

"Good lookin' Sweetie," Butter said after the exchange.

" Who are they?," she quizzed, scrutinizing the record.

"The girl singing is Tonya Hunt and the cat rappin' is Eric Capers—World's World. Make sure you request it on the radio," Butter chanted as she walked off.

Before he knew it, Butter was enthusiastically serving a slowly increasing crowd. Both male and female, ages ranging from fifteen to forty. Though he was asking five, he had no problem accepting four and even three dollars from people as they showed support for what Butter adopted as his new hustle.

"World's World! Make sure you request it on the radio!," Butter repeated with every transaction.

As the crowd dwindled away, Butter began to think about all of the requests the radio stations were going to receive if only half the people made the phone call. He quickly lost that train of thought when he spotted the candy apple red Infinity Q45 slowly turning on to 125th Street. "What up famm!," Flip said as he got out of the double-parked car.

"Oh shit!," Butter exclaimed as he and Flip slapped five followed by a rugged hug. It was no doubt in Butter's mind that behind the dark tinted windows on the driver's side was D-Mac.

"Yeah nigga! You know what it is!," D-Mac called out as he emerged from the car.

"You fly mothafucka!," Butter said as they ruggedly hugged.

Though they occasionally expressed how much they were still down for each other during periodic phone conversations, it'd been over a month since they'd last seen one another. D-Mac and Flip knew that Butter trying to get his hustle off the ground was going to take up most, if not all, of Butter's time, so they purposely stayed clear leaving Butter plenty of room to stay focused. "I'm sayin'. This how it's going down?," Flip asked while examining a record he pulled out a crate in the trunk.

"Yeah. Yeah. A little somethin'," Butter responded as he served customers.

"I thought you was gonna be on some Russell Simmons shit? I didn't know you was gonna be doing hand to hand combat," D-Mac teased. "You need a pitcher duke," he added causing the three of them to chuckle.

"Bounce nigga," Butter replied.

"I'm just bullshittin'.   But everything real.   Jake ca lock a nigga up for this right?"

"They fuck wit niggas. But it ain't like getting bagged wit the crid'ils," Butter said, referring to the selling of crack.

"They don't fuck wit us. They fuck wit our workers," D-Mac boasted. " We livin' large."

"Word. You ca' always come home if this shit don't jump off," Flip threw in.

"Yeah, I know famm," Butter said, then changed the subject, "Where you niggas headed?"

"Before we peeped ya joint over here, we was on our way to J&J variety to cop some Brucey Bee and Kid Capri tapes," Flip answered, getting back into the car.

"Word, Lisa's brother is over there."

"Damn. Y'all got it sewed up down here," D-Mac said while making his way back to his side of the car.

"Matter of fact. Let me get ten of them joints, " Flip said as he pulled out a knot of cash from his pocket. "I'll pass 'em out on the block," he said.

Butter handing him the records without taking the money, "Don't sweat that famm. It ain't nothin'."

"Com' on Duke. I' m not here to knock ya hustle. What I owe you?" Recognizing Butter's silence, Flip caught eyes with the slim, dark skinned girl that Butter was making an exchange with. "Excuse me fly girl. How much are they?," Flip asked.

"Five dollars," she answered while cutting her eyes at Butter with an innocent smile.

"Check this out Cutie," Flip said as he gestured for her to come to the Q45's window. Without hesitation she was between Flip and Butter smothering the window, "I'm sayin'. That's my manz' an 'em," Flip explained while directing her attention to Butter. "He trying to front on me. Now he aw' ready gave me ten, but my other manz want ten too."

Flip watched as her dark brown eyes scanned the interior until she found D-Mac. Flip peeled off a hundred-dollar bill and said, "Do me a favor? Tell 'em to give you ten more joints?," he said as he gave her the bill.

The girl threw her hands on her hips as she turned to face Butter. Then whimsically raved, "How you gonna take my little bit of dough and not theirs?"

"That's bad business Duke," D-Mac interjected leaning over towards Flip's window. After an amusing stare, Butter took the money and gave the girl the records.

"Thanks Shorty," Flip said, as she passed the records. He extended five dollars to her. "Now you got a free copy, " he winked.

"Thank you," she responded, standing still as if she was waiting for more directions.

"See you at the wedding Bee. We out," D-Mac and Flip chuckled while looking past the girl.

"Aight famm. Good lookin'," Butter said.

"Whomp! Whomp!" D-Mac's horn sounded as he skirted off.

Butter glanced over at the girl as she stared into the Q45's rear window and said, "World's World! Make sure you request it!" She looked at Butter, then took the record, and walked off.

Chapter Ten

Tuesday, May 1st

D-Mac and Regina were on their way to pick up Wu and
Kelly. They cruised up 87 North in his Land Cruiser. His
thoughts were on the five months Wu had been gone, and the
surprise party Lisa and Butter had planned later in the evening
for their return. He then became more excited when he
thought how good it was going to feel to have the entire crew
together again, something that hadn't been in a long time. His
thoughts instantly vanished when he noticed through his rear
view mirror, the flashing red and blue lights of a state trooper's
patrol car on his tail. "Put your seat belt on," D-Mac mumbled
to Regina, slyly putting his on as he pulled over.

Knowing the routine, he turned the truck off and watched as
the white manly-looking female trooper approached his side of
the truck. "Good morning folks," the trooper spoke in her
raspy tone, with one hand resting on her gun holster. "Do you
know why I pulled you over?," she asked before D-Mac could
respond to her greeting.

Now let me see?, D-Mac thought. *, Is it because I'm a young black
cat pushin' a fly ass truck? Or is it because you just didn't have shit
to do?* "No, not really," D-Mac politely answered.

"Your tints are too dark."

"My tints?," D-Mac repeated as if he couldn't believe she pulled him over for that.

"Yes. Anything darker than twenty percent is against state law," she stated matter-of-factly.

D-Mac, who had no knowledge of that, wasn't really up for a debate that he knew he would lose even if the trooper was wrong, so he tried to brush her off. "All right I'll take them off as soon as I get home," he said.

"May I see your license and registration?," she demandingly asked. Her eyes quickly traveled from his gold chains, to his wide gold bracelet, then over to Regina's big gold earrings before landing on the papers D-Mac extended to her. The trooper went back to her vehicle to check the paperwork.

After ten minutes of looking up at the roof of the truck, with his tilted head against the truck's headrest, D-Mac began to get irritated. "This bitch bullshitting," D-Mac said, as he glanced into the review mirror. It was then that he noticed a second trooper's patrol car coming to a stop directly behind the first one. "They coming to search ma," he warned Regina.

"I hope you're not dirty," Regina said expressing some concern.

D-Mac, knowing his paper work was in order and nothing was in the car, almost took Regina's question as an insult. "Picture that," he quipped, as he viewed the lady trooper approaching on Regina's side and a white burly male trooper moving along his side.

"Excuse me Sir," the male trooper's deep voice bellowed as he reached D-Mac's open window. "I need you to step out of the vehicle please?"

The fact that D-Mac had been through this routine several times, and the certainty of his papers being correct, caused D-Mac to protest. "You have to ask me can you search, right?," D-Mac asked.

The trooper, about to fill D-Mac in on what the lady trooper found out, raised his gun and said, "Not when there's a warrant out on you. Now Sir, please slowly step out of the vehicle."

"A warrant?," D-Mac disdainfully echoed. Hesitant and confused, D-Mac was sure there was some mistake. Nevertheless, he obeyed the trooper's order.

"Please step out of the truck ma'am," the lady trooper said as she opened the door for a distraught Regina. The lady trooper walked Regina to meet the second trooper who was placing cuffs on D-Mac's wrists.

"Mr. Turner. The federal government has a warrant posted for your arrest," the lady trooper said addressing D-Mac by his last name.

"The feds?", D-Mac jumped as his eyes jumped from Regina onto the lady trooper, then the male trooper. "What the feds want wit me?," he asked. His rights were being recited by the second trooper while the male trooper escorted D-Mac to the first trooper's car.

"I don't know. But you'll soon find out," the second trooper responded, placing D-Mac in the back seat. He then closed the door and approached the first trooper and a crying, shaken Regina. "Here's some of his property," the second trooper said as he handed Regina a large manila envelope containing D-Mac's wallet, a wad of cash, the bracelet he had to remove in order to get the cuffs on, and D-Mac's truck keys.

"Do you have someone you can call to come get you?," the lady trooper asked as her eyes locked onto Regina's tear soaked face. After realizing Regina was not with her, the lady placed a hand gently on Regina's arm and said, "Listen sweet-ie, the truck is being impounded. You can either come back to the station with us and call someone, or he can drop you off at the nearest hotel." Still unable to get a response from Regina's numbness, the lady turned to the second trooper with the, 'What do you think?' look on her face.

"Let's take her to the station," the male trooper commented. Then he watched as the lady trooper escorted Regina to the back of his car and placed her, uncuffed, inside. "Good Job," the male trooper commended his smiling fellow trooper before they got in their patrol cars and drove off.

It was the thrashing on the front door of Flip's townhouse that startled he and Denise out of bed at 6:30 that morning. Before he could reach for his underwear his room was clus-tered with gun-pointing Federal Agents. "FBI! Don't fucking move!," one of the agents barked.

A female agent hurriedly moved to Denise, gestured for her

to wrap the sheet around her naked body and stand up. The agent then escorted Denise out of the room leaving Flip's exposed body behind with the other male agents. "Get dressed," a third agent said, tossing a baffled Flip a pair of jeans from his closet.

"What about the rest of—"

"You don't need them," an agent said. "Your pants and these are good enough," the agent added, throwing Flip the first pair of sneakers he set eyes on.

"Captain. We just got word that Mr. Turner is in State Trooper custody," an agent reported to his superior while they stood around waiting on Flip.

The sound of D-Mac's last name stiffened Flip for a second as he slipped his bare feet into a pair of all white, low cut air force ones. Consumed by his thoughts of what exactly was going on, Flip could not comprehend the reciting of his rights as he blankly stared at the agent's moving lips. "So it shouldn't take long to tear his place apart," the captain retorted.

At 7:05 that morning, NYPD, FBI, DEA, and ATF, had the block looking like the police man's ball as their branded jackets and unmarked vehicles flooded the avenue from one end of the block to the other. It seemed like every civilian on the entire block was up and either out their windows, or on the street in awe as agents escorted the twins and at least one guy from every building on the block, including 1839, to law enforcement vehicles.

The ringing phone woke Lisa out of a sound sleep. She fixed her blurry eyes on Butter who was still dead to the world, then drowsily groped for the phone. "Hello," Lisa said in a barely audible voice.

"Lisa!," Denise's whimpering voice called. "Where's Butter?!"

It took no time for Lisa to recognize who it was, and the urgency in Denise's frightened voice. Lisa's heart began to skip a beat as she cleared her throat. "Denise! What's wrong?"

"The feds just took Flip!"

The news put Lisa into a sitting position, as she yelled, "What? Oh Shit!" Lisa looked down at Butter, whose eyes were trying to keep from opening.

"Who that?," Butter groggily asked.

"Denise! She said the feds took Flip!"

Lisa's words splashed in Butter's face like a bucket of ice-cold water. With widened eyes, he unconsciously snatched the phone from Lisa's ear. "Denise! What happened?," he questioned.

"The feds took Flip a few minutes ago!"

"Did they say for what?"

"I don't know! A lady cop brung me down stairs!," she sniveled. "She asked did I know anything about drugs being in the house!"

"You didn't say nothing did —-"

"I don't know nothing!," Denise said hysterically blabbering into the phone. "I don't know what's going on.

"Regina just called and said D-Mac is in Jail! She's upstate somewhere! They just tore the place up! I don't know what to do!"

"Aight listen!," Butter interrupted in his attempt to slow her down. "Cool out and stay put until I call you back!," he directed, moving about the room at a frantic pace.

"When? "

"In a little while," he responded. Butter passed the phone to Lisa and motioned with his lips for her to try and calm Denise down while he got dressed.

Butter's mind began to race a hundred miles an hour as he asked himself all sorts of questions. *Damn, are they looking for me too? Do they know where I live? Is this from when I was down? Or is it something Flip an 'em did while I wasn't fuckin' wit them that last three and a half months?*

When he spotted the three crates of records he and Mike stacked in the corner of his room the night earlier, his mindset changed. He suddenly realized that a lot of his money rested in those three crates and the crates of records over at Mike's apartment. Taking no chances, Butter thought he had better move them out of there in case the feds were coming. He signaled for Lisa to get off of the phone. Then he moved to the closet.

"What's wrong?," Lisa said as she hung up. Wearing only a pair of purple panties, she worked her way out of bed.

"Call ya brother and tell 'em I'm on my way over! Tell 'em to stay there 'til I get there!," Butter said while stuffing a Louis

Vuitton bag with his jewelry, a gun, and some cash.

Lisa, knowing Butter and her brother had been selling singles for the past few months, stood motionless at the thought that the feds might be looking for her fiancé and father of her unborn child.

"Lisa! Call Mike!," Butter roared as the strength in his tone pushed her to the phone.

In no rush to get to D-Mac's empty townhouse, the agents crashed through the door of Butter's last known address. "FBI with a warrant!," an agent barked as they rushed in the New Rochelle Townhouse.

It wasn't until the Captain saw an elderly white man frozen at the dining room table that he knew a mistake had been made. "What the hell is going on?", the skinny, gray haired man raved as he dropped his Wall Street Journal. His beady blue eyes searched the motionless agents awed expressions as he rose from the table fastening his robe. "What in heaven's name is—-"

"Just relax Sir," the Captain said as he extended a stop sign to the man while gesturing to his agents to back out. "Obviously there's been a terrible misunderstanding."

"You bet your ass there's been—-"

"Honey what's going on down there?," an elderly lady's voice leaping from the top of the steps cried out.

"Nothing honey! I'm just trying to fix something!," the old man answered never taking his cold stare off the tall dark captain. "I'll be up in a minute!"

"Listen Sir," the captain interjected, he reached in his jacket and extended a card. "I'm sorry about this mix up. You can get in contact with my office and we'll straighten this out," he said as he pointed to the busted door.

"Oh not to worry. My attorney will be in contact with you soon enough," the old man shot back as he snatched the card.

The visibly angry captain stepped out into the huddle of agents, looked around, then said, "I want a search warrant and some men over at Mr. Ryder's parent's house five minutes ago. I want every piece of paper in that house combed through until our man's address turns up!"

The orders sent four of the eight agents flying. The captain looked to the remaining four and said, "Let's go see what Mr.

Turner is sitting on."

Wu and Kelly had been sitting by the receptionist desk since 7:30 a.m. They knew discharge wasn't until 8:00, but they wanted to say their good-byes to the patients and staff members that they had become good friends with over the past few months.

At 7:55, Wu began wondering why D-Mac hadn't arrived yet. He knew he had stressed to D-Mac that he and Kelly would be ready to roll at 8:01. After spending five months in there, Wu had no intentions of spending a minute more than he had to.

"Excuse me Mr. Gray, " the tall white agent said as he addressed Wu by his last name while he and a shorter white agent towered over him and Kelly with extended I.D. "FBI, we have a warrant for your arrest."
Wu spotted the two suited men as they walked down the corridor but thought nothing of it.

"A Warrant?," Wu said in a tone louder than the shorter agent who was reciting Wu his rights as he cuffed him.

"What the hell are yall doing?," Kelly wailed, rising up from her seat desperately trying to pull Wu to her. "He didn't do anything!," she cried as a stream of tears began pouring down her cheeks.

"Ma'am. Please Ma'am," the tall agent said, attempting to restrain her. "Step away Ma'am," the agent said while gesturing for the receptionist's help.

"Bitch you betta not put your hands on me!," Kelly snapped, stiffening the petite white receptionist. "Get the hell off me!," she yelled as she wildly skirmished out of the agent's clutches as Wu was being led away.

A crowd began to gather which irritated the agent. "Ma'am I don't want to have to cuff you," the agent warned, re-capturing Kelly with a tighter grip. "He's under arrest and you're not. But if you don't settle down, I'll have no choice but to charge you with Obstruction of Justice." Though, his threat did not reach Kelly, who continued her tantrum, it caused a heavyset black staff member to emerge from the crowd.

"Kelly!," the woman said as she wrapped Kelly from behind. "No Kelly. You won't do him no good in jail," the lady said with her lips close to Kelly's right ear. Her words traveled through Kelly's body like thorezean, causing Kelly to place her hands over her mouth and sob uncontrollably.

"Everything is gonna be fine baby," the lady said as she spun Kelly around to comfort her. The lady signaled to the agent that she had Kelly under control and after a nod of appreciation, the agent hurried off.

When the agents arrived at Butter's mother's house they were met at the first door by Butter's father who was on his way to check out some real estate. "Mr. Ryder?," an agent asked as he stopped Butter's father at the open door. Butter's father nodded yes. "We're Federal Agents." The four of them extended their ID's, "And we have a warrant to search the premises."

Butter's father stood tall with a nice build. His clean-shaven face always kept a smooth look to it, nothing like it did after hearing the agent's news, "Federal Agents? Warrant?," he replied apparently befuddled. "Warrant for what? "

"Your son's involvement in illegal drug activity. If you would like to see the warrant, here it is," the agent said as he handed it to Butter's father before moving past him, followed by the other agents. When they reached the second door the agent looked to Butter's father and said, "Do we have to bust it down or —-"

"I'll open it. I'll open it," Butter's father said, weaving between them.

"Is your son or anyone else in the house Sir?"

"My wife is away and my son is not home," he responded as he opened the door.

"Does your son live here?," the agent asked. After receiving no answer, the agent firmly repeated his question. "Mr. Ryder, does your son live here?"

"You have a search warrant to my house and you don't know the answer to that?," Butter's father sarcastically stated as their stares met.

The five-minute drive to Mike's apartment was not enough time for Butter to really map out what his plans were. He just knew he had a little bit of cash, crates full of records, Mike and the two artists that had yet to see any real money, and the big possibility that the feds were after him. Butter only hoped that Mike would understand his dilemma and hold things down until he knew exactly what was going on.

When Butter pulled up to the two-story brown house that Mike's flat was in, he immediately spotted Mike's shirtless upper body hanging out of the window.

Butter motioned with his hand for Mike to come downstairs then hurriedly moved to the trunk of the Benz. Seconds later, Mike wearing a pair of black and white low cut uptowns, black Guess jeans, and a white Nike tee-shirt, was coming out of the house.

"What's up Bee?," Mike asked with an inquisitive look on his face as he watched Butter pull one crate after the other from the trunk of his car.

Disregarding Mike's question Butter said, "Yo Bee! We gotta take these up stairs!" Butter extending the third crate to him.

Though Lisa had only told Mike that Butter was on his way, Mike could tell by the urgency he'd detected in his sister's voice that something was wrong. Seeing that Butter appeared to be pressed for time, Mike grabbed the crate and rushed upstairs followed by Butter who had a crate as well. Mike placed the crate inches inside of his open apartment's door and raced back downstairs with Butter on his heels.

"Where's the rented?," Butter asked after not noticing it.

"I had to turn it in," Mike answered snatching up the last crate.

"We'll get another one later. Yo take this," Butter said as he took the Louis Vuitton bag out of the trunk and placed it on top of the crate that Mike held. "You got it?," he asked, making sure it wasn't too heavy.

"Yeah I'm good," Mike said as he was studying Butter's sweating, concerned face. "What do you want me to do?," Mike asked as he found himself feeling pity for Butter's situation, even though he hadn't a clue what it was.

"Just hold that down," Butter said, moving to the driver's door of the Benz, "I'll kick it wit' chew in a little bit."

"Aight," Mike's response missed Butter's head as he ducked in the car. Mike watched Butter sit still for a second then he made his way in the house.

Lisa's face was stained with tears as she held the phone tightly to her ear listening to the continuous rings of her brother's phone. She was left devastated by Butter's father's call informing her that not only were the feds looking for Butter, but they had also found Butter's address in his mother's phone book and were on their way.

Since Butter's father told her that it took him almost twenty minutes after the feds left to find their number, *it wouldn't be long before the feds got there*, Lisa thought. "Mike!" Lisa wailed into the phone abandoning her thought, instantly realizing the ringing had stopped, "Where's Butter?"

"Downstairs in the car. I think he left though."

"No Mike Ple-e-ase! Catch'em!," she sobbed clutching the phone with both hands.

Mike quickly moved to the window with the phone to his ear wondering what was it that had his sister so emotionally distraught, "He's gone."

"No Mike Ple-e-ase...!"

"Lisa, what's wrong?!," Mike demanded terribly disturbed by his sister's behavior. "Lisa!," he called into the dial tone. Then Mike snatched his black Nike sweatshirt and raced out the door.

After tossing the cordless phone onto the unmade bed, Lisa guided her belly through the house. Wearing some orange Reeboks and an all white maternity suit, she hysterically made her way out the front door and down a flight of steps. She stood still, surveying both ends of the long block filled with parked cars before she waddled off into one direction. Lisa knew Butter would be coming in after leaving Mike's apartment. Wanting them to be able to spot each other, she walked against the infrequent traffic in the middle of the one-way street.

As Lisa neared the corner, she heavily sobbed feeling pain in both her heart and her stomach. The cramps had begun to become too great for her, but her anticipation of Butter coming around the corner any second kept her painfully moving forward. When she finally reached the corner and looked to her right, she was flattened by the scene of Butter's Benz in the middle of the two-way street surrounded by three unmarked cars.

"Li-s-saaa!," Mike yelled, watching his sister hit the ground. His call caused Butter, who was being stuffed into an agent's car and the agents, to direct their attention to Lisa's stretched out body as her brother raced to her.

"That's my pregnant fiancéeee!," Butter raved from the secured back seat, his voice piercing through the closed window.

The captain thinking quick on his feet, saw an opportunity to stroke Butter the right way in hopes of making it easier for him and his agents later on down the line, when they approached Butter for some cooperation. "Get an ambulance here!," the captain said as his orders sent one of the seven agents diving into one of the cars. The captain watched as the agent grabbed the CB then continued, "You three drive Mr. Ryder down there!," he said while pointing in Lisa's direction. "And don't move until Mr. Ryder hears the status of his friend!" The captain then gestured to the Benz and said, "You take the vehicle and the three of you come to the house with me!"

A half-hour later, the agents relayed the news to Butter. Lisa and the baby were both alive and would be fine. Then they hauled Butter off to Valhalla, New York.

Hampstead Publishing

Chapter Eleven

Butter was delivered to the Vahalla County Jail at 9:45 a.m. He was taken into custody by a tall dark lean C.O. who escorted him from the parking lot and into the beige high-rise style building.

Butter, with his legs shackled and hands cuffed to the front, stood side by side with the C.O. while they waited for the first of two sliding glass doors to open. Seconds later they passed through the first electronically opened door. Butter watched as it closed behind them, then his attention was drawn to the second sliding door as it opened. Barely clutching Butter's arm, the C.O. turned Butter to the left to face the C.O.'s station after they stepped through the second door. Standing behind the elevated station's wooden counter was a heavy, light-skinned female C.O., a couple of feet away on her left stood a short white male C.O., and a few feet away on her right was an average height white C.O. who was fumbling with the huge control panel affixed to the wall behind them.

"Name?," the woman said more than asked, with big brown eyes drilling down at Butter.

"Sean Ryder," Butter responded, watching her gaze travel to the clipboard she held. His attention was lured away by the first C.O. as he removed the iron restraints. *Damn, thank you,* Butter thought to himself, watching as the C.O. tossed the metal into a nearby cardboard box.

"Step over here," the C.O. said as he led Butter a couple of feet to the right where they faced a tall metal detector. "Do you have any metal in your body? Fillings? Head plate? Shit like that?," the C.O. questioned.

"Nah."

"All right. Step through," the C.O. instructed. He acknowledged the silence of the metal detector then met Butter on the opposite side. "Alright, wait here a minute," the C.O. said, then stepped back over to the counter.

Butter stood facing the long corridor. His ears tuned in to the fanciful conversation the C.O.'s were having four feet behind him as his eyes scanned the first floor. Lined up along his left side were two small rooms followed by three bullpens. Straight ahead, facing him, was another bullpen followed by two more bullpens and another small room along the right side of the corridor.

Thanks to the agent's message, Butter's mind was no longer consumed with the image of Lisa's stretched out body and the fear of losing both her and the baby. His thoughts were solely on the seriousness of his situation.

"Mr. Ryder!," the C.O. called, finally able to get Butter's attention. "This ain't no place to be day dreaming," he added as he opened the door to the first little room on the left. He watched as Butter entered. "Take your clothes off and place them over there," the C.O. said as he gestured to the little table in the room—also the only furniture in the room.

Officer Cook, the name read on the C.O.'s little blue tag clipped onto his uniform's shirt pocket where Butter's eyes rested on his chest area as if he were searching for breast. He found it hard to believe that a man had asked him to strip.

After noticing Butter had not budged, Cook asked in an almost serious tone, " Do you have a hearing problem Mr. Ryder?"

"Nah"

"Well, let's go. I ain't got all day."

C.O. Cook had only been a C.O. for a couple of years, but his attitude was like most veterans he had been around. He was there to do the eight hours, whether it was bullshitting with the inmates or his fellow staff members, he made sure his days were no longer than they had to be, and he was known for his sometimes sarcastic and witty remarks towards inmates that tried to make his days long.

Butter slowly removed his white and green low cut Air Force Ones, his white Guess jeans, and a green Guess sweatshirt. He paused for a second before hesitantly removing his socks and boxers after being gestured by Cook.

"Hands up," Cook instructed as he faced Butter's naked body, frisking him with his eyes. "All right. Mouth," he said as he began looking into Butter's wide-open mouth. "'Ears," he said. His eyes quickly moved down to Butter's private area. "Lift. All right. Turn around. Spread 'em," he said then scanned the crack of Butter's yellow ass. "Alright. Bottom of your feet," the C.O. said then watched as Butter raised one foot back at a time. "All right get dressed," he said as he handed Butter an article of his clothing one at a time after searching them.

If there was a record in speed dressing Butter certainly broke it as he appeared to have slipped on all his clothing in one motion. Cook, picking up on Butter's uneasiness, held the door open and said, "Betta get use to it."

How can I get used to standing butt-ass naked in front of another man? Better yet, how did he get used to watching a nigga's nuts all day? Butter thought to himself as he stepped out into the corridor.

Through the bullpen's huge thick glass, Butter could stare back at the many eyes of young and old inmates that watched him being slowly led down the middle of the hall. Not moving slow enough to count, Butter could estimate fifteen to twenty guys in each pen he passed, most of which were standing. Butter then couldn't believe his vision when his gaze met with the six girls staring at him through the third bullpen's glass on the left. He felt bad for letting the thought of how brutal the females looked enter his mind, but it was all quickly washed away when he and Cook's attention were snagged by the light pounding on the glass that came from the bullpen on the right—directly across.

"Ayo Duke!," Wu shouted as his muffled call managed to penetrate the bullpen's thick glass. Butter turned to see Wu beating on the glass. His vision quickly focused on the few young and old faces that also plastered the glass, then back onto Wu's half grin. Butter, recognizing Wu's grin as nothing more than pleasure for the sight of a very familiar face, returned an identical grin as he neared the glass.

"Stop beating on my glass!," Cook barked as he and Butter stood facing the pen's steel door. "Where the hell you think you at?" If his roar was meant to be intimidating, it didn't show, as several guys in the pen found it amusing. "And get away from the damn door!," Cook added to another inmate after the door slid open.

"What up famm," Wu greeted Butter as he entered.

"What up," Butter responded. His eyes rapidly shook down the ten by twenty-two-foot long holding cell.

There was a ten-foot long wooden bench against the wall opposite the glass that was smothered with inmates. There were inmates sprinkled on the pen's floor, some sitting up and others stretched out. At one end of the pen sat a metal toilet, and affixed to the wall at the opposite end of the pen were two collect call only phones that were occupied. The two little vents in the pen's low ceiling circulated the dry stiff air that each inmate effortlessly fought for.

"Let's go over here," Wu suggested leading Butter to the wall by the toilet. "Pardon us Duke," Wu said to a group of three guys as he and Butter stepped over their extended legs.

After reaching their intended spot, Wu turned to face Butter with intent eyes, and in a low tone asked, "What the fuck is goin' on?"

Butter equally riddled, replied, "I don't know. Around seven this mornin' Denise called the rest talkin' about Flip and D-Mac getting' knocked by the feds. A hour and change later madd Jake rushed me. They had my whip hemmed up about a block away from my crib. They came up to the spot and bagged you?," Butter asked as if he suddenly remembered that Wu was in the rehab. He watched as Wu nodded yes, then asked, "How long you been here?"

"Since around a quarter to nine", Wu answered.

"You been in this bullpen ever since?," Butter said through widened eyes.

"Yeah. What time is it?," Wu asked, momentarily forgetting that no one was allowed to wear any type of jewelry. Realizing his own silly question, Wu then tried to line his vision up with the hallway's walls for a clock.

"The clock all the way down there," Butter said as he pointed towards the CO's station." You can't see it from here. That shit said eleven forty-five when I came in."

"Eleven forty-five!," Wu disdainfully echoed. He could hardly believe that only three hours had passed, especially when it felt like ten.

"Did you call anybody?," Butter asked, reminding Wu that he had no one but the crew and Kelly. And Kelly didn't have a phone.

"Who Im'ma call?," Wu asked him.

"I'm sayin', a lawyer," Butter clarified.

"I can't do shit on that phone," Wu said while gesturing to the collect phones at the opposite end of the pen.

At the sight of C.O. Cook approaching the door, like always, conversations were reduced to near silence as inmates desperately anticipated the announcement of their names. They all eagerly stared at the sliding door as it opened.

"Gray!," Cook called as if he was a drill sergeant. His eyes fixed on Wu making it obvious to everyone that he knew the face that matched the name, "Legal visit!"

"Pardon us Duke," Wu said as he was making his way to the door with Butter on his heels. "That must be one of them court appointed joints," he said without turning back.

"I'll get up," Butter said to Wu's back as the door closed behind him. Butter moved to the glass and watched as Wu and Cook headed down the corridor. He began to wonder how long it would be before his court appointed showed. He also wondered where D-Mac and Flip were being held?

A thin dark guy that stood next to him at the glass, distracted Butter from his thoughts. The guy was gesturing with his hands in the air to the women in the bullpen directly across from them.

"What's up!," the guy's yell ricocheted within the bullpen. The guy, Butter and a couple of other fellas looked on as three of the girls stood at their glass with their hands in the air as if they were asking him what did he want to be up? The guy branding a smile lifted up his shirt while motioning for them to do the same. , "Show us some titties!," he said while rubbing his own flat chest.

The three girls who looked like they had been rumbling amongst each other in the pen all morning, seemed to be enjoying the attention. It probably was the most attention they had received since the feds were watching them board the train with drugs. Realizing they now had at least fifteen horny niggas as an audience, they decided to do a little teasing. They stood on the bench and inched their shirts up slowly, stopping before their decent sized breast were exposed.

"Come on bitch, stop playin'!," the next guy said while, lifting up his shirt.

The girls responded with some scary smiles, then one gestured to the zipper of her pants and yelled, "Show us some dick!" Her request caused the other three girls to stand up. The sight was like witnessing an ugly pageant with six winners.

"Bitch you must be crazy if you think I'm gonna let my joint see your face," the first guy grumbled, causing the entire bullpen to laugh. "Them bitchez frontin'," he said as he fanned his hand at them before turning away. His gesture was slowly imitated by one guy after another.

The girls, recognizing the vanishing audience, studied each other for a brief second then the six of them spontaneously pulled their shirts well up above their breasts. "Oh shit!," a guy yelled causing the guys who gave up, to pile up in front of the glass. The bullpen erupted into wild five clapping and laughter. "Yeah bitchez wiggle them shits!," the guy said as they watched the girls maneuver like go-go dancers.

"Damn, them ugly bitchez got some pretty lookin' titties," a guy commented.

"Word," another guy threw in.

The guy who initially drew the girls' attention, wormed his way back to the front of the glass and again lifted his shirt up, but this time a little higher, so that it covered his face. He then motioned for the girls to do the same. When the girls appeared confused he yelled, "Cover yall fuckin' faces!" Once again the bullpen erupted into laughter causing the girls to plaster their glass with six middle fingers before ending the show.

Even while strenuously trying to remain focused on the perplexity of his legal predicament, Butter couldn't help but find the whole ordeal amusing. He laughed out loud with the fellas and still felt tickled inside as he made his way over to the occupied phones. He propped himself with his back against the wall behind two guys who were apparently next in line, and after five seconds of waiting, his humor was drowned by grief.

Wu entered the little room. *"What am I doing here? This the same room I stripped in?,"* was Wu's first thought upon entering the little room. Whether the two chairs were added or not, Wu knew he would never forget that room. He stood watching as the aging and balding lawyer sat at the small table going through some notes without acknowledging that he had entered the room. Seconds later, the thin black attorney's face was still buried in his notes. Finally, he gestured for Wu to sit in the empty chair opposite him.

While he sat patiently, Wu began thinking about a bunch of guys in the bullpen and how they kept bickering about the way their court appointed lawyers sold them out at trial. He then wondered if it were true when he heard one of guys say that the judges and prosecutors were the ones who ran the court appointed lawyers. Hoping it wasn't true, he ran his hand once over his face and asked himself, *"What the hell did I get myself into?"*

The attorney broke the silence. "Mr. Gray," he said as they stared at each other. "My name is Mr. O'Hare," his strong and confident voice stated. "I've been appointed by the court to represent you on the charges brought forth in this indictment," he said, sliding the stapled indictment to Wu for his viewing pleasure. "I don't know if you're able to afford an attorney or plan to hire one, but until someone makes a commitment to the court stating that they will be representing you, I am the attorney of record and it's my responsibility to represent you."

Wu was all ears while his eyes lay strapped to the indictment's first page. He focused down the long list of real first and last names along with their aliases that were printed beside them.

Mr. O'Hare studied Wu's bowed head as he continued. "Before we go over that indictment, let me say this," he said then paused until Wu made eye contact with him. "It's important that you be truthful with me because I'm here to help you. Whatever you and I discuss is strictly confidential, meaning it stays between you and I. Do you understand that?," he asked then watched Wu nod yes. Then he asked him, "Do you understand what the government is charging you with?"

"No," Wu said speaking for the first time. "I don't understand none of it," he honestly stated.

"Mr. Gray, you and a number of others are being charged with conspiracy to posses with intent to distribute in excess of 50 grams of cocaine base and distributing in excess of 50 grams of cocaine base. Though the indictment charges others from the summer of 1989 through April 1991, it appears that you are only being held accountable from 1989 through December, 1990. I guess that's because you were in a drug rehab", Mr. O'Hare stated while scanning his notes. "Is that correct?"

"Yeah," Wu cautiously answered, then added, "I was in a rehab but I wasn't down with no conspiracy."

Mr. O'Hare studied Wu for a second with the 'don't bullshit me' look, then said, "Well Mr. Gray, I find that hard to believe, because there are quite a few guys sitting in M.C.C. saying different..... In fact….," Mr. O'Hare flipped through his notes, his voice began soaring as if he was trying to intimidate Wu, "they said you, Mr. Ryder, Mr. Turner, and a Mr. Wheeler were the ones who put this entire crack operation together. "Is that true?," he asked him. Wu, quickly becoming uneasy, evenly replied, "Like I told you, I wasn't down with no conspiracy."

Mr. O'Hare began to look annoyed and asked, "Do you know any of these guys?" After Wu nodded yes Mr. O'Hare added, "Did you know that they were crack dealers?"

"Them niggas in the bullpen were right," Wu thought to himself before firing his own line of questioning. "Are you the fuckin' prosecutor or what?" With one eyebrow raised Wu said, "who said they were drug dealers? I don't hang with drug dealers, and anyway, why you acting like I'm guilty? You think I'm guilty?"

Mr. O'Hare studied Wu's distorted face for a second, then began tapping his pen on the note pad in front of him. Then calmly said, "Whether I believe you or not isn't of much impor-tance," "It's the jury that you need to convince Mr. Gray.... They have to believe you and not the number of people—your codefendants," he stressed," that will get on the stand and swear that you are a drug dealer." He paused letting his words linger into the air then changed his approach, ".... Do you know how much time you're facing?" He watched as Wu shook his head no. "Life. Life in prison Mr. Gray."

Like plenty of gangsters before him, Wu became numb. He watched as Mr. O'Hare's lips moved but couldn't hear a word he was saying. After about five minutes in space, Wu blurted out, "I didn't do nothing! How I'm facin' life? I didn't kill nobody?"

Not angered by Wu's abrupt interruption Mr. O'Hare calmly said, "So what did you do?" Their stares met and after Wu did not answer, Mr. O'Hare continued in an even tone. "Listen Mr. Gray, like I told you earlier, you're not here to help me. I'm here to help you. But first you have to help yourself. Now the prosecutor is willing to offer you a deal and I'm here to help you get it."

"Deal!," Wu disdainfully echoed. "Mr. O'Hare I was a crack head. I was smoking the shit not selling it!," Wu said trying to play on his recent drug addiction. "Look at the papers. You see where they picked me up. The prosecutor knows I'm a drug addict!"

"She also knows you're a drug dealer," Mr. O'Hare shot-back, unfazed by Wu's theatrics that might have won him accolades if he were at the *Grammy's*. "Mr. Gray, you're a first time offender and the DA is willing to give you three years probation if you cooperate.... That deal won't stand for long. Do you know why?," he asked then paused and continued before Wu could respond. "Because somebody else is going to beat you to it. And I'm going to warn you that any deal after that is going to be some serious hard time."

Wu watched as Mr. O'Hare gathered his pad and papers then said, "I'm not trying to do no time."

Mr. O'Hare had heard that expression from the toughest of the toughest and it always meant the same thing. His eyes burned into Wu's blank face. Then he asked him, "So what are you trying to do Mr. Gray?"

For the next few seconds, silence filled the room. Wu began to dig for reasons why he should rat on his childhood friends. Other than no jail time, the reasons weren't coming quick enough so he thought against it. Then Kelly popped up in his mind, and along with the thought of losing her to jail, came the reasons. *"This shit is all Flip's fault,"* he thought to himself. *"If he wouldn't have gotten greedy we would've been small timers and the feds wouldn't even be fuckin' wit us. And that nigga acted like he wanted to do me somethin' last Christmas night. If it wasn't for Butter, that nigga Flip would've probably left me like he did Uptown and Cookie!"*

After that thought, Wu couldn't find a reason why he shouldn't rat on Flip. The fact that Flip and D-Mac didn't show him nearly as much love as Butter and Lisa while he was in the rehab was enough for him to think *fuck D-Mac too.* Though he now felt that he could live with himself after doing what he'd have to against D-Mac and Flip, he found himself feeling totally opposite about Butter. They had been close since Uptown's murder and even closer during the rehab. Then there was the tight relationship Lisa and Kelly had developed. It all made him wonder how could he help himself without hurting Butter.

"Anytime you're ready Mr. Gray," Mr. O'Hare said breaking the silence and disturbing Wu's thoughts. "I need a couple of days to think about it," Wu replied.

Mr. O'Hare, slightly disappointed, began packing his thin brief case and said, "Suit yourself Mr. Gray. That offer might not be available in a few more days." He shut his brief case and quickly explained to Wu the procedures of the arraignment and bail hearing that were due to take place the following morning. After damn near guaranteeing Wu that he wouldn't get bail at the hearing, Mr. O'Hare gestured to C.O. Cook that they were done. "Oh, and I hope nobody beats you to it," he added just before the door was opened.

Wu was looking at the ground as he waddled out without responding. When he looked up, he was caught by the sight of Butter and someone who appeared to be Butter's lawyer sitting across from each other in the room across from the one he had exited. "Let's go. Let's go Mr. Gray," Cook ordered, getting Wu's attention. "This ain't no tour guide," he added, leading

Wu back to the bullpen.

Before Butter could use the phone, C.O. Cook called him out for an attorney visit. Expecting a court appointed lawyer, Butter was taken back when Mr. Gregg introduced himself as a well experienced Federal Criminal lawyer. He was certain to make sure that Butter understood that there was an enormous difference between a Federal Criminal Lawyer and a state lawyer who practiced Federal Law — and it was more than just the fee.

The fact that Mr. Greg was sent by Butter's father made it that much more unbelievable because Butter had no idea his parents were aware of the situation, nevertheless he was relieved and grateful.

The charges in the indictment were explained by Mr. Gregg to Butter exactly the way that they were explained to Wu. But instead of focusing on trying to get his client to snitch, Mr. Gregg's agenda consisted of strategies that could possibly get Butter the least time possible, or no time at all.

"Do you understand everything so far Mr. Ryder?," Mr. Gregg asked. Butter looked up from the indictment and nodded his head yes. Mr. Gregg acknowledged Butter's nod then continued. "Now, Mr. Ryder, your father believes that you're a music dealer and not a drug dealer", Mr. Gregg said as he was looking down at his notes. Then puzzled he stated, "But there is no mention or proof of that in any of my notes."

"I'm an independent record distributor," Butter said.

"Do you have any documented proof?," he asked, then watched as Butter shook his head no. "Okay, we'll come back to that later. What I really would like to focus on now is getting you bail tomorrow at your arraignment," he said, looking through his notes again. "You didn't complete school and you were never employed?", he told more than asked and mumbled to himself as he scanned through other pages. Then he looked up and said, "Mr. Ryder, to be quite frank with you, the only way I see you getting bail is if your parents put up most, if not all, of their real estate."

Well, Bail is dead, Butter thought. He already figured Mr. Gregg was going to cost his father a small fortune, and knowing his father, the gesture only came at the hands of his mother's persuasion. "I don't know about that," Butter disappointedly said.

Mr. Gregg, feeling Butter's disappointment as he began packing up, decided that he should leave Butter with a little hope. "Hey who knows, the judge might not ask for much," he said as he signaled to CO Cook that they were done then added, "Just hang in there young fella."

"Alright thanks," Butter flatly responded before stepping out into the corridor.

Chapter Twelve

Forty-eight hours later.

The feds had everything D-Mac and Flip owned. They had Butter's house and car, and they also took Wu's Lexus, and the deed for the town house he expected to get paid for.

At the arraignment the morning following their arrest, the four of them pleaded not guilty. The DA was able to prevent Wu, D-Mac and Flip from getting bail, however, because Butter's parents put up all their real estate, she failed in detaining Butter.

Instead of remaining at MCC where they were being detained, D-Mac and Flip were transported along with Wu, to the Valhalla jail's fifth floor where other Federal detainees were being housed. There they would stay throughout the month, until their next hearing, which was set for the first week in June.

Immediately following the arraignment, an ecstatic Butter was rushed to the hospital by Mike to see Lisa and their brand new baby boy, Sean Jr. who was prematurely born hours after Butter's arrest.

The moment he saw the little guy, his eyes welled up with tears. He could see the resemblance between him and his son instantly and knew then that he'd have to change the course of his life for sure. He became angry with himself for bringing his child into the world under such shaky conditions.

To know that there was someone who he'd now bare the responsibility of protecting from the streets and loving unconditionally, instantly became overwhelming to him. Nevertheless, he was up for the challenge and had silently vowed to spend the rest of his life doing all within his powers to provide a better way for his son if it wasn't too late. The little man staring back at him was a confirmation of a new beginning for a new generation.

After staying at the hospital for several hours, Lisa had to force Butter to leave, reassuring him that she and their son would be alright. Butter hesitantly agreed and before leaving, he kissed her on the forehead thanking her for bringing Sean Jr. into the world for him.

Stunned wasn't the word when Butter entered the apartment and spotted Kelly walking through the crib. It was explained to him that Kelly's apartment was taken from her and Lisa asked Mike to let her stay there until she could find a place. Butter was in total agreement.

On his second day home, Butter spent half the day kissing up to his parents for placing everything they had on the line, and he promised them he had no intentions of running. The other half, he spent re-organizing his music adventure with Mike, and planning some type of living arrangement for Lisa who was due home the next day. In a way, Butter felt good that Sean Jr. would not be coming home with Lisa due to the fact he had to remain in the hospital in an incubator for a few months. This would allow Butter time to find them a place of their own.

May fourth, Butter's third day home, he, Kelly and Mike were in New Rochelle having breakfast. It was sure to be a long day for Butter who had to pick up Lisa, stop by his attorney's office, then meet Mike downtown to help sell records. Though his legal woes were constantly on his mind, he knew he could not let that hinder him from trying to make sure Lisa and his son would be financially secure in the event he did have to go to jail. And the only way he could possibly see that happening was to come up in the music industry.

Mike and Butter were sitting at a small, round, wooden dining table. "What time we gotta go pick up the other rented?," Butter asked Mike.

After lowering the glass of milk from his mouth, Mike answered, "Nine-thirty," then turned to Kelly and said, "I'm not gonna front. These pancakes is ill."

"Word, I was thinking the same thing," Butter threw in.

Their compliments caused Kelly's dark tan face to glow, and she blessed them with a simple smile, then said, "Thanks."

For the most part, as far as Butter could see, Kelly was back to herself. Her features that had sparked him and the fellas to have that huge crush on her back in the days were intact. From her jet-black wavy hair that had almost grown back to its original hip length, to her drop-dead gorgeous face and wickedly curved body. Butter was glad that somebody in the family was able to win her over, because she was the type of girl that made people think any nigga around her must be getting money.

"I don't know how we gonna pull this off," Butter said, checking the cheap watch on his wrist, the one he bought from the pawn shop after selling all his jewelry. "Lisa's not getting discharged until nine. That means we probably won't be outta there 'til nine-thirty, ten o'clock," implying that he might not be back in time to take Mike to pick up the rental.

"I'll just take a cab to the lady's crib," Mike said, referring to the woman he paid to rent cars using her credit card.

Butter rose up from the table, took his empty plate and glass in the kitchen, washed them out, then returned.

"Unless you want me to drop you off now?," he asked, looking down at Mike.

"What time is it?"

"Eight-fifteen."

"Nah I'll cab it," Mike said, rising from the table with his plate.

"How far you have to go?," Kelly asked Mike as he walked into the kitchen.

Facing them from the kitchen side of the wooden counter, Mike replied, "About ten, fifteen minutes from here."

"Maybe Denise can drop you off on our way to Valhalla," Kelly suggested. "Her and Regina should be here by nine."

"Yeah I might roll wit' that," Mike said. He then realized that the pancakes were all gone. He whimpered, looked up to see

Butter easing towards the front door and whimsically said, "Oh you housed the rest of them? I see how you livin'!"

"My bad Bee!," Butter laughed as he held the door open.

Mike could almost taste one of the most deliciously famous Harlem Hamburgers melting in his mouth, "Yeah aight!"

"Good lookin' Kelly!," Butter said thanking her for the breakfast. "I'll be back in a little bit," he added before shutting the door behind him.

Kelly rose from the table and gathered her dishes, "I didn't throw the batter away," she said, placing her dishes in the sink.

"Where's it at?"

She turned the faucet water on then retrieved the bowl from the refrigerator, "I'll make them," she offered as she stood beside him over the stove.

"I got it," Mike said as he gently took the bowl from her. "I know how to put it down a little somethin' too," he added.

After flashing each other a smile, Kelly turned back to the sink, washed her dishes, then went to the back of the spacious apartment's single bedroom. As she took off the sweat pants and tee shirt she had on, she thought about how much of a gentleman Mike was by allowing her to occupy his room while he utilized the living room during her stay. Being behind the room's closed door made her feel a little more free when it came to dressing and undressing. She grabbed her robe from off the closet's hook and shot into the bathroom, which was four steps away from the bedroom.

Mike's apartment was actually the crib Butter initially rented as a thinking tank and storage. He and Mike often hung out there calculating their daily record sales and the amount of days and hours they were going to spend in each borough. It was also where they stored crates of records. Mike had become so comfortable in the crib, so one day he asked Butter would it be all right if he moved in. Butter, seeing no reason why not, answered, "No question."

At the time, the apartment was furnished with only a three-cushion sofa, a modest stereo system, a twenty-five inch color TV and a Sega genesis. Since then, Mike had added the dining table and bedroom set. Though, there was plenty of space for more furniture, Mike agreed that the whereabouts of the apartment would be between Butter, Lisa, and himself, so more furniture was not necessary.

Mike knocked off four more pancakes, cleaned up his mess, including the frying pan and stove area, then moved to the five-drawer dresser he and Kelly hauled out into the living room for his use.

After tossing articles of clothing onto the sofa, he opened the windows allowing brightness and fresh air to fill the living room. When he noticed that Kelly was done in the shower, he grabbed his things and went into the bathroom.

Minutes later, the ringing doorbell caused Kelly to come striding into the living room. The way she filled up one of her old rhinestone jean suits, demonstrated that her well- perportioned figure was in rare form. She went to the window, saw that it was Denise and Regina, then went down stairs and opened the door.

Denise, wearing some tight blue jeans with leather pockets and a matching jacket, entered first, "Hey girl," she greeted.

"What's up," Regina followed, wearing a denim skirt outfit.

"What's up yall?," Kelly responded, trailing them up the stairs.

By the time they filed into the apartment, Mike was standing shirtless by the dresser with a pair of purple denims and his black Tims. The three girls inconspicuously watched his bare toned upper body before he hurriedly covered it with a black tee shirt. They had individual thoughts but knew they were best kept to themselves. "What's up big head?," Denise said greeting Mike in the same manner she did when he and Lisa were staying at their mother's apartment.

"Nisey, what's up?," Mike asked as he turned to face the three of them.

"Mike, this is Regina. She's D-Mac's girl," Denise said.

"Hi," they said simultaneously as they flashed smiles. "*Flyy honies must come with the business*," he thought to himself as he reached for his towel. Brushing his curly hair with it, he headed towards the bathroom.

"Mike wanted to take a cab some where," Kelly said, facing Denise. "I told him maybe you could drop him off."

"Okay that's cool," Denise responded. She took a couple of steps over by the dining table and sat down. "My girl home yet?," she called out, inquiring about Lisa.

"Nah!," Mike hollered back, "Butter went to get her!"

Denise watched as Regina and Kelly flopped onto the sofa, then removed her Gucci shades and said, "Is this gonna take long flyy guy?" The girls all smirked.

"C'mon. Let's roll," Mike said, moving quickly and ignoring Denise's comment. He turned off the lights, closed the windows, then followed the girls downstairs after locking the door.

The Valhalla County Jail's fifth floor was live with Federal detainees all dressed in street clothes. Several were between the TV, phones, and the universal workout areas. Some were seated at tables playing chess, cards, and other table-top games. Six were on the basketball court, and others were in the cells either by themselves or possee'd up with friends or codefendants.

D-Mac, Wu, and Flip were huddled up by the basketball court reminiscing about their experiences of the past three days. They were recounting every incident, from the way they were busted to the fucked up tuna fish they'd had for lunch minutes ago.

"Yo that's my word. The next time my fake ass lawyer come at me wit' that rat shit," Flip said as his eyes switched back and forth from Wu to D-Mac, "I'm gonna spit in that niggas face and bounce."

"You seen mine?," D-Mac asked. Continuing before they could respond he said, "That white bitch didn't even give me a copy of the indictment. At least you niggas got that. I'm gonna scream on that ho when I see her. Then I'm gonna fire that bitch," he added.

"Fire her?," Flip mocked with an odd chuckle. "How you gonna fire her?"

"Easy. Tell that bitch she's outta here," D-Mac replied matter-of-factly. "See Money over there?," he said, directed their attention to a guy with dreads playing chess. "Me and him was kickin' it last night. Duke's back on violation. He was pulling my coat on them court appointed lawyers. Yo Bee, them mothafuckas work for us. We can take their bullshit advice, but at the end of it all, they suppose to do what we say. Just like if we paid their asses," he said then paused, making certain he had their full attention. Then he continued, "Money

116

said them mothafuckas ain't interested in goin' thru trial wit' us. For what? They ain't getting paid like that. But if they get niggas to cop, they get a little bonus. And if they get niggas to rat on their peeps, they get a bigger bonus," he said as he studied their faces. "Yo Bee, them niggas supposed to be filing madd motions, severance motions, suppression and evidentiary motions."

"Hold up Duke," Flip interrupted with confusion written all over his face. "What the fuck is a severance an sup... what ever that shit you just said?"

"My bad," D-Mac said as he realized, he had to explain it to them the way it was made clear to him. "Severance motion is a joint you ask them to file so a nigga could have a separate trial. Instead of being tried with a group of niggas like us.

"If they try us three together and the jury don't like this nigga," D-Mac said while pointing to Wu, "me and you might be goin' down on GP. That's the type of bullshit they on."

"What's the other shit?," Flip asked.

"The suppression joint is to try and get the judge to dead a lot of the bullshit evidence that sometimes have nothing to do with the case. Like it might be some shit another nigga already did time for on a different case and now the DA trying to throw that shit in our conspiracy," D-Mac said then watched Flip's distorted expression. "I'm tryin to tell you Bee. They ain't playin' fair."

"But how you supposed to know what to tell your lawyer to file?," Flip questioned.

"That's the problem. Niggas don't know shit. Well, we used to didn't know shit," D-Mac said as he unfolded a piece of paper with a sly grin. "Money gave me a list of shit to tell my attorney to file and get copies of. You niggas can copy it when we come off the V.I.," he said as he extended it to Flip.

"Money said my lawyer gonna be shook," he continued with a grin. "And if she act like she's frontin', I can just send a copy of all my requests to the judge with a letter saying I want that bitch fired because she ain't trying to do this, that, and the third."

"Money gonna get our shit bent up," Wu said commenting for the first time.

D-Mac stared hard at Wu and said, "Duke, our shit is already bent up."

Their circle was interrupted by the C.O.'s announcement. "The following inmates have visits!," he yelled as he stood by the station. "Turner! Wheeler! Gray!," he shouted then watched as the three motioned towards him.

"Turner, Wheeler, and Gray?," he asked as he was looking at their picture cards he held in his hands.

No. Moe, Larry, and Curly. What the fuck you think, D-Mac thought, then said, "Yeah," followed by Wu's and Flip's nods.

"Alright come with me," the C.O. said, leading them off.

Valhalla's visiting room was buzzing with people. Men, women, and kids of all ages were dressed to impress. Some sat around chattering with whom they were there to see, while others sat patiently waiting. Two C.O.'s sat at an officer's station equipped with monitor TV's, observing all activities, while a third officer escorted inmates from and to the room.

When D-Mac, Flip, and Wu entered the visiting room, their faces branded smiles that they had no idea still existed. All wearing yellow prison jumpsuits, they shamelessly glided to the area where Regina, Denise, and Kelly stood waiting with open arms and glowing smiles of their own.

With no hesitation, the three couples engaged in the one, intimate hug and kiss allowed before integrating a short hug and peck on the cheek with each other's mate. Though they sat in the same area, they were seated far enough apart from each other to create a sense of privacy.

Between short kisses and sly groping, Flip was informing Denise on as much as he knew about his legal situation, and what he thought could possibly happen. Not wanting to destroy any hopes she might have had, Flip chose not to tell her he was facing life. Instead his conversation stayed along the lines that the feds had nothing on him.

D-Mac's conversation with Regina was similar, except he sounded more confident thanks to Money-with-the-dreads who had enlightened him on the early stages of legal procedure.

Wu and Kelly's dialogue, however, was some place else. Though he, too, managed to get his short kisses and sneaky feeling on, he seemed to be more focused on Kelly's life on the outside than his on the inside. "So you're not gonna answer my question?," Wu remotely asked. His right arm rested around the top back of Kelly's chair while his left hand rested between her hands on her lap.

Kelly, becoming uneasy and slightly annoyed by Wu's interrogation, dropped her eyes to her lap and softly replied, "I told you I haven't thought about partying or nothing since I've been home."

"So what have you been doin'? I know after spending six months in that boring ass spot we were at had you thirsty for fun."

"See what I'm talking about?," Kelly said as she patted Wu's hand gently.

"What?," he asked while using his left hand to guide her eyes back up to meet his.

"You keep asking me that same question different ways," she answered with a fixed stare and smile. "I'm not doing nothing. I'm not thinking about doing nothing. And I just want you to come home," she sincerely added before planting yet another short kiss on him.

Kelly's statement sounded reassuring, and though it made Wu melt inside, he had one more question that had been on his mind since the day of his arrest. "This is my last question," he whispered in her ear after their lips parted.

Kelly's eyes dropped down to their intertwined fingers resting on her lap. "What?", she asked.

"Where you stayin' at?," Wu asked out loud.

The question caused Kelly's stomach to knot up. Knowing that Wu was the one who suggested that she let her apartment go because he had planned on them moving out of the Bronx on their first day home, it made sense to her that he knew she had no apartment. But because he had not brought it up, she thought there was a slight chance it might have slipped his mind. Now that she knew it hadn't, she was not about to tell him she was staying with Lisa's brother.

"With a friend," she answered, caressing the back of his hand with her free right hand.

Wu untwined his hand and once again raised her gaze to his, then asked, "What friend. Do I know her?" He watched as Kelly shook her head no. "What's her name?"

"Why? You don't know her," Kelly responded with a smirk,

brushing the tip of Wu's nose as if he was the one lying.

"You don't know who I know."

"Well put it like this. You better not know her", she shot back before attempting to kiss him again. Due to Wu turning his head, she pecked him on the cheek, and when he turned back to face her, she saw frustration quickly mounting in his face. "Nicki," she said, kicking out the first female's name that came to her. She watched as his frustration subsided then rapidly changed the direction of questioning onto him. "When you go back to court?," she asked as she ran her hand through his hair as if Wu was a puppy.

"Next month," he answered.

"What the lawyer talking about?"

"He said it looks good for me."

"What about Flip and them?," she asked as she cut her eyes over to D-Mac and Flip who were pleasantly somewhere else.

"Yeah. We all gonna be all right," he answered before commencing back to slyly breaking the excess touching rule.

Chapter Thirteen

It was going on 1:30 p.m. when Butter and Lisa entered Butter's lawyer's office. Once leaving the hospital, Butter had taken Lisa to I-Hop after she complained that she was hungry from not being able to eat much of the hospital food. They then stopped by Butter's mother's house before swinging by Lisa's mother's apartment where he had plans to leave her. Lisa began whining because she did not want to be there alone so, she suggested that he take her up to Mike's apartment in New Rochelle. When he told her that Mike was downtown, and Kelly was in Valhalla, and he had to go see the lawyer, she pouted and whimpered her way into remaining by his side.

"Good afternoon Mr. Ryder," a smiling Mr. Gregg greeted, as he sat behind a huge desk, motioning for Butter and Lisa to come further into his extravagant office. "I see you have your lovely fiancée with you," he said as he looked at Lisa, "Good afternoon Ma'am", he said.

"What's up Mr. Gregg," Butter said while returning his greeting.

"Thank you," Lisa blushed cutting her eyes to Butter then back to Mr. Gregg. "And good afternoon to you," she added.

"Thank you. Thank you. Please have a seat," he said while directing them to the twin chairs that were parked three feet in front of his desk. Mr. Gregg was one of those rare 'hard working for his client' type lawyers. Though he was expensive, his efficiency, honesty, and dedication made him well worth it.

Getting straight to the point, Mr. Gregg said, "Now Mr. Ryder, I, along with a couple of other attorneys on this case, met with the District Attorney this morning at which time she offered a ten year global plea."

He noticed the confused looks on both Butter and Lisa's faces then explained, "Mr. Ryder," Mr. Gregg said as he looked down at his notes, "that means you, Mr. Turner, Mr. Gray, and Mr. Wheeler all have to agree to a ten year prison term. If one of you declines, then the global plea will be dismissed and she'll give a twenty year plea to any individual who does not want to face trail." As Mr. Gregg lifted his eyes, he found Butter and Lisa staring at one another with incredulous expressions.

So many thoughts raced through Butter's mind. He could not grasp a single one. When he noticed Lisa's eyes becoming glassy with tears, he took her hand in his, then turned to face Mr. Gregg who had begun speaking again.

"Mr. Ryder I'm informing you... Here you go Sweetie," Mr. Gregg said interrupted himself, while extending a box of tissue to Lisa.

"Thank you," she sniveled as she was trying to gather herself.

"You're welcome," Mr. Gregg responded before he turned his attention back to Butter. "Now Mr. Ryder I informed you of the DA's offer because it's my obligation and your right to know. However, I would like to share my views on the case. Then I think we should move forward from there." He watched Butter's blank face and speechless acknowledgement before continuing, "I have before me most, if not all of the prosecutor's evidence against you. And to be quite honest, I'm not impressed," he said as he leaned back in his huge leather rocker as he folded his hand across his mid-section. "There's nothing here but statements made by drug addicts and ex-criminals," he said. "Unfortunately it was enough for the District Attorney to get a grand jury to indict you. However, in your case, I don't think there's enough here to win a conviction."

Mr. Gregg leaned forward, then stared down at a second stack of notes on his desk. "Of course there's no guarantee," Mr. Gregg continued, as he browsed through the notes, "but I strongly believe that if we could present evidence showing that you were in fact selling music and not drugs, it would create a significant amount of reasonable doubt inside the jury's minds."

Mr. Gregg could actually see hope beginning to set back into Lisa's face as he spoke. "Though you know a trial can get pretty expensive," Mr. Gregg added.

Butter paid close attention to what Mr. Gregg was suggesting. But his thoughts rested on the global plea agreement, and how his going through with a trial would leave his crew assed out. "Mr. Gregg, you said if one of us renege on the plea, it's basically trial or twenty?"

"Basically."

"How does it look for the other three if they go to trail?," Butter asked, knowing they'd rather fight than to sign on the dotted line for twenty.

Thinking about their court appointed lawyers, Mr. Gregg slowly shook his head and answered, "Not good." After a second of silence he said, "If you didn't have this music thing going for you, I would've probably been sitting here practically begging you to take a global plea. But—-"

"That's what I'm gonna do," Butter said.

His comment caused Lisa to pull her hand free. "What!," she yelled as she turned to face him.

"Wait a minute Mr. Ryder," Mr. Gregg interjected. "There's no rush here. This is something you might want to discuss with your family, your fiancé right here, and—-"

"Mr. Gregg," Butter cut in once again, "if I go to trial, my friends gonna get twenty years and who knows…life if they go to trial. I'm the only one with a real lawyer so we can count a trial for them as an automatic lost," Butter said speaking firmly. "And let's say I get off? How am I supposed to live with myself knowing my friends got life or twenty because I wouldn't take ten?," he asked. Then Mr. Gregg and Butter both watched as a frantic Lisa raced towards the door. Butter then turned back to Mr. Gregg.

Mr. Gregg honored Butter's integrity. "Like I said, talk it

over with your family first, there's no rush," he said as he motioned for Butter to go after Lisa. "We can talk again later," he said as Butter rushed out of the door.

It was clear from the many scantily clad shoppers and the open windows of vehicles that congested 125th street, that spring was in the air and summer was near. There were packs of young and old people moving at a snail's pace, in no hurry to get to where they were headed, and loud music from a number of shiny cars coming from every which way competing for their share of admirers and

listeners.

Mike had no competition though. The newest recording he had produced for his artists, "World" and "Tonya Hunt" had the streetz open. Everybody and their momma was copin' the single. There were even record shop owners from different areas pulling up across the street from the Apollo beside Mike's rental to buy either a half or whole create of records.

It had been so hectic that Mike hadn't had a chance to eat. As he continued to wheel and deal he kept an eye out for Butter's appearance. That's-how he was able to spot Denise slowly pushing her mother's burgundy Camry in his direction. Thinking that he could at least ask Denise to go get him something to munch on, he motioned to the crowd to stay put before he abruptly closed the trunk. "One minute please," Mike said. It wasn't until he stepped further out into the street that he noticed Regina and Kelly were still with her. He flagged them down making sure they recognized him, then he quickly popped the trunk open and resumed taking care of business.

"You got it going on," Denise commented as she, Kelly and Regina stood behind Mike at the open trunk

Without turning to face them, Mike ignored her comment and said, "I'm starvin'. I was hoping yall could go get me somethin' to eat? I was waiting on Butter but—-"

"Oh it's cool," Denise said. "What you want to eat?"

"Some Willie burgers," he cheered while, handing her a ten dollar bill. "About three burgers, fries and a giant mixed drink," he said.

"How you gonna do both?," Kelly questioned, amused at the thought of him juggling his food and records at the same time.

"I'll have that figured out before yall get back."

"Go ahead, you go eat. Me and Regina will hold it down, " Kelly seriously suggested.

"Word," Mike replied, liking the idea.

"Yeah we got this," Regina interjected. "How much are they?," she asked him.

"Five," he responded, stepping back allowing them room to take over. He watched as they made a few smooth transactions then hopped in the Camry with Denise, "We'll be back wit' the quickness," he uttered before Denise pulled off

"What the hell?," Butter thought to himself as he spotted Regina and Kelly handling their business out of what he already figured to be Mike's new rental. He pulled up beside the opened trunk and got out. "Where's Mike?," Butter questioned, standing behind them at the open trunk.

"Denise ran him to get something to eat," Kelly answered in the middle of an exchange. "They should be back any minute," she added as she turned to face him.

"Aight, Im'ma chill in the car until they come," he said as he turned and walked back to his car.

His moving caused both Kelly and Regina to notice a seemingly upset Lisa sitting in the car. They acknowledged her with a wave and smile, and got a wave and forced smile in return. They could tell that she was troubled by something personal so they looked at her no longer than they had to.

When Butter got back in the car, he was met by the existing silence Lisa had displayed since storming out of Mr. Gregg's office. He knew she had every right to be upset, but he also knew she had no understanding of why he felt the way that he did. He figured by now, she had enough time to cool off and hear his reasoning.

"Lisa," he called, adjusting his seat into a reclining position. "I really don't need you to be mad at me right now "I need you to have my back...hold me down," he said then watched her as she rocked with folded arms. "You have to understand, I'm not doin' this because I want to. Nobody want to just go to jail for ten years. But I can't see me breakin' out on my friends and being the one to cause them to spend the rest of their lives in prison."

"Oh but you don't see nothing wrong with breaking out on

me and Sean Jr.? And what we supposed to do the ten years you're away?"

"First of all I'm not breakin' out on you and my son. Never that. I know I won't be able to do much from there. That's why I'm tryin' to make somethin' happen now. And regardless whether I do or if I don't, my son is gonna always be looked out for. I'm not worried about that. Ma Dukes gonna handle that on the strength... I'm sayin' what's up with you?," he asked then watched as she began to brush the tears away from her reddened cheeks, then continued, "Lisa, you heard what the lawyer said. He can't guarantee Jack. What happens if I lose? No tellin' when or if I'll ever see the streetz again. At least this way I know for sure that in ten years from now this will be behind us, or me, or which ever one you decide?"

Lisa sobbed as she was drowning in her emotions, turning to finally face Butter before collapsing into his arms burying her head in his shoulders. "I'm sorry," she whimpered as she began squeezing him tightly. "You know I got your back."

"I know Boo. I know," he said, fighting to keep his tears from piling up as he consoled her. Butter noticed Denise and Mike pulling up in the rear view mirror and began detaching himself, "Okay, here come your brother and 'em," he said while wiping Lisa's tears.

"You need to be wiping your own tears," she responded with a smile. Using her thumbs she brushed his tears away then laced him with a kiss.

The second Mike bowed down at Lisa's side of the window, he could tell that something was wrong. Not knowing whether it was the baby, the case, or their relationship, he was concerned. "What's up?," he asked as his eyes searched their faces. "My nephew aight?"

"Yeah," Lisa responded as she playfully began running her hand through his hair. "Nothing's wrong," she added before pecking him on the cheek.

"Ayo Bee," Butter interjected disappointedly, "I can't really get wit' this record shit today."

Mike easily detecting sadness in Butter's voice, replied, "Yo, I'm aight Bee." Mike looked over at Kelly and Regina then said, "Me and my little crew got this." After they shared a grin, he added, "Just give me a couple of your crates."

126

Butter returned Denise's hello as she made her way to speak with Lisa and he made his way to meet Mike at the trunk. They each carried a crate to the trunk of Mike's rental, then stepped back over towards the trunk of Butter's rental. "Mike I hate to seem like I'm unloadin' everything on you, but I need to ask one more favor."

"You're not unloadin' on me. I understand what's goin' on. I'm wit'chew Duke."

"Thanks man, that's good to know," Butter said as he and Mike gave each other five. "You know with me goin' thru this bullshit and your sister not being able to bring the baby home for a minute, she's really not tryin' to stay at your momz crib by herself. and I don't like—-"

"Oh you want her to stay wit me?," Mike told more than asked. "C'mon man. That ain't no favor. It's your crib," he whimsically stated.

"I'm sayin, it's your crib Bee."

"Check this out," Mike said then put his hand on Butter's shoulder. "That crib big enough for all of us. In fact I'm gonna swing by the army and navy and pick up a couple of them inflating beds and we can camp out up that mothafucka," he sincerely added.

Butter, flattered by the offer, smiled and said, "Nah, I'm straight at Ma Duke's crib. Good lookin' out though."

"I'm sayin Bee, whatever," Mike replied as Butter ducked into the car. Mike tapped the trunk in response to the peace sign Butter held out the window before accelerating into traffic.

About eight o'clock that night, Butter and Lisa were let into Mike's apartment by Kelly. They instantly became slightly amused at the sight of the two inflated beds puffed up on the living room floor. The sofa and dresser had been arranged so that the two beds looked roomy in the middle of the floor. It appeared like a pajama party was about to jump off.

"What the hell...where that nigga Mike at?," Butter asked as he fumbled for words.

"I don't know," Kelly chuckled. "He was yelling something while I was in the tub. I couldn't hardly hear him."

"My little brother is crazy," Lisa said. "I hope you don't mind sharing that big ass bed?" Lisa watched as Kelly gave her an inviting smile, "Cause I'm not sleeping on that," she said as she and Kelly moved to the bedroom.

Butter, still amused, flopped down one of the thick air mattresses and after feeling its puffiness, yelled out, "This shit is soft!" He remained stretched out on it, watching as Lisa and Kelly returned.

Seconds later, they were stiffened by the ringing phone. "I got it!," Butter said as he got up from the mattress. "Hello." After a few seconds of silence Butter said, "I accept."

His answer indicated to Lisa and Kelly that it was a collect call from Valhalla and they quickly motioned for Butter not to mention anything to Wu about Kelly's being there.

"Aaaayo!," Butter called into the phone as he nodded his head as if to say I know. Then he motioned for Lisa and Kelly to back off.

"Yo," D-Mac said, recognizing Butter's voice. "What up baby?"

"What up," Butter excitedly replied. "You called my momz crib?," he asked figuring that's how he knew where to catch him.

"Yeah, she said you was up here."

"Where's Wu an' 'em?"

"Wu is up stairs in the rack and Flip is on the jack wit Denise."

"Aight, you niggas straight?"

"Yeah, no question. Our peeps dropped off that dough when they came up earlier...Good lookin' Bee," D-Mac said as he thanked him for the money.

As they conversed, Butter could tell by the number of pauses that D-Mac wanted to inquire about something. He figured it to be the global plea so he pushed it by asking, "Did any of you niggas speak to yall lawyers?"

"Mine's supposed to come tomorrow, but these niggaz lawyers came up."

"So yall know what time it is?"

"Yeah," D-Mac sorely replied, then added, "Yo Bee, we was kickin' it, and we understand that you're the only one wit a real lawyer...I'm sayin'. If you're takin' that bitch to trial, we ain't gonna be madd at'chew Duke."

"Check this out," Butter said, making it clear, "If it cost me ten years to save three of my manz lives—fuck around, four including mine, that's nothin', and so you niggas know, my lawyer even thinks it's a good plea."

Ecstatic that Butter felt that way, D-Mac said, "Word!" Your lawyer said that? My man wit' the dreads said that shit too. He said that shit would be a blessin' if we all took it. Word, he said niggas in the feds ain't seeing dime pieces no more, niggas gettin' slayed wit' thirty and better."

"Word!," Butter surprisingly said.

"No bullshit, these niggas playin for keeps. My man was like the only reason we getting' any rhythm must be because your lawyer. Damn, just imagine if we all had lawyers like that goin' at that bitch."

Butter quickly thought about all the money they wasted, let out a short sigh, and said, "Word."

Ready to spread the info, D-Mac said, "Yo let me go hit these niggas up wit the," four one one. You the realist!"

"Nah. You niggas the realist," Butter replied before they hung up.

Hampstead Publishing

Chapter Fourteen

The ringing phone, chirping birds, and sunlight that seeped through the windows all played a part in waking Butter out of his sleep. He checked his watch which displayed 6:45 a.m. so he sprung up from the air filled mattress. It was then that he realized he had never left Mike's apartment. His eyes scanned the living room for evidence that would indicate if Mike were, or had been there, and when he saw none, his attention was drawn again by the phone. Fully dressed, Butter drug himself to the dining table. As he picked up the phone, he noticed Lisa groggily coming out of the bedroom apparently to answer the only phone in the house.

"Hello," Butter answered in a raspy voice, as he signaled Lisa to go back to bed. After a few seconds he answered, "Yeah, I accept."

"Hello!," D-Mac uttered, in a loud and urgent tone. "Yeah," Butter drowsily responded.

"Ayo Bee, Wu left!"

"I know this nigga didn't call me early in the morning to tell me that," Butter thought. He remained silent waiting on more.

"Hello!", D-Mac called out into the silence.

"Yeah," Butter replied.

"You heard me?"

"Yeah I heard you," Butter said still unaware of why D-Mac was so riled up.

"The C.O. said they came and got him at 3:30."

"Who came and got him?"

"The Marshals!"

"And?," Butter said like, 'What's that suppose to mean?' Then he asked, "Where'd they take him?"

"Ayo wake up Bee!," Butter snapped getting irritated. "We think that nigga Wu is flippin'!"

"Just because the Marshal's came?"

"Listen!," D-Mac interrupted, pleading for Butter's understanding. "Check this out! The nigga been in the cell stressin' for the last few dayz. He played the jack a couple of times yesterday... Matter of fact when you see Kelly, ask her when is the last time she spoke to Wu on the phone. That's who he told us he was kicking it wit'," D-Mac suggested before he continued. "And then the nigga rolled out three-thirty in the morning. C'mon Duke, tell me that shit ain't shaky? Even my man wit' the dreads said he think that nigga switched teams!"

Now wide-awake, Butter moved down the hall towards the bedroom. His heart and mind raced as he tried to make sense of D-Mac's allegations. He was only certain of one thing, and it was that he was steps away from finding out if Wu lied to them. "Hold on," Butter said to D-Mac before tapping on the room's door. After being told to come in, he opened the door. "When the last time you spoke to Wu?," he asked Kelly. He stood halfway in the door with his stare on Kelly.

Half sleep, puzzled, and holding the sheet up to her neck, she answered, "Yesterday," in a scratchy tone.

Figuring she was referring to the visit, he asked, "on the phone?"

"No," she watched his distorted face, then asked, "Why? Is something wrong?" Her questions hit the closed door.

"That was Kelly?," D-Mac asked.

Butter, pacing back to the living room, answered, "Yeah, her and Lisa stayin' here wit' Mike for a minute."

"What she said?"

"She said no."

"Oh shit!," D-Mac shouted. There was no doubt in his mind what Wu was up to. "That rat mothafucka!"

Butter, still willing to give Wu the benefit of the doubt said, "Yo we don't know for sure, don't—-"

"Yo Bee! That niggas mind is weak!," D-Mac charged. "You forgot that nigga was smokin'? We should've known his ass was weak from the jump!," D-Mac fumed.

Before Butter could respond, there was the clicking sound that indicated someone was trying to get through on the other line. Thinking it was Mike, Butter thought that he needed to answer it.

"Yo D, hold on," Butter said as he clicked over to the other line where he was asked by the operator if he wanted to accept a collect call from Wu?

"Yeah!," Butter answered without hesitation.

"Hello," Wu said.

"Where you at?," Butter asked.

"MCC."

"What you doin' there?"

"I don't know," Wu lied. "They just came and got me early this morning,

He don't even know what's going on himself," Butter thought, as he quickly deciding to hold off from telling Wu that D-Mac was on the other line. Butter said, "Hold on a second, some body on the other line. "Butter clicked back to D-Mac's line and said, "Ayo that's Wu!"

"Where that hot mothafucka at?," D-Mac raved. It was Butter's first time hearing the term "hot" but he was sure that it meant a rat, something he still wasn't convinced that Wu was. "MCC," Butter answered. "He said he don't know why they came and got him."

"He's a fuckin' liar!," D-Mac shouted. "Tell that coward mothafucka I said he betta shut the fuck up!"

"Hold on," Butter responded. He clicked back to Wu's line and said, "Wu, I got D on the other line. They think you on some bullshit."

"Bullshit?," Wu said while playing dumb.

"Niggas think you rattin'," Butter bluntly stated.

"Rattin'!," Wu responded dejectedly. "Nah Bee. Don't

believe that shit! Tell them don't believe that shit. That's my word. I don't know why they moved me!," Wu said sounding as sincere as possible.

"Wu I hope that shit is true, word," Butter sighed. "It'll be fucked up if you go out like that," he added.

"C'mon Bee, don't even talk like that, that's not for us — -"

"Hold on a sec," Butter said before clicking back to D-Mac's line. "Hello."

"Yeah," D-Mac stressed. "You told that rat ass nigga what I said?"

Butter, becoming irritated with D-Mac's slurs and unsure if what D-Mac was saying was true, said, "Yo D, cool out wit' all that shit. If the feds would've came and took you and left Wu and Flip, or took Flip and left you and Wu, would that have made you or Flip a rat?"

"Oh my fuckin' god!, " D-Mac yelled before pulling the receiver from his ear and looking at it as if he was trying to see Butter's face. It was hard for him to conceive that Butter could not see the same picture as he and Flip.

After a few seconds of silence, D-Mac regained his composure and attempted to slowly guide Butter through it. "Butter," D-Mac spoke evenly, "check this out. You said he's in MCC, right?"

"Yeah."

"Aight, where the fuckin' twins and all them other rat-ass niggas at?," he asked becoming heated as he mentioned them. "MCC!," D-Mac shouted answering his own question before Butter could respond. Then he continued, "And why he lied about the phone calls? Because he called his lawyer or the fuckin' DA!", D-Mac said as he began shouting again. He became so vexed that he could not and would not speak to Butter any longer. "Yo hold on," he said passing the phone to Flip.

"Butter," Flip spoke into the phone, "That nigga Wu goin' out on us. Trust me, it's hard for me to believe too but it's real. And since you got him on the other line, let him know that it's fucked up."

"Hold on," Butter said before he clicked back over to Wu's line. "Hello." After no response, Butter called into the phone again. "Wu!" There was still no response. Wu's line was dead. Butter then clicked back over to Flip's line, "Hello," Butter said.

"Yeah," Flip replied.

"He got cut off."

"He probably hung up," Flip commented.

"I don't know, but he's gonna call back," Butter stated with confidence. He watched as the bedroom door opened and Kelly, followed by Lisa, made their way down the hall, killing the conversation. Butter said, "Yo, I gotta go, make sure you niggas call me back later."

"What time?," Flip asked.

"Tonight, around eight aight?"

"Later," they both said before hanging up.

Butter quickly racked his brain for the answer to the question he knew Kelly was coming to ask. Not wanting to make things more complicated, he knew there was no way he could tell Kelly what D-Mac and Flip thought. At least not until he was certain of it himself.

"What happened to Wu?," Kelly asked wearing a light blue robe and matching scarf identical to Lisa's pink one.

"Nothing," Butter placidly answered. "They moved him that's all."

"Moved him? Moved him where?," Kelly quizzed with concerned eyes.

"We don't know yet," Butter lied, buying himself some time. "I guess we can find out later. It's too early now," he replied.

Without any further questions, Kelly about-faced and headed back towards the bedroom. Butter could not tell whether or not Kelly was satisfied with his response because her face showed no expression. But when he turned to look at Lisa, she stood still staring at him. He could tell by her incredulous glare that she knew he was holding something back, so before she could ask, he said, "Walk me down stairs." He had intentions of telling Lisa, but not while Kelly was present.

When Lisa returned from seeing Butter off, she couldn't make it past the living room's sofa. She sunk into it and began thinking about everything she and Butter discussed moments earlier. Butter told Lisa everything, including D-Mac and Flip's thoughts. He also told her that it would be best kept from Kelly for now until they knew for sure.

Later that morning, Mike entered the apartment and spotted Lisa stretched out on the sofa. He wondered why she hadn't used the mattress. Being extra careful not to wake her, he floated to his dresser and began quietly gathering his things with thoughts of showering, changing, and heading back out to sell records.

As Mike browsed through his underwear drawer, he was stiffened by Lisa's barely audible call. "Mike," she said, fixing herself into an upright position.

When he turned his head to the right to meet Lisa's blurred vision, she continued, "What time is it?"

Hunched over the next to last drawer, he checked his watch. "Nine-thirty. Why? You late?," he added whimsically.

"Late for what?"

"Just kiddin' Sis. What you doin' sleepin' on the sofa?", he said while pointing to the airbeds. "What you think those for?"

"I slept in the bed with Kelly. I fell asleep here after I walked Butter downstairs this morning," she explained re-adjusting her scarf. "Come here. I wanna tell you something," she motioned for him to have a seat next to her.

Though Butter had told her not to tell Kelly, he said nothing about telling Mike.

Studying the urgency Lisa's face displayed, Mike stood straight up and said, "What?"

Lisa, eager to get it out, said, "They think Wu is snitching."

It took a few seconds for what Lisa said to register, and once it did Mike still showed little emotion. He replied, "Who? Who think Wu's snitchin'?"

"Flip and D-Mac," she answered.

"Word," Mike responded sorely. "What Butter think?," he asked her.

Lisa motioned her head uncertainly and said, "Wu told him he wasn't." She saw the confused look on Mike's face then added, "They called this morning."

"They still together?," Mike interrupted.

"No. Listen," she sighed before explaining. "The feds moved Wu to MCC three thirty this morning. Butter was talking to them on two different lines early this morning. Wu kept saying he wasn't and D-Mac kept saying he was."

"What Kelly thinks?," Mike asked. As Lisa began to answer,

Kelly, who emerged from the hall, startled Mike.

"Kelly don't know. And don't tell," Lisa said then froze as if Mike's face was a mirror and she could see Kelly through it. She turned to meet Kelly's piercing stare.

"Don't tell Kelly what?," Kelly questioned as her eyes were shifting back and forth from Lisa to Mike and back to Lisa.

Mike looked on as Lisa cut her eyes to him. "*What should I do?*," her eyes questioned. Already figuring that Butter told her not to tell Kelly, Mike wanted no part of it. He casually continued collecting the rest of his things and slid off to the bathroom leaving Lisa and Kelly ogling each other.

"Don't tell Kelly what, Lisa?," Kelly asked with a little attitude.

Lisa could tell by the look on Kelly's face that if she told Kelly anything other than the truth, it would only make things that much worse later on, so for the next ten minutes, Lisa told Kelly everything. She explained why Butter asked when was the last time she spoke to Wu, to why Butter thought she would be better off not knowing. Lisa assured Kelly that they were only keeping it from her until they were sure the things that were being said about Wu were true.

Kelly had had relationships with hustlers before. In fact, all she got down with were hustlers, so she showed no hostility towards Lisa, nor was she upset with D-Mac and Flip for thinking what they thought. She knew in the game it was common for friends and relatives, no matter how close they were, to turn on each other. Still, Kelly felt she needed to be sure. She thought because she knew from back in the days what Butter, Flip, D-Mac, and Wu meant to each other, that Wu deserved the benefit of the doubt, and she was satisfied that Butter thought so as well.

"I'm going to MCC," Kelly said, breaking the short silence between them.

"Do you think he'll tell you?," Lisa asked.

"I don't know, but it's only one way to find out."

"Do you want me to come with you?"

"Would you? "

"Sure," Lisa said before Kelly disappeared towards the bedroom. Lisa's eyes locked into Mike as he emerged from the same direction. "Mike, you going downtown?," Lisa asked him.

"Yeah," he answered as he set-up the ironing board.

"Good," Lisa responded, then sprung up. "You can drop us off at MCC."

"MCC?", he questioned. "Don't you think you should call Butter and let him know that you ran your mouth?"

"I didn't run my mouth. She overheard," Lisa shot back with slight attitude. "And I am gonna call Butter, Mr. Know it all."

"Yeah, thanks to you," he shot back with a sly grin. Lisa sucked her teeth, fanned her hand, then walked off towards the bedroom. Her gesture caused Mike to let out a short chuckle.

The twin visiting rooms on eleven south in MCC's high rise jail were separated by a glass bubbled corridor where two vending machines and the guard was stationed. The small room on the right hand side of the corridor had chairs lined up in a U-shape along its walls identical to the room on the left hand side.

Both rooms were cramped with inmates and their visitors, mostly Spanish and blacks ranging from eighteen to thirty-five. Some inmates sat entertaining their visitors with the latest development on their legal predicament, while others slyly got their groove on, taking advantage of the single guard that mainly stood in the bubbled area where it was easier for him to view both sides.

Kelly and Lisa sat on the right side near the back corner of the tight room. They were both wearing nylon Reebok wind breaker suits and matching Reeboks. Both spotted Wu as he appeared from the corridor into the bubble and both were staring hard at him. He wore the customary white tee shirt, blue khakis, and jelly sandals.

Kelly immediately recognized the disturbed look on Wu's face. She wondered if it was because Lisa was with her? Or was it because she surprised him?

"What are we doing here?," Lisa asked herself, noticing the angry look on Wu's face as well. Wu was making his way over. At that very moment, Lisa wished she had been able to get in touch with Butter when she tried earlier, and maybe he would've told them that going to see Wu wouldn't be such a good idea.

"What's up?," Wu said coldly, as he and his chip on his

shoulder sat in between them. Wu's entrance was the total opposite of what happened in Valhalla's visiting room. There were no smiles, hugs or kisses between he and Kelly.

Kelly, instantly detecting Wu's apparent attitude asked, "What's the matter with you?" Kelly leaned away from him with a raised eyebrow, as if Wu smelt of a foul odor.

Wu ignored Kelly's question and expression. Then fixed an unpleasant look at Lisa. "Where's Butter? Is he downstairs?," he asked her.

"No," Lisa said, coming close to duplicating Wu's facial expression.

"What. Yall think I'm a sucka or somethin'?," Wu asked them while shifting his angry stare from Kelly to Lisa, and back on Kelly.

"What?," Kelly responded. Neither she nor Lisa had a clue as to why he was carrying on the way he was.

"You heard what I said! You think I'm a sucka?," he repeated keeping his stare on Kelly.

"Wu, what is you talking about?," Kelly asked him. Their tones began drawing a little attention from people within earshot.

"What the hell is you doin' fuckin wit' Lisa's brotha, Mike?," he snidely asked.

His question wiped both Kelly and Lisa's minds blank. Although, his information was not accurate, it was close enough for them to know that it was coming from a reliable source. After a few seconds of silence, Kelly's wheels began to slowly turn again. "What?," she asked.

"Who told you that lie?," Lisa jumped.

Wu turned to Lisa and said, "A kid came to my dorm this morning from Valhalla. D-Mac gave him a message saying that my girl was livin' wit' a nigga named Mike and that he was diggin' her back out!" He then turned back to Kelly. "Is it true? You fuckin' Mike?," he demanded.

"No I'm not fucking Mike," Kelly refuted.

"Why is you trying to break on her?," Lisa said, jumping in again. "If she was fucking my brotha her ass wouldn't be here!"

Wu, becoming irritated with Lisa's two cents, faced her and said, "Lisa you know what? Mind ya fuckin' business!"

"It is my fucking business! You talking about my brother!," she said as her face reddened.

With thoughts of mushing Lisa, Wu turned his stare back to Kelly. "D ain' t gonna say it if it ain' t true! Is it true?!," he demanded.

"D also said you're snitching!," Lisa jumped in–once again. "Is that true?," she shouted at Wu's back.

Wu, ignoring Lisa's comment, leaned closer to Kelly with fire in his eyes and asked a second time, "Is it true?"

"I told you no!," Kelly responded, as her eyes were quickly checking the sly stares coming from around the room.

"Do you stay with him?," Wu fumed.

"Are you snitching?," Lisa jumped in again.

"Why won't you answer Lisa's question?," Kelly replied.

"What! Bitch I'll—-!," Wu snapped. In one motion he punched Kelly in the face and hovered over her with his hands clutched around her neck.

Everyone in the room frantically rose to their feet and moved towards the door, watching as Lisa jumped on Wu's back. She began swinging wildly, kicking and biting Wu all at the same time along with Kelly who was also swinging and scratching with all the life she had.

Seconds later the guard, followed by a number of other guards, charged into the room ripping through the group. "I need all the inmates to line up along the chairs over there!," one guard shouted as he instructed the room to get to the wall inside of the opposite room from where the other guards were trying to pull Wu out of the middle of Lisa's and Kelly's wild swipes. "And please everyone else step out this way!," he said while motioning in the direction of the bubble outside of the room.

After the guards were finally able to untangle them and some what gain control of the situation, two of them held tight grips on each of Wu's cuffed behind the back arms. They held him almost motionless in the room while another guard attempted to clear the people that were bundled up in the corridor.

"Yeah! I don't know what you smilin' for!," spat Lisa who was in the hands of another guard, in response to the devilish grin Wu branded. "Ya shit is all wepted up mothafucka! Yeah you rat mothafucka!," she yelled then turned to the lined up inmates. —"Yeah that mothafucka's a rat!," she continued. "Yall betta not fuck with him! He a fucking snitch!," she yelled.

"Ma'am please," the guard interrupted. "You need to calm down," he said.

"Ya boy friend is the rat!," Wu shot back while trying to save face .

"Shut up!," one of the guards that held Wu snapped.

"Nah fuck that! Yall lettin' that bitch call me a rat!," Wu yelled as they began leading him off.

"That's right!," Lisa barked. "Because they know it's true. You rat snitch mothafucka! And my man ain't snitchin'! Never that!," Lisa managed to squeeze in before Wu was escorted out of the room.

Lisa looked over at Kelly who was also being restrained by an officer and noticed the finger prints around Kelly's neck and the slight swelling of her left eye as her tears began to trickle down at a steady pace. "Don't cry for his bitch ass!," Lisa said.

Later that afternoon while wheeling and dealing in front of the Apollo, Butter noticed Lisa and Kelly getting out of a cab that had pulled up on the opposite side of the street. He knew where they were coming from because at Lisa's request, Mike had told him that he dropped them off at MCC. Trying to make things lighter on his sister, Mike also told Butter that Kelly had over heard Lisa telling him about Wu, and that Lisa had tried calling him before they left the apartment.

Though it all seemed innocent, Butter was crazy heated with Lisa. He was calling her all kinds of stupid asses the entire afternoon. Lisa had him so uptight, he swore he was going to curse her ass out something silly. As they crossed the street, he had begun rehearsing.

Butter quickly served a few more customers out of the group that lingered, then closed the rental's trunk and politely direct-ed the small remaining crowd to go around the corner in front of J&J Varieties where Mike was located. By the time Butter turned his focus back toward the street, Lisa and Kelly were close enough for him to notice Kelly's black eye and bruised neck and Lisa's busted and slightly swollen lower lip. His rehearsing came to an instant halt and his anger towards Lisa vanished. "What happened?," Butter grimaced, surveying their faces as the three of them stood in the street between the rental's truck and the front end of the vehicle parked behind it. "We were fighting with Wu up in M.C.C.," Lisa matter of fact-ly answered. She watched as Butter's incredulous stare locked onto hers with a look that asked, **"What** the hell were you and Kelly doing fighting Wu in M.C.C."* Breaking the silence, Lisa, with much attitude and tears of fury forming in her eyes added, "He tried to choke Kelly out and I jumped his ass!"

Butter, not sure which one he was most upset with, Lisa or Wu, let out a harsh sigh, and as he blew past them, he said, "Yo get in the car." Lisa sucked her teeth real hard and followed Kelly onto the sidewalk, and they got in the car.

Chapter Fifteen

That evening when Mike entered the apartment, the sight of Butter sitting on the sofa with his focus drawn to the Street Fighter video game he was playing, caused Mike to race to Butter's side.

"Yeah! Let's do this!," Mike said as he excitedly retrieved the other joystick.

Butter, who was still upset, hadn't spoken to either Lisa or Kelly during their entire ride home. When they entered the apartment, Lisa and Kelly marched straight to the bedroom while Butter, trying to funnel his frustration, flopped on the sofa and began playing the video game, something he decided he would do until eight o'clock, which was the time Flip was supposed to call back.

"Nah I'm about to bounce," Butter sorely replied. "I'm just waitin' on a phone call."

Mike, recognizing the rue in Butter's voice, felt it was the perfect time to try and shine a little light on the situation. He dug in his back pocket, pulled out a small white and gray business card then extended it to Butter. He watched as Butter hit the pause button before taking the card.

"Karen Styles. CEO. Universal Records?," Butter mumbled as his eyes scanned over the address and phone number. "Who's she?," Butter asked nonchalantly handing the card back to Mike.

"That's who we gotta meet with on June third," Mike said, holding back his excitement as Butter drew back his extended hand.

Butter finally grasped what Mike was insinuating, "Say word!," he exclaimed while examining the card closely.

"On everything."

"Oh shit!," Butter shouted jubilantly as he and Mike rose up off the sofa.

"It's about to be on, Duke!," Mike cheered as they carried on ruggedly embracing one another. They were happier than a faggot with a bag of dicks.

Their raucous fete caused Lisa and Kelly to come flying into the living room with alarmed expressions on their faces. Mike, taking instant notice of their bruises, quickly abandoned the celebration and said, "What the hell—?" He moved over to them and asked, "What happened?"

Before anyone could respond, the phone rang.

Knowing it was for him, Butter said, "I got it!" and rushed to answer it. " Hello!" After a few seconds he said, "Yeah I accept."

"Hello," came D-Mac's voice.

While moving to the kitchen, Butter spiritedly said, "Yeah, what up money?!" He watched from the kitchen side of the counter as Lisa and Kelly appeared to be explaining the M.C.C. story to Mike.

"What the fuck is wrong with you?," D-Mac questioned, rec-ognizing that Butter was far more amped up than normal. "You had some leaky nigga?"

"Nah," Butter answered. D-Mac's question reminded Butter of how long it had been since he last smoked any weed. He then thought about telling D-Mac the good news. But changed his mind due to the fact that it was still premature. Instead Butter said, "I'm just glad that my niggas called. Where's Flip?"

"Takin' a shower. We getting' ready to watch the Knicks

game."

"Ah-h' ight"

"Did that nigga ever call back?," D-Mac asked, referring to Wu.

"Nah…"

"These kidz came from M.C.C a little earlier," D-Mac said. "Niggas runnin 'round here giggin' on some Chinese kid that supposedly got fucked up by two black ba-ad bitchez."

"Yo, watch ya mouth bee," Butter playfully interrupted.

"Watch my mouth?"

"Yeah nigga. That was Lisa and Kelly. They jumped Wu," he added.

Butter's statement took a second to hit D-Mac, and when it did, he dropped the phone and cried laughing. Seconds later he picked up the phone and said, "Sa-ay word!"

D-Mac's uncontrollable cackling was amusing Butter, so he chuckled and replied, "Word to miz."

"Yo what happened?"

"I don't know. I was so heated when I found out, I never even asked," Butter answered.

"Are they there? Let me speak to them!," D-Mac said.

"Chill Duke…"

"C'mon Bee, don't do that to ya manz," D-Mac said.

"Aight, aight," Butter conceded. "Who you wanna talk to?," he asked looking into the living room.

"Both of 'em," D-Mac answered.

"Aight," Butter said, drawing Lisa's attention with a waving hand then motioning for her to come to the phone. "D," he said, extending the phone to her.

"Hello!," Lisa answered with a tone displaying much attitude. "Who this?"

"Lisa nigga! And why you did that bullshit?," she asked then watched as Butter's face twisted.

Her anger instantly extinguished D-Mac's laughter as he replied, "What bullshit?"

"You know what bullshit! That message you sent to M.C.C. about Kelly!"

It took D-Mac two seconds to figure out what happened, and he couldn't help but resume laughing. "My bad. I know that shit ain't funn…oh shit!"

"That shit ain't funny!"

"I know! I know!"

"We could've gotten our asses kicked!," she said as she motioned for Kelly to come to the phone.

"My bad. My bad," he replied with more control over his laughter. "Where's Kelly?"

"Right here! Hold on!," she said and passed the phone to Kelly. She took Butter's hand and led him to the bedroom.

Displaying more calmness than Lisa, Kelly put the phone to her ear and said, "Hello."

His laughter totally subsiding, he said, "Kelly, on everything I love I didn't think no shit like that was gonna happen."

"So what you thought was going to happen?," she asked.

"Word up. I don't know. I was just tryin' to stress that rat-ass nigga out. I know that's ya man and everything, but he ain't playin' fair. My bad though," D-Mac apologized before stating frankly, "You do know he's a snitch right?" After no response, he realized she wasn't going to answer him, so he continued. "That's aight. I understand. But...Hello? Kelly, you still there?," he called into the deadness of the phone.

"Yeah. I'm still here," she responded.

"Oh good. Kelly let me say this, then I'm gonna let you go aight?"

"I'm listening."

"I'm sayin'. We all knew each other for the longest. You know what time it is. You know that shit Wu pullin' is foul. And I don't know if you love him or not, but that nigga don't deserve you. Niggas like him don't deserve to have cuties like you ridin' wit' 'em. They going for self so they should ride by they self 'til they die by they self. No friends, no family, no girl, no nothin'!" D-Mac said emphasizing the word nothing.

Though Kelly was now far less upset with D-Mac than she had been earlier, and could also understand and feel his pain, her only response into the silence of the phone was, "That's it?" Her focus turned to Butter and Lisa coming into the living room.

"Yeah put Butter back on."

"Alright bye," she said then gave the phone to Butter as he walked over.

While they were in the back, Lisa told Butter everything that happened. She made sure to stress the comment Wu made about Butter being the snitch. Then she apologized for moving faster than he thought she should've and he apologized for appearing not to be interested in anything she or Kelly had to say down on 125th Street, before they genuinely kissed and made up.

"Ayo," Butter said as he put the phone to his ear. "That was some cold bullshit," he said regarding what Lisa told him D-Mac said to Wu.

"Man, fuck that hot ass nigga!," D-Mac snidely retorted. "I mean, I'm fucked up that he hooked off on Kelly an' 'em but…any way, I told you that coward was hot. Besides he got his ass kicked!," D-Mac amusingly added. "Ayo I gotta go tell Flip this shit. We'll hit chew back later."

"Aight Duke," Butter said then hung up the phone.

Though he was now convinced that Wu was in fact snitching, he was not going to let the thought of what it meant to the case ruin the best news he had heard in months, years even. He floated into the living room where Lisa, Kelly and Mike were gathered and announced, "It's time for us to celebrate!"

Lisa and Kelly, who were still in the dark about Mike's good news, stood looking at Butter as if he was bugging out. "Celebrate what?," Lisa asked.

"Oh you didn't tell 'em?," Butter asked, then watched as Mike shook his head no. Butter pointed to the sofa and said, "Okay I think yall betta sit down for this." He studied the curiosity in their eyes after they were seated, then pushed the TV and Sega Genesis back. "Let me move this game and shit. I don't want yall to tear nothin' up."

"Butter", Lisa warned, as if to say 'Would you stop bullshitting'.

"Aight, aight, aight," he said as he clapped his hands and rubbed them together like he was warming them up. Then he put his arm around Mike and pulled him close. "We have a meetin' with the CEO of Universal Records!"

Realizing they were momentarily stuck, he added, " We might be getting' a multi-million dollar deal!"

Lisa's solo reaction was louder than Butter and Mike's initial celebration earlier. She jumped up and all over the two of them. Kelly, however, was unsure what it meant for her, but showed genuine happiness for them as she remained seated laughing and clapping at Lisa's reaction.

Butter, showing Kelly that what was going on between Wu and the crew had nothing to do with their family-type relationship. "Oh, you not down wit' the click?", he asked Kelly then watched as Kelly nodded yes. "Well get dat ass up and act like it!," Butter laughed.

Kelly rose up and they stood around hugging one another for a few minutes. After settling down a little, Lisa asked, "When is the meeting?"

"June third," Mike answered.

His answer reminded Butter of his court date. "Aw shit. Hol up," Butter said as his face sunk in his hands.

"What's wrong, Boo?," Lisa asked *as her face showed concern.*

"My hearing is on the third," Butter answered with disappointment. Knowing it was just the first of many to follow, he wasn't concerned about what was going to happen at the hearing. He wanted to be present for the Universal meeting, 'What time is the meetin'?," Butter asked Mike.

"One o'clock," Mike answered.

"Oh I might be aight. My hearing starts at nine-thirty. Mr. Gregg said them shits don't take long. Yeah, we good," he said giving Mike five. "Aight let's roll," he suggested.

"Where we going?," Lisa questioned.

"Out. We gotta go celebrate!"

"Unh unh," Kelly moaned as she pointed to her black eye. "I'm not going out like this."

"Just throw your shades on," Mike *quipped.*

"And what about me?," Lisa gestured to her lip.

"Put crazy lip stick on it," Mike suggested, appearing to have all the answers. He and Butter were now amused, and watched slyly as Lisa and Kelly studied each other's faces while pondering Mike's suggestions.

"So?," Mike asked, "What's it going to be?"

"Unh unh!," they both responded, causing Mike and Butter to laugh.

"Oh it's funny now?," Kelly asked.

"Nah, nah," Mike chuckled, causing them all to laugh.

So instead, they celebrated in the apartment. Mike and Butter went out and picked up some weed, Moet, pizza, Chinese food, seafood, and a bunch of other shit they knew they couldn't eat all in one night. They also brought back a couple decks of cards, and the four of them played monopoly and spades into the early morning hours.

Over the next two weeks, the days flew by quickly. Mainly, because everyone was busy. The fact that they had a meeting set up with Universal Records didn't prompt them to party and bullshit. Instead it caused them to push harder. Wanting to present the 'Big Wheels' of Universal with an indomitable, dynamic package, Mike and Butter felt that they would have to strengthen their team. In order to do that they needed more artists and more demos to add to their roster — something that would leave them no time to sell records.

When Lisa and Kelly suggested that they, along with Regina and Denise, hold down 125th Street, the idea turned out to be the ultimate solution.

Within days, Mike and Butter found three more promising artists; two young rappers named Sweat and Lyrics, and another R&B chick they nicknamed Summer. Not only because it was nearing that season of the year, but also because she was as pretty as a summer day. Knowing they were going to need some crazy tracks, Mike and Butter also pulled in an old friend of Mike's. Joe Maldonado, the super producer and track maker who had the underground on lock. Together, the three of them worked around the clock to prepare what they considered an exclusive, no nonsense package for Universal Records.

Hampstead Publishing

Chapter Sixteen

Lisa and Kelly were in the kitchen at Mike's apartment finishing up the dishes that were left from the big dinner they both had spent half the day preparing. It was sort of like a complimentary meal to make up for the fast food meals the four of them had been eating over the past couple of weeks.

Lisa finished the dishes. "All right Boo, I'm ready," she said as she came into the living room and stood over Mike and Butter who were totally engulfed in their joysticks.

"Damn Lisa!," Mike whimpered.

"Yeah boy! I told you, you can't fuck wit' me!," Butter boasted.

"Move ya ass out the way!," Mike said as he brushed Lisa to the side. "You made me lose the damn game!"

"Don't push me!," she replied as she mushed Mike's head. "And c'mon Butter, it's six-thirty!", she added with attitude.

"Nah, nah, one more!," Mike pleaded as Butter began to rise. "You know if she wouldn't have gotten in my way…"

"Fuck outta here! Ya ass was out, aight! C'mon, I'll buss ya shit again!," Butter challenged, motioning for Mike to sit back down.

"Unh- unh Butter," Lisa said as she tugged on Butter's arm.

"Why don't you go sit your ass down somewhere!," Mike scowled, watching as she attempted to take the joystick from Butter.

Ignoring Mike's irritation, she said, "C'mon Butter, we have to make it to the hospital to see Sean Jr. before visiting hours are over!"

"Oh word," Butter jumped up. "I'll do you tommara on some big screen shit," Butter added with a wink, implying after they had signed the deal.

"Nah, we gonna do this tonight when you get back."

"We ain't comin' back," Butter said with a sly grin. "We gonna stay at my momz crib. You know a nigga gotta go to court early in the mornin'."

"That's dat bullshit shit," Mike shot back with a grin.

"Play Kelly," Lisa called out as she and Butter moved towards the door.

Mike, still upset with her for costing him the game, gave her a grim look, then said, "Get ya stupid ass outta here."

"Your mother's a stupid ass," she shot back.

"She's your mother too."

"So. She's still a stupid ass for having you after me," she said then laced him with a middle finger.

"C'mon, I'll play you for a little while," Kelly laughed. Kelly's challenge caused Butter to stop in his tracks as he and Lisa neared the front door.

Mike looked up to see the amusement in Butter's face then looked back at Kelly. "Scram. This ain't for you," he said rising off the sofa.

"I'll bet'chew fifty dollars she'll beat you!," Lisa cut in, walking all the way back to Mike with her pinky out and thumb up.

"Don't do it!," Butter warned. "They been playing that shit on the low!"

Mike surveyed all their faces. He seen a grin on Butter's, a serious stare on Lisa's, and the slyness that Kelly's bore, then said, "Bet!," locking pinkies and touching thumbs with Lisa before sitting back down.

"And I want my money," Lisa said as she headed back towards the door.

"Ayo, if she beat you Duke..."

"Imagine that!" Mike said cutting Butter off.

"I'll see you tomorrow Kelly!," Lisa cut in.   "And kick his ass!"

"Bye!," Kelly responded.

"Yeah, get the hell out!," Mike said to the closed door.

A half an hour later Mike was down a hundred and fifty dollars. It turned out that Kelly was an even better player than Butter. No matter which fighter she used he stood no chance. The only reason why he kept betting it back was because he had no intentions on paying anybody a coin.

"Last game," Mike said, reaching for the reset button.

Kelly was becoming bored with beating on him, so she set the joystick down, reminding Mike, "You said that last game."

"Nah, c'mon. Double or nothin'," Mike resisted, taking her hand as Kelly moved to walk off.

Turning around, she placed her stare down onto his and said, "Face it baby. You got no wins."

"I told you about doin' that," Mike said, referring to her waggling tongue—a gesture she made every time she put his man down.

"What?," she innocently replied.

"That tongue move," he said, firmly increasing his grip on her hand.

"Why? It bothers you?"

He studied her face for a second, focused on her eyes as if he was trying to find a trace of the black eye she had, then trickled to her waistline. His dick was hard as a pot of overnight grits, and though he wanted to make a move, he was unsure what it would do to his close relationship with Butter being that Kelly was still considered Wu's girl.

Kelly's nipples were pushing through her bra as well. Because there was no sex allowed in the rehab, Kelly hadn't had any in six months. The more she thought about it, the more her hormones raced wildly inside of her. She wanted Mike to make the next move just as bad as he wanted to make it. When she noticed he was hesitating, she figured that he was contemplating whether or not it would be all right with Butter, so to let him know that it was up to her if they fucked or not she moved closer to him and placed her free left hand on his head as he buried his face into her stomach area.

The softness that he felt through the cotton of the long orange tee shirt that over lapped her curve-hugging spandex pants sent an inviting message through his body that drove him to free his right hand from hers and move both hands onto her thighs. Working them underneath the shirt, he traced her curved hips and she responded by throwing her head back while biting down on her bottom lip as she combed her fingers through his curly hair.

Seconds later, she pulled her shirt off allowing his face to meet with her flesh. Now firmly palming her ass, he began tracing her belly button with his tongue. The tingling feeling it created quickly became unbearable. She firmly caressed the sides of his head and guided him up to meet her height. She undressed him as their tongues swam inside each other's mouths. He unfixed her bra and massaged both of her firm breasts. The gesture caused her
to let out a heavy sigh. Seconds later they were both naked.

While still passionately kissing and exploring each other's bodies with uncontrollable hands, he slowly backed her around the sofa and gently guided her down onto the airbed. Yearning to soothe the burning sensation inside of her, she spread her thighs and with both hands took a firm grip of his ass cheeks as he penetrated.

"SSSSS!" she inhaled, driving him deeper and deeper inside of her with every slow grinding stroke.

In rhythm, they casually increased in speed. Like a back catcher, Mike was catching every fast and curve ball Kelly was throwing at him. After several minutes of continuous stroking, Mike's eyes locked onto the raised eyebrows of Kelly's closed eyelids. He could feel her warm juices pouring down on him. The thought of her cumming caused him to explode inside of her. They flowed like two faucets in a stopped up sink, quickly filling up, then over running into the sheets. Depleting everything within him, Mike collapsed on top of her before rolling over beside her. For the next few minutes they lay staring into each other's eyes.

"What you thinking about?," Kelly asked in a low sexy tone. She witnessed him slowly shake his head then she said, "I know what you're thinking about." Slowly stroking her hair with his left hand he shook his head no again. "Yes I do. You're thinking about how complicated things are with me being in the middle of what's going on with Wu and Butter and them. And how what we just did might have made things that much more complicated."

He flashed a smile, then said, "If all of that meant 'do you still love him?' Then you're right."

"Yes," she said.

"Yes what?"

"Yes. That's what all of that meant."

"And?"

"And yes. I still love him but...," Kelly paused, then shook her head indicating she didn't want to talk about it.

Mike moved his free right hand and placed it over her left hand that rested on his chest and asked, "But what?"

After letting out a short sigh, she said, "We all grew up together. I mean I'm a year or two older so I guess I can say I watched them grow up together. And they watched as I grew as well. They stayed in the hallway of 1839 day and night. Shooting dice, smoking weed, starting trouble. They were bad. And they stuck together. The whole block loved them though. They kept it safe too" she chuckled. "I mean they all had this crazy crush on me."

"That's understandable," Mike said seductively.

She blessed him with a smile then continued, "Every boyfriend I had, not that I slept with all of them," she quickly added, "it was like those four were waiting for every guy I was with to try and play them so they could do something to him," she chuckled.

"Anyway, if what Wu is doing to them is hurting me I can imagine what it's doing to them. And what he's doing will never be forgotten by them or himself. He'll never be able to part with that. And I just can't see myself being with someone who has to carry around a chip like that on his shoulder for the rest of his life."

"I can't see you being with anyone like that either," Mike responded with a fixed stare. "In fact I can't see you being with anyone but me," he added boldly.

Mike was definitely Kelly's type. A fly guy, and though it wasn't drugs he was moving, he was a witty hustler. And the fact that he was possibly less than twenty-four hours away from being a millionaire didn't hurt either. Kelly was happy he felt as he did about her.

With her head resting in her palms, she stared down at him and seductively asked, "So what are you saying?"

Mike eased her over until they were on top of the dry sheets of the second air bed. "Exactly what I said", he replied as he saddled up behind her and rode off like an outlaw.

As Butter and Mr. Gregg sat at the long dark brown wooden table on the left side of the courtroom, Butter's eyes scanned the room as if he was making sure everything was exactly like it had been a month earlier at his initial arraignment. He glanced to the right at the dyke looking prosecutor and her team that consisted of two agents one black and one white. Both of whom Butter remembered from one of the vehicles that had surrounded his Benz. Butter then shifted a few feet over to the prosecution's table where he viewed the young, white court clerk setting things up at her little table. Straight forward, Butter saw the empty witness stand next to the elevated Judge's station, and further to the left he spotted the huge, mean looking black guard who stood by the door of the Judge's chamber like he was guarding Fort Knox.

As Butter moved off of Fort Knox and continued looking to the left, he saw the door that the detainees were escorted through and prayed he would never have to walk through there again.

Yearning for more pleasant thoughts, Butter looked over his shoulder and winked in response to the kiss Lisa blew to him from the first distant row of seats behind him.

At that moment, he was glad he hadn't been able to persuade her not to come, like he was able to persuade his parents, who were taking care of business.

The Judge's entrance drew Butter, and everyone else's, attention to the front. Every single person rose to their feet, then sat down immediately following the clerk's chant that all should be seated and come to order.

"Good morning every one," said the old, balding black judge. He acknowledged their return greetings as he fumbled with some papers. "All right," his strong, demanding voice said. "It's going on ten-fifteen and I know we're running late. For

that I deeply apologize. Now, having said that, let's move on
with the proceeding," he suggested strongly as he studied both
Mr. Gregg and Mrs. Bailey, the prosecuting attorney. "Oh,"
the judge said, "before we get started on the evidentiary suppression and severance issues, Mrs. Bailey, it is my understanding that there is an entirely different issue you would like
to bring before the court?"

Mrs. Bailey stood. "Yes Your Honor," she said while remaining on her feet.

"Well if it's all right with both counsels I would refer to hear
what that issue is and see if it can be quickly resolved before
we go into suppression motions?"

Mrs. Bailey, still standing, replied, "That would be fine Your
Honor."

"Counsel?," the Judge said as he zeroed in on Mr. Gregg for
a response.

Ah…this is not good, Mr. Gregg thought as he rose up, eager
to find out what Mrs. Bailey had up her sleeve. He looked
down at Butter's puzzled face then met the judge's stare and
said, "Yes Your Honor. We have no problem with that."

"Thank you Sir," the judge said as he nodded for Mr. Gregg
to be seated. The judge then zeroed in on Mrs. Bailey and said,
"Very well, you may proceed Mrs. Bailey."

"Thank you Your Honor," she said.

Mrs. Bailey's focus aimed down at small piles of papers scattered on the table. Selecting a thin stapled stack, Mrs. Bailey
looked at the judge and said, "Your Honor, at this time I would
like to serve Mr. Ryder with a copy of a superceding indictment that charges Mr. Ryder and others mentioned with intent
to commit murder." Mrs. Bailey sternly continued as she
flipped through the pages, "Count one charges that Mr. Ryder
and others mentioned, on and around the second week of June
in 1989 conspired to commit a double homicide. And count
two charges that Mr. Ryder and others mentioned, on and
around the last week of January in 1991 also conspired to commit a triple homicide." Mrs. Bailey glanced at the bewildered
looks on the faces of Mr. Gregg and Butter.

The attention of everyone was then snagged by the judge's
announcement, "Well Mrs. Bailey, if permission to serve Mr.
Ryder and his counsel with a copy of that indictment is what

you're asking, you are most certainly welcome to do so."

Nodding she said, "Thank you Your Honor."

The judge and the rest of the room watched as Mrs. Bailey strode over and extended a copy to Mr. Gregg, whose face was still branded with a look of disbelief.

Mr. Gregg stood holding up the indictment. He stroked his tie and said, "Your Honor, if I may, I'd like to have a few minutes to look this over with my client."

After a few seconds of consideration the judge said, "You certainly can."

"Thank you Sir," Mr. Gregg replied before he sat down.

As Mr. Gregg browsed through the pages, a confused and speechless Butter looked on. He recognized D-Mac, Wu and Flip's names as the others mentioned on the double homicide charge. On the triple homicide charge, Butter saw his name along with Flip, D-Mac and the twin's names. It only took a second to figure out how these indictments had come about. Wu told about one, and the twin's had ratted about the other. What Butter couldn't grasp was why Mr. Gregg hadn't just told him that the DA was looking into murder charges. And even more importantly, how could the DA just come out of the blue and charge him for some shit that happened way back when?

Butter and Mr. Gregg scanned through the last page together and just as Butter was ready to question him, Mr. Gregg met his eyes and beat him to the punch. In almost a whispering tone, Mr. Gregg said, "You never told me about this."

You never asked, mothafucka, Butter thought with a distorted expression. ***And** if you would've asked, I would've told you the same shit I'm about to tell you now*, Butter's thoughts screamed. "I don't know nothin' about no murders. Where this shit came from?," Butter said in a tone that was a tad louder than Mr. Gregg's.

Pressed for time Mr. Gregg replied, "Well, we'll have to discuss this later." Without waiting on Butter's response, Mr. Gregg rose. "Excuse me, Your Honor?," he said asking if he could speak.

"Yes counselor?"

Holding up the pages with one hand and stroking his tie with the other, Mr. Gregg said, "Now that Mrs. Bailey has enlightened us with this superceding indictment, I think it would be appropriate that I ask the court to postpone the evidentiary hearing that was to follow until Mrs. Bailey provides me with the evidence she has pertaining to these particular charges. Because I'm almost certain that there are issues I would like to suppress in it as well."

"Any objections Mrs. Bailey?"

"No Your Honor," Mrs. Bailey answered.

Now splitting his focus between the two standing counsels, the judge asked, "Will we be set for next Monday?"

"My office will have a copy of the evidence to Mr. Gregg by this afternoon Sir," Mrs. Bailey stated.

Shifting his focus, the judge said, "Mr. Gregg?"

"Yes Your Honor. One week from today would be feasible," Mr. Gregg responded.

"Well then. If that's everything?"

"Excuse me, Your Honor," Mrs. Bailey interrupted.

"Yes counselor?," the judge responded.

"There's one more thing I would like to add."

"Be my guest."

"Well Your Honor," she said as her focus shifted from her papers on the table to the judge, "due to the seriousness of the current charges against Mr. Ryder," her frigid glance flashed on Butter as she continued, "I would ask that the court reconsider and revoke bail that has been set forth in an earlier proceeding."

"Mr. Gregg," the judge turned his focus, "I'm sure there's something you want to say?"

Mr. Gregg stared down at Butter's awed facial expression, then lifted his eyes back to the judge, "Yes Your Honor," he said. Then he cleared his throat before continuing. "I would like to object and add that my client has already been out on bail for a month and has demonstrated no interest in fleeing. Secondly, I would just like to remind the court that my client's family has put up a substantial amount of property which clearly shows their trust in his obligation not to flee."

The judge momentarily studied both attorneys, then looked at Butter, and said, "The court is aware of the amount of property your client's family stands to lose in the event your client does decide to flee. And I might add that Mr. Ryder here, " he said while gesturing to Butter, "ought to be thankful to have parents that trust and care for him as much as they do. However, as Mrs. Bailey has stated, conspiracy to commit murder is a very, very serious charge and so I would have to agree with her and order that Mr. Ryder's bail be revoked. He is to remain in custody pending all hearings."

Chapter Seventeen

Later that morning, Butter sat motionless in the tiny eight by eight holding cell that was on the other side of the court room's door. It was the same door he had prayed he would never have to walk through again. As Butter waited for what he guessed would be the Marshals coming to escort him to one of the jails, his mind continuously played back the conclusion to the morning's events—the light pounding of the judge's mallet, the flurry of tears he witnessed running down Lisa's reddened face, and the big black Fort Knox guard uncuffing him after he was escorted to the cell.

As if he could erase it all, Butter slowly ran his hand over his face and continued to do so until he spotted Mr. Gregg entering from the same door he came through. "Mr. Gregg!," Butter shouted. He rose up from the bench and gripped the steel bars tightly as if he was about to rattle a cage. "This is some bullshit!," he raved. "How they gonna lock me down? I ain't runnin' nowhere! I didn't kill nothin'! That bitch come in here wit' some bullshit beef...!"

"Listen Mr. Ryder," Mr. Gregg cut in sharply, he stood inches from the cell with a folder in one hand and his brief case in the other. Calm down for a second. Now what we need to do is try and go over a few things before they come and get you. I'm not sure, but you'll probably be going back up to Valhalla," Mr. Gregg said as he placed his brief case on the floor. "So, if I can get this done here, I can maybe save a trip," he added as he opened the folder.

Ain't this a bitch? I'm tryin' to save a fuckin' trip too, Butter though as he grilled the top of Mr. Gregg's bowed head with thoughts of cursing his ass out. But, knowing he needed Mr. Gregg on his side more than ever, Butter quickly abandoned the thought.

"Okay Mr. Ryder," Mr. Gregg said as he met Butter's stare. "These murders...do you know about them?," he asked. Mr. Gregg acknowledged Butter's negative head movement, then continued. "Did you know any of the victims?," he asked Butter as he handed him a piece of paper that had the real names of Uptown, Cookie, and the three Jersey boys.

"No," Butter answered scanning the paper then handing it back. "How she came up wit' some shit like that?"

"Well, I can almost assure you that it's not just coming from one person. And with my knowledge of the twins cooperation I can imagine where the information for the triple homicide came from. But I'm not so sure about the double homicide."

Since Mr. Gregg hadn't mentioned having any knowledge about Wu snitching, Butter thought for a split second, "**Maybe because he wasn't?**" Then thought better after realizing the twins knew nothing about Uptown and Cookie. "What about Wu umm Gray?," Butter asked as he quickly corrected himself. "Is he rattin'?"

Mr. Gregg looked as if he gave it some thought and answered, "No. I don't recall hearing or seeing anything about Mr. Gray cooperating. Why? Does he know about these murders?"

"*Nice try*," Butter thought before he answered, "I don't know."

Ready to bring things to a close, Mr. Gregg said, "Okay. Well Mr. Ryder, I'm afraid these new charges add an entirely new dimension to both this case, and my fee," he bluntly stated. "Now I will get in touch with your father as soon as I get back to my office, and I suggest that you speak with him as well."

"How much are we talking?"

"If I have to deal with these new charges in addition to the original ones? Were talking a minimum of forty-five thousand a week for trial, and even a plea deal may cost that."

"That's everything my momz and popz been working for," Butter thought before letting out a harsh sigh. Their attention was then drawn to the two laughing marshals who had entered the area and were startled by Mr. Gregg's presence.

"Morning Sir," the first marshal spoke after recognizing that Mr. Gregg was an attorney.

"Morning," Mr. Gregg responded as he and the second marshal greeted each other with a nod. Mr. Gregg looked at Butter and said, "Oh, Lisa asked that I tell you to call her at her mother's house. She said she'll be there until you call." Mr. Gregg then watched as one of the marshals knelt down in front of the outside of the cell, stuck his arms between the bars and began shackling Butter's ankles. "Is there anything you would like me to relay to her? She's out in the lobby waiting on me to return."

"Nah, just tell her I'll call," Butter sorely replied. "Thanks," he said.

"Sure thing," Mr. Gregg said before disappearing out of the door.

Thanks to all the legal info D-Mac had continuously acquired from his man with the dreads, as well as constant threats of writing to the judge, he and Flip were able to keep madd pressure on their public defenders to do less talk about cooperation and more filing of motions. It turned out to be pretty effective, because they, too, were scheduled for a severance and suppression hearing on June third. In fact theirs had been held at nine o'clock...an hour before Butter's. And like Butter, they were first served a copy of the superceding indictment. However, their hearing had continued on as scheduled, though the suppression motions were put off until the following Monday also. Their severance motions were heard and denied.

By ten thirty, fifteen minutes after Butter's hearing started, D-Mac and Flip were already back on Valhalla's fifth floor. After finally coming to grips with what went down at the hearing, they stepped to D-Mac's man for a better understanding.

While checking out the new indictment, the dred became puzzled as to why Wu's name was listed as a codefendant on the double homicide and not the triple, and why the twins were listed as codefendants on the triple and not the double. He asked them if they had any idea why that was?

Trying not to indicate that the charges were true, D-Mac mentioned something about Wu being in rehab around the date specified. Not needing to know much more than that, the dread concluded that Wu snitched about one and the twins ratted about the other. The dread then shared his theory with them but it was something they had both already figured out.

What Flip and D-Mac couldn't figure out was how could the murder charges be brought against them on the words of three rat ass niggas who were nowhere around when the murders took place? When D-Mac hypothetically put the question to the dred, his answer was the fucked up grand jury system. He explained to them that all the DA did was sat them niggas in front of the grand jury and let them run their mouths.

When D-Mac asked why they weren't informed of the proceedings by their public defenders, Dred told them that their lawyers most likely had no idea. The dread then explained that the grand jury is a panel that prosecutors and their rat-ass witnesses secretly go before to tell their side of the story. The dred continued about how fucked up the process was because the accused are never present to defend themselves. In summing it up, the dred really messed their heads up when he told them not even expensive lawyers like the one their man Butter had would be able to detect when their clients are about to get hit with an indictment. Or, like in their case, a superseding indictment, and that he, the dread, wouldn't be surprised if the new charges got Butter's bail revoked.

It was a quarter to twelve by the time the dred got through schooling them, and after being challenged to a game of chess by a friend, the dred pardoned himself and left D-Mac and Flip standing around the basketball court area. The two of them continued to carry on the conversation about the unjust tactics of the prosecutors, which they consistently labeled as "bullshit."

Knowing the lunch trays were coming up, their focus periodically rested on the elevator located in the corridor outside the

sliding glass doors next to the C.O.'s station. When the elevator finally opened, the sight of a guard followed by Butter carrying a bedroll, silenced and stiffened them. The first thing that
popped into their heads were Dred's statements about Butter's
bail being revoked.

As oxygen began to flow to their brains again, D-Mac and
Flip's stares met. They then moved towards the station where
Butter now stood and greeted him with thug hugs and fives.
The three of them then marched into Butter's assigned cell and
kicked it while Butter made his bed.

They started talking about that morning's court proceeding,
but were interrupted by the arrival of the lunch trays.
Knowing their next hot meal wouldn't be coming for another
five to six hours, they collected their trays and returned to
Butter's room to continue their conversation.

After learning that D-Mac and Flip had been in court an hour
before him, Butter was awed at the way the fucking judge
played it off like he didn't know what Mrs. Bailey had in store
for him. It also made Butter realize that the revoking of his bail
was possibly decided before his hearing even started.

They finished eating, returned their trays, and while D-Mac
and Flip watched TV, Butter called his momz crib. He spoke
with Lisa who told him that his momz had to go somewhere in
Brooklyn and his popz went downtown to meet with Mr.
Gregg. She also told him that she called Mike's house and no
one was there. It wasn't until then that he had begun to feel
stressed about not being able to attend the meeting at
Universal Records.

They chatted a while longer then hung up. Wanting a little
time for himself, Butter didn't bother letting D-Mac and Flip
know he was done on the phone. Instead, he went to his cell,
collapsed on his bunk, and let the thoughts of his legal woes,
the Universal meeting, and the fact that he might have to get
used to spending the rest of his life in a cell, consume his mind
until he dozed off.

Later the next morning, Butter was awakened by D-Mac and
Flip who informed him that it was almost time for the lunch
trays to come up. Realizing he had fallen back to sleep after
breakfast, Butter jumped up, quickly washed up, and told the
fellas he'd be right back. Then he raced out the door to the

phone. Desperately wanting to know how the Universal meeting turned out, Butter anxiously dialed Mike's number. While the phone rang, he wondered where Mike and Kelly had been the entire time he was trying to get in touch with them the night before and earlier that morning? He also wondered why Lisa hadn't left a message with either his parents or her mother before she disappeared.

"What the fuck is goin' on?," Butter mumbled to himself as Mike's phone continued to ring. He finally hung up and tried Lisa's mother's apartment where he got no answer. Figuring his parents had surely heard from Lisa by now, he called home, but was disappointed when no one answered the phone there either. He snickered ironically at the thought of no one being home while he was locked up. Then on his last desperate attempt to speak to anyone with any type of important information, Butter dialed Mr. Gregg's number with the intention of finding out how the meeting with his popz had turned out and whether or not Mr. Gregg was still representing him. But even that fell short after Mr. Gregg's secretary informed Butter that he was out of the office.

Left feeling mystified, stressed, and frustrated, Butter slammed the phone down. It wasn't until afterwards that he noticed D-Mac and Flip standing by the basketball court several feet away.

Realizing his action had drawn their attentions and not wanting them to think he was crackin' under pressure, Butter slowly moved towards them while racking his brain for an explanation to his gesture, but it turned out not to be necessary because as he neared, all of their attentions were snagged by the guard who appeared by the C.O.'s station.

"Ryder! Wheeler! Turner!," The C.O. shouted. "You all have visits." Nearly stunned, the three shot each other a dubious stare as they filed up behind the C.O.

Though the three of them were undoubtedly thrilled to have visitors, as they neared the section Lisa, Kelly, Mike, Regina, and Denise had monopolized, perplexed thoughts began to cast down on them. D-Mac and Flip wondered why Denise and Regina hadn't mentioned that they were coming to visit them during their phone conversations the night before? And Butter wondered why Lisa, Kelly and Mike's facial expressions didn't look like a million bucks?

The three of them exchanged what appeared to be consoling hugs and kisses on the cheek of Kelly's and each other's mates, greeted Mike with fives, then planted their own mates with a firm hug and long wet one.

"What's up?," Butter asked, surveying all the visitor's faces as they sat down. "Why everybody looks like they just left a funeral?"

"Word!," Flip agreed, throwing his arm around the back of Denise's chair.

They watched as the girls responded by staring at Mike. Seconds later D-Mac, Flip, and Butter's eyes followed. Immediately suspecting something had gone wrong with the deal, Butter fixed his stare on Mike and asked, "What happened?"

Trying to maintain the seriousness in his expression Mike sorely answered, "Twenty million." He watched the confused look on Butter's face. Then with more enthusiasm, Mike said, "They gave us twenty million, Bee!" Mike and the girls were finally able to let out the excitement they had been working so hard to hide.

Forgetting about the twenty questions he had for them, Butter rose to his feet and in an exultant fashion, kissed all the girls on the cheek, gave Mike, who met his height, a rugged hug, then turned to D-Mac and Flip who were surveying the faces like everyone was high, and said, "Universal gave me and Mike's label twenty million!"

"Fuck outta here!," Flip replied, astonished.

"Sa-ay wor-rd!," D-Mac said before they rose up and congratulated them.

"Ayo Duke," Butter said, looking D-Mac square in the eyes, "remember when you said 'imagine if we had three lawyers like mine goin' at that bitch'?" He watched as D-Mac nodded yes then said, "Well now we're gonna see."

During the remainder of the visit, Mike and Butter sat next to each other discussing the next moves that were to be made as far as the production of their label. Butter stressed to Mike how important it was to him that he, — Mike — go with Lisa to see Mr. Gregg and inform him that their label was now documented. He also told Mike to tell Mr. Gregg to find two more high-powered lawyers for his two codefendants, D-Mac and Flip.

The next day Mr. Gregg brought in two top notch lawyers he knew, and within one day he had them updated on the entire case. Mr. Gregg discussed all of the government's evidence, which consisted of statements made by agents, the three look-outs, the twins, a lab technician, crack head Ike and his smoking sidekick, the pitcher and Wu who was the person Mrs. Bailey labeled as her star witness. Mr. Gregg was sure to mention that everyone had already agreed to testify. In addition, Wu and the twins would also be testifying about the murder charges.

Lastly, Mr. Gregg talked about Butter's record label and how he planned on building his defense around it. He suggested that since Mrs. Bailey would most likely attempt to portray Butter, D-Mac and Flip to the jury as close friends who started a crack enterprise, it would probably be in their clients' best interest if they acted as a team, presenting a defense that showed their clients were close friends who started a record label.

Liking the idea, the two attorneys agreed and for the next few days they were on a mission. Knowing that they had to prove the government was not meeting its burden of proof beyond a reasonable doubt, the lawyers sent out a team of private investigators to dig up dirt on all the rats and agents involved in the case.

With the help of Lisa and Kelly, the P.I.'s were able to gather a list of people from each borough that recognized Butter's picture as the guy who sold them records out of the trunk of a car, and for a couple of hundred which Lisa and Kelly offered at Butter's request, they even remembered D-Mac and Flip's faces. But the shocker came when they were able to get a large number of people on the block to sign statements saying that they never witnessed Butter, D-Mac and Flip selling drugs in the area.

By the time the following Monday's hearing rolled around, the defense had obtained and equally divided over two hundred sworn statements from record buyers and a hundred and fifty from the neighborhood, giving them over a hundred and sixteen witnesses a piece. The defense also shared a stack of evidence discrediting most of the DA's witnesses, including a couple of agents that had lied on several occasions during a number of previous drug trials.

After hearing suppression arguments from all counsels, the judge, in an effort to avoid a long drawn out trial, reduced the defense team's witness rosters considerably. However, he allowed Mrs. Bailey's evidence to remain the same. Lastly, the judge encouraged them to try and reach a plea agreement before the trial date which he set for the first week in September.

As the weeks continued to roll by, the government's witnesses were studying and rehearsing their statements and the defense team was narrowing down their rosters to the twenty witnesses apiece that the judge was allowing. It was a far cry from the hundred and sixteen they really never intended on using, but actually a bit more than they expected.

During the second week of July, Mrs. Bailey, feeling her case was still solid, offered each of them fifty-five years. A number she felt was more than reasonable considering murders were involved. When she received a disagreeing response, in an effort to oblige the Judge's request that they reach an agreement, she reduced it to

forty-five in early August. When that, too, was rejected she refused to make another offer, and by mid August she began making preparations for the trial.

Chapter Eighteen

Monday, September 15th, 8:30 a.m.

D-Mac, Flip, and Butter, were escorted into the courtroom's detainee holding cell. After having their restraints removed, trying to prevent from wrinkling their suits any further, they stood around eagerly waiting on nine o' clock, the time the trial was set to begin.

"You look funny as hell in a suit," D-Mac kidded with Flip, trying to ease some of the tension they all felt.

"We all look funny in these shits," Flip nervously chuckled. "The last time any of us wore one, was at your grandfather's joint. May he rest in peace."

"Word," Butter sorely agreed before changing the subject. "Yo , what yall think?"

"About what?," Flip and D-Mac replied at the same time.

"About this. The trial. Goin' all the way to the door wit' it?," Butter asked as if he was unsure whether they made the right decision.

"We ain't had no choice, Bee," Flip responded. "You heard what the lawyer said. We lose our right to appeal and the whole shit if we would've copped to the forty-five. I mean I understand we'll probably get life if we lose, and I don't know how you niggas feel, but I'll be sixty-six in forty years. That cop was life to me. And never will I sign mine on the dotted line."

"Word," D-Mac agreed. "I'll be sixty-five my mothafuckin' self. The only niggas that's gonna recognize me is you two old bastards," he added, causing them to chuckle.

Their laughter quickly eased and their faces turned to stone as they placed steady stares on the two marshals coming through the door. "It's show time, fellas," one of the Marshals said as he opened the cell.

They glanced at each other as if to say, 'This *is it!*', then filed out of the cell before being led straight into the courtroom. Upon entering, they met the stares of family and friends, and of all defendants. Some were there to show support. Others were there being nosey.

They focused their sights on the section behind the defense table where Lisa, Kelly, Mike and their parents were all seated. Flashing them appreciative smiles, they each took seats next to their lawyers who were set-up at individual tables. Flip faced the empty jury box, Butter and D-Mac faced the empty judge's chair and witness stand. They each took turns glancing at the court clerk, Mr. Fort Knox, and the prosecutor's table where Mrs. Bailey sat with her team.

"All rise!," said the clerk as the judge emerged from his chambers. Everyone immediately rose to their feet and quietly watched as the Judge took his seat. "You may be seated," the clerk instructed shortly thereafter.

"Is everybody ready to begin here this morning?," the judge asked as he surveyed the faces of the defendants, counsel and court clerk.

"Your Honor, I am going to have to change my witness order slightly," Mrs. Bailey stood up and stated. "Mrs. White, the lab technician, won't be able to make it until late in the week due to a slight illness."

"All right," the judge responded. Then turning to Fort Knox he said, "Bring the jury in, thank you."

The courtroom watched as Fort Knox moved to the door by the jury box, disappeared and returned seconds later followed by the jurors; eight whites and four blacks, ranging from their late twenties to late forties in age. They filed into the box, took

their seats, and instantly began fixing their glares on the defendants. Already warned by their attorneys not to look away, D-
Mac, Butter, and Flip hardly blinked an eye.

"Good morning ladies and gentlemen of the jury," began the
judge, drawing everyone's attention before proceeding with a
minimum of formalities that included a quick overview of the
trial process. Prosecution witnesses, with defense cross-examination would follow opening statements.   Finally, closing
statements and the judge's explanation of the law. The judge
reminded the jury that opening statements were not evidence,
then turned the courtroom over to the prosecutor.

Mrs. Bailey moved smoothly to the lectern in front of the jury
box. She was wearing a smoke gray pinstripe suit that fit tightly, exposing the flatness of her scrawny body. The back of her
was all that D-Mac, Flip, Butter, and their attorneys could see.
They each slyly maneuvered their heads in hopes of getting a
glance of her facial expression while she spoke, but before she
uttered a word, she turned to face them with an extended arm
in their direction.

"Those three men!," Mrs. Bailey's charged in a voice that was
alarming and snide with her extended finger pointing at
Butter, then D-Mac, and onto Flip. "Those three men stand
accused of conspiracy to possess with the intent to distribute
cocaine base crack. And conspiracy to commit a number of
murders. The evidence that you will hear in this court room
will show you that those three men were malicious drug dealers who robbed and murdered in order to prosper and enjoy
the lavish life styles you and I would have to work an entire life
time to achieve!"

She stared at the jurors, surveying them for a few seconds
before she continued. "The evidence will show that those three
men left lifeless young bodies in a Bronx apartment with bullet
wounds to the head and face of a young married couple. And
the evidence will show that they gunned down three young
New Jersey residents while they were at a light, blocks away
from where their operation was established."

Having seized the moment, Mrs. Bailey turned back to face
the jury. "As the days pass, ladies and gentlemen, and we
hope there will not be too many, but you'll understand our
need to tell you the whole story — you will see and hear this

evidence from the people who witnessed it. You will hear first from undercover narcotics and DEA agents who have had this case under heavy surveillance. The police officers who answered the call to nine-one-one and went to the Bronx apartment of a young married couple where they discovered the bodies of Eugene "Uptown" Simmons and his wife Cookie Simmons lying in a pool of blood. Also in the apartment was a hysterical baby. And then ladies and gentlemen, you will hear from two homicide detectives who were the first on the scene of the triple homicide and questioned numerous people." After a pause Mrs. Bailey continued, "There's a lab technician who's going to tell you that the drugs in question is cocaine base. Better known as crack. But you're not just going to hear from police officers and a lab expert. You're going to hear from Mr. James 'Wu' Gray, a co-conspirator and very close friend of those men," she exhorted, pointing in the direction of the defense's table. "You're also going to hear from a set of twins and a number of other coconspirators as well."

Mrs. Bailey broke to fix a drink of water. The attorneys at the defense tables knew she didn't need it. It was just a way to underline what she just said, letting it settle into the juror's minds. Though they were not moved by her words, Mrs. Bailey managed to mesmerize her intended audience. She was also able to tighten the stomach muscles of the three defendants.

She went on, "I have an obligation, ladies and gentlemen," Mrs. Bailey said as she took a sip of water and continued after placing the glass on the prosecutor's table. "One I have accepted willingly and with enthusiasm. An obligation to prove that those three men are not the entertainment moguls their defense will try and make them out to be. Those three men are nothing but drug dealing murderers who are guilty beyond a reasonable doubt. And you too have an obligation. Your obligation is to follow the law as the judge explains it to you, and to consider the evidence you see and hear presented in this courtroom. And if you follow that obligation according to the evidence that will be presented here, you will…you must, find those defendants guilty as charged!," Mrs. Bailey said as she sternly ended her statement, then stood motionless for a moment before taking her seat at the prosecution's table.

Had it been a play, Mrs. Bailey would've received a standing ovation, but being that shit was real and considering where they were, the silence of the courtroom was deafening.

"Mr. Gregg?," the judge said breaking the silence.

Mr. Gregg sporting a double-breasted, tailor made dark gray suit, quickly studied the uneasy expressions of all three defendants. It was something he always did. Mr. Gregg figured that if by the time he was done and their expression didn't change, it meant he hadn't convinced them, and if he couldn't convince his clients, then that meant to him that he had also failed with the jury as well.

Knowing that his opening statement was going to be the most important of the three, Mr. Gregg shot his constituents a look of confidence, a look that said, '*It's on!*'

Mr. Gregg rose up and gallantly moved to the lectern, then said, "Ladies and gentlemen, my name is Anthony Gregg, and I represent Sean Ryder," he gestured to Butter while continuing to face them. "One of the defendants in this trial," he said as he stroked his tie, then guided their attentions to Mrs. Bailey by pointing at her. "Now that lady!" his voice vigorously traveled throughout the courtroom, "That lady has told you that she has the burden of proving the charges made against Sean Ryder. Proving them beyond a reasonable doubt. And indeed she does have that burden. A heavy burden. A burden she will not bear successfully, because her evidence will not support it.

"You see, there's a flip side to that coin. Yes ladies and gentlemen. The side that says the defense does not have to prove anything. We don't even have to put any witnesses on the stand if we don't think it's necessary. I'm not here to play Matlock and figure out who really done what. All I'm here to do is to help you see that, that woman," he gestured to Mrs. Bailey again, "has not met her burden of proof. That the evidence does not and will not say the things she says it does." He studied the juror's faces for a while as if he was checking out how many had grasped what he'd said. When he saw no puzzling looks he continued. "So, ladies and gentlemen, here is what the evidence will really show and tell you. That an apparent drug deal gone bad left a married, drug dealing couple, dead in their Bronx apartment where no murder weapon has been found. You are also going to hear about the gruesome triple homicide of three young Jersey residents whose car was ambushed in the Bronx. And again no murder weapons were found.

"The evidence is also going to tell you that there was a major crack operation going on in the Bronx. One that has made hundreds of thousands of dollars. But not only will the evidence show you all of this, it is going to show and tell you all the ones who have admitted to these crimes. And not because their conscious drove them to come clean. Oh shucks no," he added with an animated nod and grin, "but because they were caught red-handed," he said losing the animation. "And now they're looking to point the finger at anybody....do or say whatever they must, to avoid going to prison."

Mr. Gregg, taking a page from Mrs. Bailey's book, moved to the defense table and fixed himself a glass of water while letting his last statement linger. He surveyed the defendants faces a second time and could see hope settling back in. He then took a sip of the water and glided back in front of the jury.

"Ladies and gentlemen," Mr. Gregg continued, really getting into a rhythm, "A Supreme Court Justice once said that a prosecutor could get the grand jury to indict a frog that leaped too high. And I wouldn't doubt that. Sean Ryder is not a frog. He's a young man who has a good family behind him," he motioned to people sitting behind the defense's table. "He is a young man who has just started a family with his fiancée," he said while pointing to Lisa who was holding Sean Jr., who'd been home for a month. "Sean Ryder is a young man who, unfortunately, lived in a drug infested neighborhood. But that's no crime. If it were, how many of us would be sitting over there?," he said while pointing towards the three defendants. He paused for a second, then continued, "Sean Ryder never sold drugs with, or for, the guys that are going to come up here and tell you that he did. Sean Ryder sold music. That's right ladies and gentlemen.

"When Mr. James, 'Wu' Gray, gets up here and tells you that he was selling drugs and committing murders, you have to believe him. But don't believe for a second that Sean Ryder was doing it with him. Sean Ryder wasn't into bringing sorrow and grief to families. He was into bringing happiness, that's what he did. And through his music he brought happiness to families in Queens, Brooklyn, Manhattan, and the Bronx. He brought happiness, and that is what the evidence is going to show and tell you."

Mr. Gregg stopped, realizing that he was in full control as he moved with silence towards the defense table. In his mind, he could not only hear the standing ovation, he could also hear the jury calling for an encore. He fumbled with some papers and without picking them up, returned back to the lectern.

"I submit to you," he pointed at an annoyed Mrs. Bailey, "that the prosecutor will not offer you convincing proof of anything other than theatrics," he said while surveying the faces of the jurors individually. Then he continued, "Listen to the testimony. Listen to it all, carefully and critically with an open mind. Most of all, do not draw any conclusions until you have heard all the evidence, all the arguments, and until the judge has fully explained the law to you. If you do that, you will have no choice but to find Sean Ryder not guilty of any charge, not guilty of anything except living in a bad neighborhood."

Mr. Gregg then gave the floor to D-Mac's lawyer and like a lead off batter hitting a single, he waited on first. Not wanting to wear down the jury, D-Mac's attorney said the same thing differently, followed by Flip's lawyer who loaded the bases.

Immediately following the lunch recess, the prosecutor started presenting her case. Mrs. Bailey's first few witnesses were two NYC undercover cops, two DEA agents, and two homicide detectives, all in whom got up on the stand. One after the other, they swore to tell the truth but did nothing of the sort, and that fact was proven by the grilling cross examination by the defense lawyers, led by Mr. Gregg. When the court retired at five-ten, the defense packed up feeling good about that session's outcome.

Tuesday morning Mrs. Bailey came out swinging. Not wanting to sag too far behind, she put her star witness on the stand.

"Would you state your name for the record and members of the jury please?," Mrs. Bailey stated.

"James Gray," Wu replied, barely audible. His eyes were scanning everywhere except the defense table. He had pictured this day coming over and over again, but never imagined that so many eyes would be glued onto him. The stares had caused him to feel uneasy, but nevertheless he had a job to do, and it was his ticket out of jail so he was determined to do it.

"Could you speak up so the jury can hear you Sir?," Mrs. Bailey said.

Wu cleared his throat and in a more boisterous tone replied, "James Gray!"

"Thank you. And how old are you Mr. Gray?," Mrs. Bailey continued.

"Twenty one."

"Mr. Gray, do you have a nickname?"

"Yes, I do."

"For the record, please state your nickname," she said.

"Wu."

"Are you familiar with individuals by the names of D-Mac, Flip, and Butter?"

Looking at them for the first time he answered, "Yes, I am."

"When did you first have occasion to meet D-Mac, Flip, and Butter?"

"Summer of '80."

"That's the year, 1980?," she asked him.

"Yes."

"And where did you meet them?"

"On University Avenue. The block I live on."

"And where on University do you recall meeting them?"

"In the hallway of 1839. The building I live in."

"Do you see D-Mac, Flip and Butter in court at this time?"

Wu fixed a cold stare on them and said, "Yes, I do."

"Point them out, please," Mrs. Bailey said. The court watched as Wu extended his pointing finger over at the defense's table. Then, as if he was trying to touch their noses, he pointed them out one by one.

D-Mac, Flip, and Butter, being sure not to make eye contact with each other as they were told by their lawyers, kept their stares on Wu, and because they knew better than to say anything, they kept their thoughts to themselves.

Look at this bitch-ass nigga, D-Mac thought.

I can't believe this shit, Butter thought.

Damn, I should've killed this nigga. Flip thought

"Let the record show that the witness has identified the defendants," the judge interjected, before Mrs. Bailey continued.

"Mr. Gray, at the time that you met the defendants, were you involved in the sale of drugs?"

"No, I wasn't."

"Were they involved in the sale of drugs?"

"No."

"At what time did you become involved with the selling of drugs?"

Wu appeared to be giving it some thought, then answered, "Around '89."

"And in '89, what drug were you selling?"

"Crack."

"And were D-Mac, Flip, and Butter selling crack?"

"Objection your honor," Mr. Gregg charged as he rose to his full height. "Counsel is leading the witness," he admonished.

"Sustained," the judge agreed.

"Mr. Gray, were you selling crack by yourself?," Mrs. Bailey asked as she reformed her question after the damage was done.

"No."

"Who, if anyone, were you selling crack with?"

"I sold it with D-Mac, Flip, and Butter."

For the next forty-five minutes or so, Mrs. Bailey went into specifics of the 1839 crack operation. The jury listened as Wu told them how the crack was made, sold, and how much they sold them for. After being sure that the jury had heard enough about the crack operation, Mrs. Bailey moved on to the murders. Though Wu truthfully testified about the drug activities, his accounts of the murders were far from the truth. Wu fabricated. He stated that he was in Uptown's apartment with Butter, D-Mac, and Flip when Flip murdered Uptown and Cookie. That was the statement that almost caused D-Mac to charge the stand. Wu also stated that one day while visiting him and Kelly at the rehab, Butter told him about the execution of the Jersey boys.

Wu was doing so well for the prosecution that Mrs. Bailey kept him on the stand for another hour. The jury seemed to be intensely listening as Wu even recounted the '85 gold chain, '86 Starter jackets, and '88 Triple Fat Goose-robberies he and the fellas committed.

Of course the defense attorneys interrupted several times with objections, and though many were surprisingly sustained by the judge, it was after the jury had already heard the stories. Wu's testimony was so chilling, it stiffened D-Mac, Butter, and Flip like icicles as they sat next to their lawyers. Mrs. Bailey was so proud of Wu's performance, that when she finally finished, she nearly winked at him before sitting down.

The defense had gone over Wu's statements months prior to his testifying, and they knew the only chance there was of him not being a good witness, would be if he appeared fidgety and nervous. Though Wu started out that way, his overall demeanor displayed calmness and confidence, making him an excellent witness.

On cross-examination, Mr. Gregg started off trying to cross Wu up on his accounts of his drug testimony, but when he saw how well Wu was handling himself, he flirted a little with the murders. He then put full pressure on Wu's reasons for testifying.

"Mr. Gray," *Mr.* Gregg's voice vigorously soared as he rested an elbow on the lectern, "in your plea agreement, Sir you pled guilty to conspiracy," Mr. Gregg demandingly asked.

"Yes."

"You don't deny possession and distributing crack, or murder?"

"I didn't murder nobody," Wu stated firmly.

"Okay, well you don't deny being a conspirator to murder? Is that correct?"

"Yes."

"And as part of your plea agreement, the counts charging you with murder have been dismissed haven't they?"

"Yes."

"Even after you admitted to selling this crack, and taking part in murders. It's all going to be wiped away, right?"

Wu, beginning to unravel, looked at Mrs. Bailey uneasily before answering, "Yes."

"And it is your plea agreement that you're going to plead guilty to one count. Is that correct?"

"Yes."

"And as to the rest of the counts against you, the government—to your understanding," he gestured to Mrs. Bailey, "is going to recommend they be dismissed. Is that right?"

"Yes."

"And you understand that if you give substantial assistance, that is, if you aid the prosecutor in this case, that you're going to help reduce your sentence?," Mr. Gregg stated as he purposely blocked Wu's view of Mrs. Bailey.

"Yes," Wu said.

"That's what you're trying to do?"

Wu hesitated and then answered, "Yes."

"You understand that if you please the prosecution in this case, they will make a recommendation for reduction of sentence?"

Mr. Gregg's question caused an enraged Mrs. Bailey to rise to her feet and howl, "Objection! Your Honor, I object to the form of that question!"

"Sustained," the judge agreed.

"Your honor, I request a curative instruction!" Mrs. Bailey interjected, wanting the judge to reduce any damage Mr. Gregg's last question might have done.

"Ladies and gentlemen," the judge addressed the jury, "Remember that questions are not part of the evidence in the case, it is the answer to the questions. But I would ask you to disregard the question that has just been posed." The judge shifted his stare to Mr. Gregg and said, "Mr. Gregg, you may restate your question please, Sir."

"Mr. Gray," Mr. Gregg continued, "You know that the reason you haven't been sentenced yet, is that the prosecutor is waiting until after you testify in this case?," he stated for the jurors' knowledge.

"No."

"You do understand that your sentence does depend on your testimony in this case, don't you?"

"I understand they can knock some years off."

"And you're trying to work it down as low as possible," Mr. Gregg stated as he continued to block Wu's view of Mrs. Bailey.

"Yes, I am."

"That's all, Your Honor."

After the lunch recess, D-Mac and Flip's attorneys continued attacking Wu's plea agreement. Though it might have helped, it was inevitable. Wu had done major damage to the defense's case.

Next, Mrs. Bailey brought out one twin after the other and the jury listened as they corroborated Wu's accounts about the drugs and murders. They testified that they helped set-up the Jersey boys, and they often heard Flip bragging about the triple homicide. Though they weren't as solid as Wu, their testimony still appeared to be damaging, even after the defense attorneys were through roasting them.

The next few days of the trial breezed by. Mrs. Bailey put Mrs. White, the lab technician, on the stand. She testified how the drugs that were confiscated were delivered to her lab by agents for testing, which she performed and found to test positive as crack.

On cross examination, the defense felt because she was only testifying to the type of drugs being crack, there was no reason to keep her there long, so they brought to light that it was the same lying, untrustworthy agents they grilled earlier who delivered the drugs to her agency. Then she was dismissed.

Mrs. Bailey followed by letting the jury hear from the three lookouts, crack-head Ike and his smoking partner, the pitcher, who all corroborated Wu's and the twins' run-down of the drug operation. After the shrill cross-examination from the defense lawyers, by late Friday Mrs. Bailey rested the government's case.

The court recessed at four-fifteen and wasn't due to resume until nine a.m. Monday morning. After the defendants were taken back to the holding cell and the court began to clear out, Mrs. Bailey casually walked over to the first defense's table where Mr. Gregg stood alone packing his brief case.

"Anthony," she said, addressing him by his first name like they had been long time friends. "I think those defendants got themselves some pretty sharp attorneys," she said as she referred to D-Mac, Flip, and Butter.

Almost certain that she hadn't come over just to tell him that, Mr. Gregg played along. "Thank you. I'll be sure to tell the other two how you feel about us," he responded as he flashed a wry smile.

"You know there doesn't have to be a Monday," Mrs. Bailey said as she eased in with a wry smile of her own.

"Meaning?," he retorted as he shut his briefcase.

"The magic number is twenty-five," she offered.

"I wasn't expecting to hear another offer from you at least until half of my witnesses got up on the stand and told the jury what my client was really selling."

"Don't kid yourself Mr. Gregg," she responded in a more persuasive tone. "You know just as well as I do that all twelve jurors are not going to bite. And it doesn't matter how many old ladies from the neighborhood you bring in here next week," her wry smile returned before she added, "the twenty-five expires in seven hours."

There'll be another offer, Mr. Gregg thought as he watched her disappear out of the courtroom. Hoping that his client was still in the holding cell, Mr. Gregg hurried to the door that led to it, but was disappointed after opening it and noticing that the Marshals had apparently already taken them back to Valhalla. Though Mr. Gregg doubted that they would entertain such an offer, he knew he had to tell them of it and let them decide, but not before he relayed the message to his constituents.

Chapter Nineteen

Twelve days later.

The jury was in its third day of deliberation. After their
clients rejected Mrs. Bailey's third offer of twenty-five years, it
took Mr. Gregg and his team six days to present all their evidence. They ran through witness after witness. Despite the
few objections and meager cross-examination by Mrs. Bailey,
who didn't want to seem like a vulture to the jury, Mr. Gregg
felt their witnesses had done well. He was also pleased that the
jury appeared to show no signs of boredom while he and his
team gave their closing arguments. Even though they were
equally receptive to Mrs. Bailey's witnesses, he felt that he had
more than a couple on his side.

It was a quarter to four, and for the past three days Mrs.
Bailey had begun to grow a little uneasy. Not only had the jury
not returned a guilty verdict—one she felt they should have
returned two days earlier, they also had been requesting to see
more of the defense's witnesses testimonies, something they
hadn't been doing in the last two days.

"It looks like there's going to be a tomorrow," Mrs. Bailey
said, as she stood in front of the defense's table towering over
Mr. Gregg who sat between the other two lawyers. She

watched as the three slightly nodded while maintaining their game faces. "Of course you know, it won't be long before they persuade the one that's holding out to come to their senses," she said.

"Maybe there's six trying to convince, six," Mr. Gregg shot back, "or maybe that one is yours."

Mrs. Bailey, already having thought of that, displayed a supple grin and said, "I can do away with the murder counts."

Knowing that the jury hadn't asked one time to see any murder testimony, Mr. Gregg replied, "Come on, Carol. We both know that the jury might have already done away with those counts on their own."

"You know what?," Mrs. Bailey's calm and even tone questioned as she hovered over them with both hands on the table. "One of two things is going to happen. They're going to return a guilty verdict, or they're going to hang up. Which means we'll be here next month either holding a sentencing hearing or another trial. However it turns out, it's not good for your clients."

Mr. Gregg knew she was right, but wasn't about to let her know it. He maintained his calmness and asked, "Is there another magic number coming?"

Not really wanting to go through another trial, Mrs. Bailey said, "One final offer." Her glare surveyed all three faces before she continued, "You see Mr. Gregg, my team," she gestured towards her table, "and I think that the jury might be caught up on not whether they should convict, but who gets convicted. And we think they're having trouble convicting your client. Which might very well lead to a hung jury for all three defendants. So here's the deal. I'll give your client three years probation and a healthy fine, but the other two get ten."

"Ten?," D-Mac's lawyer chided in. "Excuse me, but am I missing something here?," he asked.

"Listen counsel," she fixed her stare on D-Mac's attorney, "two of them are going down. Now which two— I'll leave that up to you and your clients," she added before stepping off.

"What a bitch," Flip's lawyer commented.

Mrs. Bailey had figured out that D-Mac and Flip were riding Butter's coat tail, so she thought if she offered a global plea, it would possibly encourage one to convince the other two to take a harder fall. It would make her job easier at getting three guilty pleas, which wouldn't be as good as three convictions, but a whole lot better than a hung jury.

For the past three days, D-Mac, Flip, and Butter had been rotating every two hours. One would stretch out on the bench while the other two would sit on the floor as they restlessly waited on the jury's verdict from the holding cell.

"This shit is fucked up," D-Mac commented while looking up at the paint-chipped ceiling from the bench. "Everybody is out there chillin' while we cramped up in this little mothafucka. Why can't we sit out there and wait for the verdict? We sat out there for the trial," he added before Butter and Flip, who were mentally fatigued, could respond.

At the sight of the door opening, the three of them did as they'd been doing for the past three days. They rose to their feet, feeling numbed at the thought that a verdict had been reached.

"No, not yet fellas," Mr. Gregg said, recognizing their expressions as he and the other two attorneys stood inches away from the cell.

"What time is it?," Butter asked.

"Four O'clock," Mr. Gregg answered.

"I guess we'll do it again tomorrow," Butter sorely replied.

"I don't know," Mr. Gregg responded, drawing inquisitive looks from three of them.

"What that means?," Flip interjected.

"The prosecutor has made another offer," Mr. Gregg said as he got right to the point, "And I really believe this is her final one." He watched as the three stood motionless with looks that showed they were eager to hear the rest. "She wants you to cop to three years probation," moving his stare off Butter and onto D-Mac and Flip, "and you two have to cop to ten."

"Ten?" The three of them said, seconds apart.

"What type of shit is that?," D-Mac added.

"She's made it clear that everybody's not walking from this one."

"What's up with the jury? That's not lookin' good?," Butter questioned.

Mr. Gregg faced him and said, "Well that depends on what you consider good. My guess is that the jury is hung. And if that's the case there'll be a second trial..."

"Let us get a minute," Flip interrupted.

Mr. Gregg checked his watch, gestured to the two attorneys, then said, "We'll be back in ten minutes."

Flip waited until they were out the door then turned to D-Mac and said, "Yo, what the hell are we thinking about?" His tone was mild, "We know what we did. And we know ten years is nothing close to what we supposed to be getting', or what we're gonna get once these loaded dice stop rolling," Flip said, implying the court system. "A few months back we were all excited about taking the ten and just putting this shit behind us..."

"Yeah, until Wu fucked that up," D-Mac interrupted.

"He did, but us three stuck together," Flip continued. "Remember fifty-five years? Forty-five years? And the quarter she offered us? We rode this shit all the way to the door. And we've been waiting four days for the door to open," he said then paused while studying their faces. "Guess what? That shit opened, and we betta haul ass out of it."

Before anyone could respond, the door opened and their attention was drawn to Mr. Gregg who entered followed by two marshals. "There's a verdict," Mr. Gregg said, watching all the life drain out of them. "But," he paused, "it doesn't have to be read." Mr. Gregg's eyes studied all three faces. "So, what's it going to be?," he asked them.

"The cop", Flip blurted out. He didn't have to think twice. Then Flip looked to D-Mac for a response.

"What if the verdict is not guilty? Then we all outta here today," D-Mac's eyes answered. He then remembered when the Dred told him that ten would be considered a blessing to the niggas who's only choice was twenty-five and better. "I'll take the cop."

"Go home Duke," Flip said as he and D-Mac fixed their stares on Butter. "You got wifey to marry, a shorty to raise and money to get."

"Who else gonna hold it down for the team?," D-Mac added.

Without words, Butter hugged both of them at the same time and with his head between both of theirs he said, "You niggas are the realest."

"Yo Duke, you the realest," D-Mac replied.

"Word!" Flip added.

Epilogue

Three months later.

Following their guilty pleas, D-Mac and Flip were sentenced to ten years and twenty-five hundred dollar fines. Butter, who'd been out on bond, received three years of probation and, as promised, a healthy fine. One hundred and fifty thousand. Though his fine was excessive and could have easily been challenged, Butter as well as everyone else wanted this stressful nightmare situation behind him and he strongly suggested Mr. Gregg not oppose. Mr. Gregg, happy to oblige since courthouse rumors had it that the verdicts were guilty, let it ride.

A week following the trial, Wu, the twins, Ike and his smoking partner, were all sentenced. LA received a year and a day. The combination of him ratting, his squeaky clean criminal record, and his minor role all played a part in his 'slap on the wrist.' His brother, Al, wasn't as fortunate though. The prior conviction that landed him on Riker's Island back in the days came back to haunt him. It placed him in Category II, which offset his minor role. Despite his snitching, Al still got smashed with eight years. Ike and his partner were sentenced a year and a day each, and because of their apparent drug abuse, they were also ordered to participate in the Bureau of Prison's five hundred hour drug program.

Wu got the worst end of the stick. Despite working with the government and testifying against his family-like crew, he never received the immediate freedom that he expected and so desperately wanted. Instead, he received a four-year sentence and was also ordered into the drug program. In addition, he not only lost Kelly, who was pregnant by Mike, but he lost his integrity and the love of his crew. Living with the fact that he'd betrayed his only true friends was in itself a life sentence.

Coming next from Hampstead Publishing, another Joe Black Anecdote...

SQUEEZE
Prologue

Troy Boogie was a legit, hard working employee by day, but a grimy, illegal drug dealer by night. Me and my partner, Trigga, didn't know him personally but the fact that he a price tag of forty G's over his head most likely meant that a mothafucka felt he was on some bullshit, and whether he was or not wasn't as important to us as that forty G's.

At first, Trigga and I thought Troy would be just another routine hit—you know, get the drop on him on some dark street, peel his wig back, then catch the wind. But after tailing Troy for a couple of dayswe discovered that once Troy punches the clock and leaves work, he's met at the 34th Street train station by a couple of members from his click and is hardly ever by himself from that point on.

Even though my crimey and I knew trying to body Troy on a busy 34th Street would be not only crazy, but dumb, we had no choice because—one; we had already received twenty thousand, and two; we knew better than to renege on a hit.

Twenty-West 36th Street was the building Troy worked in. It was one of the many high rises that stood towering on the long, narrow block. Exiting the building to its left was a slew of other high-rises that continued for about a half mile, ending at the furthest corner from Twenty West. In the opposite direction was a high-rise building with an adjoining underground parking lot, followed by a doughnut shop and a meager womens' thrift shop that stood on the corner.

From our previous observations, Troy noticed that they always exited Twenty West at precisely the same time every evening—ten past five—and he always made the left which was the scenic route to the 34th Street train station.

Our plan was simple. When Troy exited the building, my crimey was to slyly pace along with him from the other side of the street, and before Troy could reach the corner, Trigga was to flash across the street and dump two hot ones from the nickel-plated Lady Smith into Troy's melon, then flash toward the opposite corner.

My job was to watch Trigga's back and blast anyone who tried to play Super Hero, but if everything went smooth I was to blend in with what we anticipated to be an awed crowd and provide the police with a fucked-up description of the shooter.

As I slowly and inconspicuously moved up the same side of the block Troy would be coming down, my eyes quickly and continuously scanned the surroundings for uniformed cops that periodically roamed through the block, either by foot or by vehicle. I could tell that it was after five-o'clock because as I approached or passed each building, packs of what appeared to be restless employees were gallantly emerging. The brisk wind had some moving more swiftly than others as sweaters and jackets were being adjusted.

Meanwhile, I held a steady stroll underneath the warmth of my oversized navy blue hoodie. I checked my watch and saw that it read twelve minutes past five and then lifted my gaze expecting to see Troy. Like clockwork, there he was. His thin, tall frame casually waltzed in my direction with all his attention obviously occupied by the conversation he was having on his cell phone. My vision then locked onto Trigga as he made his way from the other side of the street with his head buried in an oversized black hoodie and his right hand tucked in its front pouch. I looked over my left shoulder, taking a last split-second glance at the scenery behind me and turned back just in time to see the shining piece of chrome Trigga retrieved from his pouch as he boarded the sidewalk a step or two behind Troy.

In what seemed to be one motion, Trigga raised the gun to the back of Troy's head and dumped two hot ones through Troy's purple Yankee fitted.

"BOOM! BOOM!" the roar of the pistol turned the sedate scenery into frenzy, causing innocent passers-by to hysterically scatter every which way. Like many others who stood frozen, I witnessed Troy's body crumble to the ground in slow motion-like fashion—as if he were a life-sized blowup dummy that had just been deflated.

As Trigga made the dash in the opposite direction

from me, my ears were consumed by the frantic screams of devastated women.

One distinguished male's voice barked, "Freeze! Police Officer!" He drew his gun before taking off after Trigga while blabbering into the radio that was clutched in his other hand.

Never anticipating an undercover to be right at the scene, I had no time to even think about what had to be done. Trigga and I weren't just partners, we were like brothers, so in my mind that undercover cop was just a plain 'ol wanna-be Super Hero that was in hot pursuit of Trigga.

Because I was absolutely sure that Trigga would have done the same if the tables were turned, I took off in hot pursuit of the cop. The three of us, several feet apart from each other, hastily weaved through the busy sidewalk pushing, and even knocking down people as they desperately tried getting out of harm's way.

"Move!" the cop yelled, moving through the pack like a running back on first and ten. Following in the open path, I could see the cop gaining ground as Trigga breezed past the building with the underground parking lot. Out of the fear of striking one of the many innocent bystanders, the cop had no intention of taking a shot at Trigga's dodging motions. However, without remorse or hesitation Trigga abruptly turned and fired in the cop's direction.

"BOOM! BOOM!" the shots caused both the cop and I to momentarily take cover before continuing in a forward motion from a nearly squatting position.

Still going unnoticed by the cop, I picked up speed with a spur of the moment plan that I formed out of instinct. The exit to the garage that was underneath the building next to Twenty West was on Thirty-Fifth Street. I figured if I dropped the cop anywhere near the garage's entrance, I could dip into the garage on Thirty-Sixth Street, exit out Thirty-Fifth Street, then get ghost from there. As Trigga neared the corner, the cop was steps away from passing the garage's entrance. I knew it was now or never. I turned on the after burners, crept up on him and showered him with hollow tips from my blue-steel forty-five.

"BOOM! BOOM! BOOM!" I watched as the lead

ripped into his right shoulder blade, neck, and head before he collapsed hard on the ground. I wasn't sure if he was dead, nor was I about to check, but I was certain that if he wasn't, his condition would never surpass vegetable status.

I looked up, caught a glimpse of Trigga's back before he vanished around the corner in the direction of Thirty-Fifth Street, then jetted through the parking lot. As I neared the exit, I slowed down and removed my hoodie. I flung it underneath a parked Audi, quickly gathered myself, then emerged out onto Thirty-Fifth Street as cool as Kiza Sosa rockin' a pair of British walkers back in '84. I could tell by the missing sense of urgency that the people who strolled up and down Thirty-Fifth Street hadn't a clue as to what had just gone down one block over.

Full of anxiety still, I neared the corner hoping to either meet up with Trigga or at least spot him flying by. Just as the thought of us pulling it off successfully popped into my head, it was washed away by the thundering sounds of distant gunfire that dangled in my ears.

"Oh shit!" I said to myself as I viewed the horrific looks on the faces of people who were scrambling in my direction from around the corner.

Maintaining my poise, I continued toward the circle with the unthinkable on my mind. I was devastated when I witnessed a gang of uniformed cops cautiously moving closer to Trigga's stiffened, blood-stained body that lay lifeless up against the lower half of a department store's wall.

As the tears mounted in my eyes, I desperately wanted to do something. But what? Deep inside I knew there was nothing I could do. I painfully looked on along with the large number of innocent bystanders as the police hovered over Trigga's bloodied body.

My watery vision shifted from Trigga's body, up along the store's blood-stained, shattered glass, then onto the uniformed cop that was gesturing for the crowd to move back. I suddenly realized that it was a wrap, and because I knew my 187 on the undercover would soon shut down Manhattan, I forced myself to walk further down the block where I hopped in a cab and was out.

Special BIG UPS From The Author...

All my real niggas on lock, stand da fuck up! I'll never forget you and neither will da streets! Where's Brooklyn at? My mothafuckin' man Ernest Bynum (Big June, what up baby?), Ayo Calvin Klein, what's really good? I owe you kid, it was your peep talk that made me take matters into my own hands, love is love! Ayo Derrick Williams (Drack, get at me son!). Randy "Moe-Deezy" Kearse (ya STREET TALK dictionary is official!), Omar Reeves and Tyrone Hunt (yo Big O and Twin, you niggas are the realest!) Dee Blind, what up kid? I have to give the crazy big up to my Ecuadorian man Flaco Idrovo, and T. Jefferies (ayo Shake, I had to do it big, you know how me, you and Flaco roll!), Capone and Noodles, they wanna know how I did it! Queens, where ya'all at? Ronald Tucker (ayo Tuck, love is love, get at me famm), Joe Hogan, my brother from another mother, you know how we do! To Micheal (ayo Twin, real recognize real, gangsta!), Malik, yeah coach, I'm still winning championships. T. Coleman (Ayo Teddy, who get down like us!) Harlem world, what's really shakin'? Ronnie Love, where you at famm? G. Scott, how big you trying to get baby boy? Silver D. from 102nd and Douglas, I see you kid!, Ron Jordan (Ayo Abuser, I continue to write for gangstas like you!), Pup, Ed, Wu, I know you niggas think I was gonna forget! B.X. niggas, stand da fuck up! My Cody Raymond Franklin (Marly Marl, real niggas do real things, it won't be long kid!), Peter Shue, you the realest, love is love son! Big Bump, you know what it is. Joe Maldanaldo, (Ayo little Joe, who's realer than us?), Danny "Green Eyes", it's always great to run into a good nigga like you, keep it gangsta!, Eric Capers, yeah, and my man Rap (Ayo world, me and Shake doing the fifty dollar cup, yeah its' serious!), Rodney Montgomery (Ayo Booney, yeah, I'm takin' it back kid!), Rodney Risper reppin' Mt. Vernon (Ayo Candyman, what up flyy guy?), C Bates from Burke Ave. (Ayo Sharky, you did the shit real niggas do!) Leyton Wint (Ayo Choco, you got madd skillz on the editing tip, now you just gotta get focused!). These niggas may not be from my town, but the way they repp theirs, lets me know that there are real niggas all over the world. Elizabeth gangstas, Shawn Hartwell, the youngest in charge, tell those haters to fall back! Rajah Miller, you too smooth for me kid! S. Johnson reppin' Trenton (Ayo InF you know how we do, love is love!), Ramsey Thomas and Santos reppin' Albany (Ayo Rock and Sandman, yeah it's real!), Big Ponch Fontanez reppin Youngstown, Ohio, I like the way you move kid! Big Earl Pearson, reppin' Rhode Island, damn kid, you get any bigger you won't fit on the island! Ernest Floor reppin' Philly (Ayo Ern, put it in your collection!), T. Rek and Hawk reppin' Newburg, okay, you niggas gangsta!, Big Lump, Jonsey, J.K. and Cheeks, I heard New Haven just aint the same without you niggas, and how could it be!!! Oh Shit! Can't forget my man Seth Ferranti. Ayo Seth, let them muthafucka's know you move with real live niggas!!! Of course there's scores of other real niggaz on lock that I didn't have room to mention, but yo, I got you on the next joint!

ABOUT THE AUTHOR...

Born in the Bronx, New York, Joe Black was found guilty in 1993 of participating in a large-scale crack trafficking conspiracy and sentenced by a North Carolina judge to a lengthy federal sentence. Over the past decade Joe has served portions of his bid in a number of different federal institutions. Throughout his travels he's been known to entertain scores of inmates with his gritty street and jail tales.

To contact Joe Black, please write to:
         Joe Black
         c/o Hampstead Publishing
         P.O. BOX 33
         Keasbey, NJ 08832

or visit him at:
www.illstreetz.com or www.hampsteadpub.com

COMING SOON FROM
Hampstead Publishing Inc.:
Squeeze by Joe Black
Moving Violation by Joe Black
Down In Da Dirty by J.M. Benjamin
Deep In Da Game by Robert Booker
Elizabeth's Finest by the Eport Posse
and other books by
Michael "Minkah" Norwood
Corey Ford
Derrick Phillips
Derrick Willliams
William Jackson

For more information log on to:
Hampsteadpub.com